ZENANI DEORDHI:
THE LIFE AND JOURNEY OF A PRINCESS

Santosh Singh

ISBN 978-93-90463-94-7

First published in India 2020 by Inkstate Books
An imprint of Leadstart Publishing Pvt Ltd

Sales Office:
Unit No.25/26, Building No.A/1,
Near Wadala RTO,
Wadala (East), Mumbai – 400037 India
Phone: +91 969933000
Email: info@leadstartcorp.com
www.leadstartcorp.com

Disclaimer: The views expressed in this book are those of the Author and do not pertain to be held by the Publisher.

Editor: Cora Bhatia
Cover: Ami Parekh
Layouts: Victor Patali

To my life-lines
Pratap, Shivangi
and Varun

ABOUT THE AUTHOR

Dr. Santosh Singh secured her triple Masters in Sociology, English, and Education from Lucknow University and Agra University, respectively. She holds a doctorate in Sociology from Rajasthan University. She was also awarded post-doctoral fellowship by ICSSR, New Delhi. After a stint of teaching in BDKM Post-Graduate College, Agra, she was assigned a prestigious assignment of imparting training in secretarial work to the future bureaucrats of Namibia, under the aegis of Internal Security Academy, Mount Abu, Rajasthan. She has been associated with Institute of Social Sciences (ISS) New Delhi since 1996.

Her published works are – 'Passion for Flames', 'Learning Societies - Shifting Patterns', 'Combatant Women', 'Violence against Rural Women.' 'Dynamics of Inclusion and Exclusion in Uttar Pradesh' in 'Inclusion and Exclusion in Local Governance, 'Women Empowerment and Civil society' in 'The Indian Women's Journey- the last Five Decades.

She has contributed a number of research articles and stories to national journals, magazines and newspapers. She is focusing on women empowerment, water and sanitation, conflict and gendered violence, Panchayati raj and civil society. Currently, she is a senior fellow of the Institute of Social Sciences, New Delhi.

She can be reached at singhsantoshchauhan@gmail.com

www.authorsantosh.com (http://www.authorsantosh.com)

ACKNOWLEDGEMENTS

It is a pleasure to acknowledge the support I have received from many quarters. It is within the cosy climate of my fraternity that the present book has come to fruition. The book would not have been possible without their extraordinary support.

I have to begin with my parents who inspire me – my father Dwarka Singh and my mother Lakshmi Devi, the persons who did not compromise with their principle even under the most trying circumstances. I always have a feeling that they have been constantly protecting me from their heavenly abode and keeping me blessed.

My daughter Shivangi for all her academic inputs and emotional backup. As always, she reads the first draft.

My son-in-law Varun for his unconditional support in all of my endeavours. His support is invaluable.

Yashraj, my nephew, a budding genius, for all his valuable inputs to the story.

Pratap Singh, for going through the draft with utmost care. My discussions with him are enlightening. He helps me in building sub plots, which weave well into the story.

I want to express my gratitude to my Editor Cora Bhatia. At each stage, she has been insightful, meticulous, and supportive. In sum, she has been an ideal editor.

Big hugs to the outstanding team – Malini Nair, Puja Dutt, Devanshi Doshi, Trupti and Kshitij Dhawale at Leadstart publications. I have no words to say how grateful I am to the wonderful Leadstart team for turning my daydream to reality. I am tremendously grateful.

Over the past many months, while grappling with the issues of Royal women, I worked with many people whose inputs and valuable suggestions need special mention – Dr Alka Singh and Archana Singh,

Ashok Singh and Vinod Bhardwaj, a gentleman like my brother. Mrs.Rajbala Singh needs special thanks as she provided me with the relevant material and historical texts. I am extremely grateful to all of them.

Special thanks to the REVAMP, the Digital Marketing Agency, which has taken upon itself to showcase the "Zenani Deordhi" to its readers.

I express deep gratitude, in advance to the readers expecting that they will steal some moments from their precious time to pick this book and go through it. In fact, I am highly motivated by my precious readers to undertake this work.

This book offers a glimpse into the feminine side of history that is more humane, yet not without the gory tales of blood. I hope this will be interesting for all of you, as it was for me.

Big thanks to all of you.

CONTENTS

FOREWORD

Indian women, especially the Rajput women, enjoy a dualism of image and perception. On the one hand, they exhibit courage, velour, and determination, and on the other, they are tradition abiding, civilisation carrying, and custom following. There have been countless women in history on both sides.

There were Rajput queens, who dove into battle with courage and determination, to fight for their lands, homes, honour, ideals, or territory. They did so under great odds. There were also Rajput women, who were loyal to the tradition, grasped the exigencies of the situation, and acted quietly but heroically to save a royal custom or crisis. Even they were consumed by the cultural practices of the time. But they did so with commitment and conviction. Be it Sati or Jauhar, for the sake of chastity or royal duty.

Dr. Singh tells the story of a royal woman through (Zenani Deordhi) with sufficient sprinkling of description of royal scenes and surroundings marked by grandeur, glitter, gaiety, and opulence etc. The reader will be guided into those environs by Dr. Singh's narration, and will feel a part of the proceedings.

I would not discourage the readers for making their own interpretation and evaluation. I enjoyed going through the story as narrated and saw the characters as they were.

Dr. Singh is presenting a life as it unfolded, an institution (Zenani Deordhi) as it operated, a history, as it should have been.

I congratulate her for digging deep into a slice of history, and correcting the historical fault line of the feminine side of royalty, and treating the readers with fascinating, at times jaw-dropping tale.

Dr. D.K. Giri,
PhD (New Delhi), PhD (England)
Professor, International Politics
JMI, New Delhi
Political analyst and Author.

Dated - 15 March, 2020

NOTE ON THE NARRATIVE

'Zenani Deordhi – the Life and Journey of a Princess' weaves the period when most of the principalities abandon the rule based on principles and dharma. Their greed and lust engulfed them completely that ultimately drove them towards annihilation. Lust and greed, be it for power, be it for money, be it for women, it makes a person a devil. Lust is the mother of all kinds of social evils.

The narrative trails the shadows of Fateh Kanwar, queen of late Maharaja Jagat Singh of Jaipur, whose life was engulfed in myriad images, right from an innocent teenaged princess to a devoted wife; later, labelled as a cunning and cruel regent queen.

They were two young lives converging on a deadly course: one an innocent twelve-year-old princess of Bikaner, who was living an idyllic life in royal corridors, the other, a young crown prince, who had spent all his life defying the traditions and Raj dharma, even after ascending the throne of Jaipur.

We only know that she was the princess of Bikaner and was married to Jagat Singh, the crown prince of Amber. Still, there are quite a few questions about her life, which are shrouded in mystery. At what age did she get married? Where was the marriage solemnised, at Bikaner or Amber? How was the marriage negotiated? In addition, was the wedding a fall out of political alliance or the marriage gave rise to a political alliance? How did Fateh Kanwar deal with the entry of her rival queens? Later, how did the tumultuous relationship with her husband survive? How was she treated by the king? Was she duly respected by other queens who joined after her? How did they all handle human emotions of jealousy, rivalry, hatred, admiration etc.?

In some of the descriptions, there is a reference of Rani Bhatiyani and her deordhi, during the period from1818 to 1834, when Fateh Kanwar was the regent queen of Jaipur. That's all. Fateh was a princess of Bikaner of Rathor clan, who was married to the Kachwaha, Prince of Jaipur. Some texts mention her as the daughter of Ratan Singh, Thakur

Saheb of Lathi Jaisalmer. As per the tradition of Jaipur royalty, she was to be known as Rani Rathorni. As the date of the demise of Rani Bhatiani and Fateh Kanwar was the same, and the period of regency was also the same, it led to some ambiguity. Thus, it can be inferred that the Bhatiani queen and Fateh Kanwar were no different persons. These were the two identities of one person.

Sawai Maharaj Jagat Singh of Jaipur died at an early age, a well-documented fact, but what happened to the large number of queens and concubines, he left behind remains a mystery. History is silent on it. Many such unanswered questions were lost in obscurity. However, one thing can be stated with certainty that Fateh Kanwar was the first queen of Jagat Singh and the first of his many queens to enter the Jaipur palace.

The story of Fateh Kanwar spanning the period of 1800 to1835, is not completely fiction. It is a creative depiction of history. The life of regent queens of Rajputana was extremely difficult. They seldom crossed over thresholds of the zenana or interacted with the public, although they remained very active within the periphery of the palace and managed the state with the help of a few trusted advisors. Unfortunately, this very loyal support system exploited the situation, where regent queens were placed in, to serve their own vested interests.

It is believed that Fateh Kanwar, too, was merely a puppet in the hands of her own badaaran, a female assistant of queen in administrative matters, who having come very close to the queen, virtually ruled Jaipur on her behalf, while some others believed that she was hand-in-gloves with her trusted badaaran.

The persona of Maharani Fateh Kanwar impelled me to visit her deordhi. Women have, largely, always been the underside of history, Fateh Kanwar like her other counterparts was left completely unnoticed by the historians. The reign of her husband was as intriguing as the life of Fateh.

Fateh Kanwar, who was the Maharani, subsequently became Maji Sahib, the regent queen, after the demise of Jagat Singh. Her confidante Rupan badaaran, Rajmata RathorniJi, and she herself were the three women who were different from each other, but stayed together through all the vicissitudes. The intriguing politics in the house of Jaipur prompted me to peep into the lives of these women. How did these women stand and assert themselves against the brutal currents of fate and achieved miraculous feats in the days of restricted freedom? It is startling, just incomprehensible.

As I leaf through the history of Jaipur, I find that many sheets have been attributed to Sawai Maharaj Jai Singh II, grandfather and Sawai Maharaj Pratap Singh, father of Jagat Singh, by most of the historians like Jadunath Sarkar, Malcolm, and in the texts by the authors like Devi Singh Mandawa, Chandramani Singh, Bhatt, Mathur and Nath Shashtri. Jagat Singh generally finds mention in the books for two incidents of his notoriety – one, for his lustful relationship with a dancer, named Raskapoor and two, his meanness contributing to the brutal death of Krishna Kumari, the princess of Udaipur. Colonel Tod refused to give him any space in his 'Annals and Antiquities of Rajasthan', dismissing him as 'the most dissolute prince of his race or age'.

Kachwaha Rajputs used to rule over Jaipur that was earlier known as Dundhaar region then Amber. In 1727, Sawai Jai Singh shifted his capital from the valley of Amber and settled in a new town in a sprawling plain area surrounded by hills. It was named Jaipur after him.

The history of Kachwahas, their arrival in Dundhaar is a long story. There are many serpentine lanes and by lanes – some illuminating, while others are dark; stone pavements that were trodden by power hungry hawks; some led to the world of *pothis* (books). Eunuchs who controlled zenanas, kings who renounced the throne and the king who willed half of the kingdom in the name of a dancer – all weave the tale of Kachwahas. It is complex and chaotic.

Fateh Kanwar belonged to the Rathor principality of Bikaner, a sandy plateau covering a large area of 23,317 square miles, as large as Belgium and Holland combined today. She grew up in the hills of Gopalpura and Sujangarh. Her favourite hunting site was a black stone hill, at Silwa.

Jagat Singh ascended the throne of Jaipur in 1803, when he barely completed seventeen years and died at the age of thirty two, thus, reigning only for fifteen years. It is believed that he expired because of excess consumption of medicines and liquor made of rice for arousal of libido. He fought many battles in the short span of his rule. He was fond of arts. However, he was madly in love with Raskapoor.

Raskapoor was perhaps a Muslim dancer. Her entry into Jaipur royal court is also shrouded in mystery. Colonel Tod only refers her as a concubine of Jagat Singh. In 1985, Dhyan Makhija penned her tale as pulp-fiction focussing on Raskapoor, as a dancing girl, exquisitely beautiful with an extraordinary melodious voice and her relationship with Maharaja Jagat Singh.

Whenever the king visited a particular queen, she would make elaborate preparations – apply sandalwood paste on her body, decorate the room with fragrant flowers, make arrangements for dance and singing if required, and she would adorn herself splendidly for the evening. However, it was not a cherished moment for every queen. If a dancer, a singer, or a *daavari* could please the king, she stood a chance to become a concubine. Special rooms in some zenanas were decorated with paintings of erotic themes, where the king could satiate himself with such women.

The interiors of the deordhi were lavishly decorated, but the buildings were designed to prevent outside view. Gardens complete with flowering bushes and fountains were incorporated into the royal zenana. Women could have had glimpses of the outer world through *jharokhas*, overhanging latticed windows, or from roofed balconies, located at great heights.

Zenana would be incomplete without its concubines. This segment has always been highly volatile with upward mobility. They could own a chamber and a fixed amount. Varsha Joshi in her research, (Polygamy and Purdah: 1995), highlighted that a Rajput ruler could neither take women from the Brahmin community as concubines nor as queens in pursuance of a standard north Indian practice, restricting hypogamous marriages

Joshi maintains that women from ruling Rajput clans were also not to be initiated as concubines, a method practised to maintain the superiority of their lineages. Also, women from social groups ranked lowest in society were not taken as concubines by Rajput rulers. The women who became concubines were thus drawn mostly from secondary social castes. The records reveal the existence of Muslim women as concubines in some Rajput houses, like Raskapoor and in one rare instance, in the early eighteenth century Ajit Singh (1707–24) of Marwar accepted an inferior Rajput caste woman as a concubine

In the books of history, the zenana rule of Jaipur state is described as years of decay and decline at all levels, full of mismanagement, corruption and conspiracies. Whatever may be the reasons for the failure of the zenana administration, none of the regent queens could put forward an ideal model of woman-statesmanship.

The storyteller does not present the history as it is. He/she illustrates the facts as per his/her sentiments of love and hate for the incidents. History has never been neutral or impartial. Unlike a mirror, history has never presented the images from the past as they were or used to be. To me, history is somewhat like a court verdict based on obtained and presented facts. To me, the story is often hidden between the lines of the verdict.

As I chose to portray the adventures of the amazing life of Fateh Kanwar in this book, I felt burdened with a sombre responsibility to discard the superfluous information so that she could be presented as a real human being in all her pain and glory, so that prevalent stereotypes woven around her could be dispelled.

Once I was convinced that I should pen the remarkable journey of Rani Fateh Kanwar, I carefully scanned all the credible texts and literature I could lay my hands on. My hope is that by uncovering the intricate life of Fateh Kanwar, I would be able to dispel many stereotypes attached to the Indian women as such. At the same time, by bringing Rani Fateh Kanwar from the underside to the forefront, I do not intend to debase any practice or a community. I have narrated the story, presented the facts, dispassionately and objectively. It is my belief as a student of Sociology, culture and gender studies that facts should speak for themselves.

15 March 2020

Santosh Singh

PRINCIPAL CHARACTERS

- Gaj Singh: Maharaja of Bikaner

- Raj Singh :(son of late queen of Gaj Singh, RajawatJi.) The eldest son of Gaj Singh ,who became Maharaja of Bikaner at the age of 42 years.

- Pratap Singh: Six-year-old, the eldest son of Raj Singh; Maharaja of Bikaner at the age of six years, killed by his own uncle.

- Surat Singh: Half brother of Raj Singh; ascended the throne after Pratap Singh, the minor king of Bikaner

- Sultan Singh: Half brother of Surat Singh, son of Akhe Kanwar

- (Sultan and Raj Singh were half-brothers)

- Ajab Singh: Real brother of Surat Singh

- Akhe Kanwar Devadi: Maharani of Bikaner

- Chandra Kanwar: Queen of Gaj Singh; mother of Surat Singh

- Fateh Kanwar: Daughter of Ajab Singh, later the Queen of Jaipur

- Padma Kanwar: Mother of Fateh Kanwar

- Pratap Singh :(The king of Jaipur)Sawai Maharaja of Jaipur; father of Jagat Singh

- Jagat Singh: King of Jaipur after the demise of his father Pratap Singh

- Jai Singh: Minor king under the regency of his mother Fateh Kanwar

- Chandrawati: Wife of slain Prince Jai Singh

- Maji Sahib Rathorni Ji: Mother of Jagat Singh

- Sireh Kanwar: Sister of Maharaja of Jodhpur married to Jagat Singh

- Anand Kanwar and Suraj Kanwar: Sisters of Jagat Singh; Anand

Kanwar married Bhim Singh of Jodhpur; Suraj Kanwar wedded with Man Singh of Jodhpur.

- Rupan Bai: A daavari, who later became Mukhtiar, during the regency of the queen Fateh Kanwar

- Juntharam: A Jain Sanghi trader; Minister

- Rawal Berisal: Rajput thikaanedaar; Minister

- Chandra Singh: Thakur of Duni

- Jayraj: Head of Gunijankhana

- Pandit Sheonarayan: Chief Minister

- Mohanram: Chief Nazir (Chief of Security)

- Mohan Singh: The minor prince of Nurwar

- Shyam Singh: Thakur of Bissau thikana

- David Octerlony: The British Resident

- Roper: The Political Agent

- Captain Low: The Political Agent

- N. Alvis: The Political Agent for Rajputana

- Blake: The British official

- Rana Bhim Singh: The King of Mewar

- Man Singh: Maharaja of Jodhpur

- Krishna Kumari: The Princess of Mewar

- Raskapoor: The concubine of Jagat Singh

'O Mother, auspicious be thy woodland,
thy snow-clad mountains and thy ever-running streams.
May the Earth pour out her milk for us,
a mother unto me her son."

-Prithvi Sukta,

Tāmagnivarnām tapasā jvalantīm vairocanīm'
karmaphalesu justām;
Durgām devīm śaranamaham prapadye sutar-
asi tarase namah.

(I take refuge in you Goddess Durga, fiery in her luster and radiant. You, the Supreme power, who manifest in diverse forms, in actions and their results. You steer us expertly across difficulties; I salute you. I bow before you.)

-Taittriya Aryanayk , 10.1.65

CHAPTER 1

1787 – Bikaner
The Bloody Throne

It was a pleasant, breezy evening of the first quarter of March, in 1787. Maharaja Gaj Singh was taking a stroll on the terrace. Chandra Kanwar, his beloved queen was walking along with him. He stopped for a while, leaned against the railing, and glanced around sprawling fields, and the high ramparts of the fort.

Maharaja's health had been plagued by prolonged illness for the past few months. His prolonged sickness had taken its toll on him, mentally and physically. But today, there was no visible sign of its presence, albeit he was completely bed ridden for over a fortnight.

The rosy golden rays of the setting sun made his face glow. His fine cotton *jama*, a flared skirt like garment, made his stout silhouette look a bit bulky. Well fitted on his chest, the *jama* was tied at the waist with twisted strings of pearls. The long sleeves of his *jama* were crushed in multi folds at his wrists. A silk stole of grey, with a golden border was draped over his shoulders.

Two large pearls in his earrings took swings, with every movement of his head. His *Bikaneri* turban, considered a mark of the Maharaja's dressing sense, was kept neatly on the side table beside his armchair. Blue coloured beetle wings were neatly encrusted on his turban ornament screwed on to the front of his headgear, on the sheath and the hilt of his sword.

Gaj Singh was so possessive of his sword that he never stepped out without it. Even for a brief moment, when he relaxed on the terrace, the sword would be firmly placed in his right hand's fist.

In the morning, the Maharaja had visited the temple of his family Goddess *Naganechi*, built on a high mound with white marble, red and lime, stone. In the sanctum, he stood before the silver idol with folded hands, and prayed fervently for some time.

The king and the queen spent half an hour on the terrace together, enjoying intimate moments in each other's company. He softly caressed his extended moustaches, in between, while attentively listening to his queen Chandra Kanwar. This half an hour brought lot of hope and joy for them, after a tumultuous fortnight.

✳

The sun was about to set. The vast stretching desert had turned golden orange under the crimson rays of the setting sun. Maharani Akhe Kanwar Devadi seated on an armchair had been staring in the horizon for very long. Her eyes were fixed on the setting sun. There were furrows on her forehead. Her green shawl slipped from her head. Kneeling against a velvet cushion, she continued to gaze far away. What was she brooding over? Her mind was engulfed into myriad thoughts.

Maharani Akhe Kanwar, the senior most queen was crying her heart out. She decided to go to *Gaj Mahal*, the residence of Chandra Kanwar, the Bhati princess of Jaisalmer. Since the day Gaj Singh had tied the knot with her, he had been living with her in *Gaj Mahal*, which was specially constructed for her well before the marriage.

Chandra Kanwar had drawn strict boundaries around the king. Entry to the *Gaj Mahal* was forbidden both to the royals and to commoners for securing privacy of the King and the Queen. For her, *Gaj Mahal* was her private and exclusive place.

Akhe Kanwar never tried to cross the barriers. Never ever encroached their privacy. 'Why must I go to somebody's house to see my own husband? Why I must seek permission of a queen so junior to me to meet my husband? Why blame someone else, when the Maharaja himself never expressed his desire to meet me? He never remembered me! Had he invited me, no one would have dared to stop me? Deeply aggrieved, she sobbed; her eyes were wet. Her wounded pride began to flow incessantly on her cheeks.

✳

Covered with a thin silken quilt, leaning against the velvet cushions of his bed, Gaj Singh stared blankly out of the window for some time. As he reminisced about his old glorious days, a faint smile perched on his face.

The bright morning, when Shah Alam the Mughal Emperor conferred an esteemed title – *Sri Raj Rajeshwar Maharajadhiraj Maharaja Shiromani* on him, in the presence of other kings and nobility in the royal court of Bikaner; was the day when he was allowed to mint his own coins, perhaps, the only king in the entire Rajputana to have this privilege.

Yet, Jodhpur, his permanent adversary, flashed through his mind over and over again. Rathores of Jodhpur had unleashed a wave of attacks on Bikaner, but he successfully pushed them back every time.

Engrossed in a spate of flashbacks, his hand spontaneously caressed his moustache, and his eyes brimmed with pride. Memories of the good times, surging like ocean waves, overwhelmed him with happiness, though shortly. Today, he sighed with despair, thinking about his current illness.

Rathores of Bikaner have been as rough as its terrain and as prickly as its patchy soil. For years, worn and torn by the Thar Desert, its fiery winds, shifting sand dunes extending miles and miles without an oasis in sight, Rathores were turned into hard rocks, not to be cracked easily. They became as hard as granite and as menacing as a cobra.

Immersed deeply into his past with his eyes fixed in the sky, Gaj Singh did not utter a single word for a long time. Finally, a moan was released from his lips.

Chandra Kanwar gave him a puzzling look. She was settled in a carved wooden chair beside his bed. He gestured with his hand, indicating that there was nothing serious. Chandra Kanwar got up from her seat, poured some water in a silver tumbler from an urn, and gave it to the king. Maharaja gulped down half of the glass, then rested his head against the pillow.

✳

Every day, Gaj Singh greeted the Sun with a hope to recover soon, but as the evening descended, his yearnings turned into gloom. His deteriorating health filled him with deepening sadness. He was aware that his days were numbered, but he hoped against hope that it would not happen soon. The eternal truth, nevertheless, is that no one has ever escaped the lethal paws of *Yama!*

Gaj Singh had married several times in his life. First, he tied the nuptial knot with the Rajawat princess of Mahar, who met an early death, after giving birth to a male child. Then he wedded with Akhe Kanwar Devadi, princess of Sirohi. The infant, born of the late queen, was brought up under her motherly care and she proved herself a worthy queen in every respect. After marrying Akhe Kanwar, many women entered in his life – Baghel Princess Rambha Devi, Panwar Princess of Jhadol, Chundawat Princess Swaroop Kanwar of Amber, Princess Fateh Kanwar of Kama, Princess Phool Kanwar of Jhalai and the Bhati Princess Chandra Kanwar of Jaisalmer. Besides the above, the palace had a large number of women - *pattars* (dancing women) and *paswans* (concubines) to keep his spirits high.

Gaj Singh, however, enjoyed the company of the young and exquisitely beautiful queen Chandra Kanwar the most, which was in her late thirties and exercised absolute control over her husband. As was the usual practice in royal houses, other queens were left to lead their solitary life in closed premises of the zenana.

Gaj Singh fathered sixty-one children, but only a few of them were his legitimate progeny. Raj Singh was the son of late Maharani Rajawat Ji. Sultan Singh was of Akhe Kanwar. Surat Singh and Ajab Singh were from Chandra Kanwar. Chattar Singh, Shyam Singh, Udai Singh, Jagat Singh, and Mohkam Singh were from other queens.

✳

During the later years of life, Gaj Singh was not happy with the way his sons were leading their lives. No spark! Living comfortably under the towering persona of their father, they had turned into placid waters of a lake.

One day, sitting in a gloomy mood, he ruefully told his wife, 'People are right when they say that nothing grows under the banyan tree. Just look at my sons, they have no energy, no desire, no plan to extend or strengthen the kingdom! My sons, spending their days in namby-pamby activities, are no different.'

The queen buoyed up the Maharaja, 'All the fingers in a hand are not of the same size. I do not know about others, but I know, for sure, my son Surat. He stands apart amongst his brothers. Given an opportunity, he, a sure fire, will make you proud. Trust me, Maharaj!'

Gaj Singh sensed what the queen really meant. However, at the same time, he was resolute not to deviate from the time-honoured custom and deprive his eldest son Raj Singh of his right to the throne. He did not know what to say when he looked into the anxious eyes of the queen. He deliberately changed the subject without giving an inkling of what was going on in his mind, to the queen. She judged the mood of her husband and decided to let go of the issue, as obviously, she did not want to annoy the king.

✳

It had been warm all day, but the night was just pleasant and peaceful. It was the last week of March. Summer had marked its beginning. Gaj Singh had a sound sleep. His wives and sons were relieved, as he seemed a bit better. But by the noon of the next day, he suffered a severe ache in his chest and his face turned pale. The courtiers rushed to summon the royal medicine practitioner, who administered some medicine that gave temporary relief to the Maharaja.

The hope of his recovery dwindled with every passing day. Finally, on 25th of March1787, Gaj Singh lost the battle of his life. The news of the Maharaja's death spread like a wild fire throughout the state. *Gaj Mahal,* the sprawling palace was engulfed in moans and groans.

After the last rites, it was decided by the elders that the eldest son, Raj Singh, who was number one in line must ascend the throne soon.

'4th April, the tenth day of the waxing moon fortnight, being the most auspicious time has been chosen for the coronation of the new king,' the royal priest pronounced.

As Akhe Kanwar initiated the preparations for the coronation of Raj Singh, cracks began to appear in the apparently smooth surface of the royal floors. Fangs of rivalry among the brothers had completely ruined the bonds of brotherhood by the time Gaj Singh breathed his last. The princes, twisting their moustaches, were ready to test their strength for the throne, but in the absence of enough solid support for their stand from the courtiers and nobles, they remained dormant. As per the tradition, the crown was bestowed on the eldest son and as such, Raj Singh was clearly the winner in the race for ascendancy.

Among his brothers, Raj was close to Sultan, his stepbrother and son of Akhe Kanwar. They knew what was brewing under the royal carpet of power corridors.

'Surat is completely a foolish man. He does not realise what he is doing,' Sultan said curtly, keeping his voice very low.

'I understand that. But he is our younger brother. I am not for power or crown. I am ready to step down, but I do know that mother and the elders cannot allow me to discard the tradition just like that,' Raj lowered his eyes as if he tried to conceal his pain.

'I am not a soft-hearted man like you. And, I can never ever trust him. His foolhardy way of working and greed had driven me to leave Bikaner long ago for my own good. He has taken some of the personality traits from his over ambitious mother,' Sultan replied gruffly.

'Come what may, we are brothers. The same blue blood flows in our veins. Every royal house has one or two problem children. I will manage him after the coronation. Don't forget, we have blood ties,' Raj tried to calm down Sultan.

For the last six years, Sultan had made Udaipur his permanent abode, as the Rana of Udaipur had granted him a large piece of land under the territory of Mewar. Nevertheless, Sultan kept visiting Bikaner off and on. This time, he prolonged his stay due to his father's ailment and eventual demise.

✳

Raj woke up with the dawn chorus. Aurora riding in her golden chariot had spread her rays to dispel darkness. Rousing life was all set to shift the stillness of night.

Raj enthusiastically completed the last minute preparations for his coronation. He took a quick look at himself in the mirror, which his wife, Chandan Kanwar was holding in her palms. Looking deep into his eyes, she smiled lovingly. He smiled back, but she noticed a streak of uneasiness in his dark brown eyes.

'You look perturbed. What is bothering you?' She questioned anxiously. Raj just waved his hand indicating nothing and walked towards the door. He headed straight for *Kanak Mahal*, the palace meant for ceremonies, adorned with colourful flags.

As Raj, dressed in an off-white and yellow *jama* for the occasion, headed for the coronation hall, smiling encouragingly, Sultan joined him. He was virtually Raj's shadow, vigilantly watching his security.

Surat, desperate to grab the throne, somehow or other was equally watchful. He was very hostile to the idea of Raj's ascension to the throne. He had nurtured a strong feeling for some time that, none other, but he alone, deserved the throne of Bikaner.

Sultan passed this information over to Raj, while they were heading for the coronation hall. Although Surat applied all his brain and consulted his loyalists to usurp the throne by any means, nobody supported him except Ajab Singh, his real brother.

Raj was disturbed, yet, he quietly absorbed this unpleasant news, albeit, he failed to hide his penitent expression. His happiness was marred by this revelation. With a curt nod, he turned away and headed for the room of *Maji Sahib*.

Would this throne break the bonding between brothers?

He wondered.

*

Akhe Kanwar had taken over the responsibility of the crowning ceremony. She could hear the heavy tread outside the door. While welcoming them, she noticed the grim faces of her sons, as they came to seek her blessings.

She spoke in a sweet voice. 'I know what is bothering you, Raj! The squabbling amongst your brothers because of the throne! Our birth determines our position in the family hierarchy. Time of birth decides what you will get in life, but our deeds determine our destiny and status in the society. We all come into this world with pre-drawn lines on our palms...' she paused, gazing directly at Raj, and then she continued, 'why do you worry about something that is not under your control? Each person treads on the path he chooses for himself. You follow your course, let others follow theirs.'

Raj heard her attentively, closed his eyes for a moment. Inhaling deeply, he touched her feet. She blessed him and prayed for his well-being.

The coronation began in a solemn environ. At the main door of the coronation hall, the priest welcomed them. Raj offered him salutations and touched his feet.

The priest showered his blessings, 'Long life, and fame to the crown prince of Bikaner! May you rule the State with sagacity and astuteness! May you imbue your people with happiness and contentment! Rathores are known for their rule based on the premise of courage, velour, dharma, and truth. May you make your judgments based on the same as well as empathy and honour, just like your fore fathers?'

Raj felt better after hearing the priest's blessings. He entered the hall and paid reverence to all other priests, who were assembled there. He was made to sit near the altar meant for the *havan*, a sacred fire, made for offerings. Priests settled themselves in a semi circle opposite him, with the head priest facing him from the centre. He dipped *kusha*, the sacred grass, in the bowl, sprinkled pious water collected from the river, all over his body, starting from his feet and moving up to his head.

Raj looked at the grass and asked, 'What is so special about this grass?'

The priest answered with a smile.

'This pious grass has many names – *kusha, kusa, durva,* and *dharbai.* It has been considered pious for use during rituals since ages. As per our puranic scriptures, Lord Vishnu in the form of a tortoise supported the Mandara Mountain on his hard shell, when the ocean was being churned in search of nectar. In this process, the hair on the shell came off and drifted towards the shore. When the gods were carrying the pot filled with nectar, a few drops dropped on the hair and turned it into grass, having healing properties. When it dries, it is used to make a seat such as the one you are sitting on…'

As he listened to the story, Raj's fingers slightly caressed the seat.

The rituals were complete. The head priest made Raj Singh sit on the throne, and then placed the crown firmly on his head. Sunrays piercing through latticed window brightened the glow of the crown.

Conches blared. Drums were beaten. Slogans were raised. People assembled in the court premises chanted in a chorus –

'Sri Sri Raj Rajeshwar Maharajadhiraj Maharaja Shiromani Sri Raj Singh Bahadur ki jai. Jai ho!'

'Long live Maharaja Raj SinghJi! Jai! Jai!'

✳

Raj came to Akhe Kanwar, bent down, and touched her feet. His six-year-old son Pratap observed his father wide-eyed and instantly followed suit. Akhe Kanwar hugged her grandchild tightly. Her heart was throbbing with joy.

'The crucial part of the ceremony is done, my son. Today, I am happy and so would have your father,' she said.

'I felt as if my father was right there all the time with me,' Raj confided.

Before she could answer, a young girl holding the hand of her mother entered the chamber. Fateh Kanwar was a nine-year-old beautiful girl, the only daughter of Raj's stepbrother Ajab Singh. Her gorgeous looks coupled with innocence captured the hearts of everyone around the place.

Akhe Kanwar extended her arms and she flew into her embrace.

'*Dadisa*, how do I look in this dress? *Masa* had it stitched specially for me.' *Maji Sahib* looked at her from head to toe.

'You are my little doll. My *gulabo* (pale red faced)! Pink *chunar*, pink *lehenga*, and pink *mojris* (footwear).'

So overwhelmed was *Maji Sahib* that she could not hold her tears of joy for long. She loved the innocent Fateh deeply. There was a strong bond between *Maji Sahib* and her granddaughter. Fateh enjoyed listening to tales from her, when her siblings spent time in playing games.

✳

On the next day of the coronation ceremony, began the inevitable battle, a covert contest, for the throne. Loyalties were divided among brothers. They chose to plunge into this battle of power without having any inkling of game-winning nuances, with Surat in the lead. His sole ambition to rule over Bikaner was fuelled by his coterie. But his dreams could be fulfilled only by shrewd mind and crafty scheming. He knew it well because he was fourth in the line of succession. He was not prepared to live at the mercy of the new king.

The brothers were distraught at the lust of Surat for the throne. They talked in a hush-hush manner that Bikaner was no more a safe haven for any of them. That Surat cared for none but himself; that he would not live peacefully, nor he would allow Raj to rule for a longer period. That court and courtiers were taking advantage of the internal conflict, which had turned Bikaner into a breeding ground for greed, lust, and evil.

One day, Ajab Singh, the real younger brother of Surat, reasoned with him.

'Brother, why are you nurturing a wild dream? Had God chosen you to rule over Bikaner, you would have been the eldest son and an heir to the throne? I request you to live peacefully. When we are unable to yield our greed, we become a slave of our own desires and never hesitate to use evil means to usurp them.'

Surat dismissed his plea. 'Please do not rake up this issue any more. You may do whatever you like. Let me do what I think is right for me.' Surat warned him and headed straight to *Gaj Mahal* with heavy footsteps.

For Surat, it was the end that matters most not the means. He had set his heart on Kendramani fort, citadel of Bikaner.

✳

Kendramani, a square-shaped walled fort, was one of the best military garrisons in those days. It was a repository of artistic excellence, comprising more than twenty-five different structures. The exteriors and the interiors of the fort premises displayed scenic beauty. The structured and artistic hanging balconies, long corridors based on rows of elaborately carved brackets were exquisite features of the fort palaces. These palaces were so designed that every part fulfilled its function. The   rooms were devised for seclusion, its terraces for the cool air or opening, its corridors for convenience, each compartment, court, hall, and passages had its own use, and were introduced to suit   the requirements of the kings and queens. Pavilions inside the fort had splendid stone carvings. It was encircled with a forty-foot-high boundary wall, and had a thirty-foot-deep gorge around it for protection. Almost every ruler who lived in this fort added a new composition with his unique style.

As the cool breeze blew from the west, Surat stopped for a while on the steps of *Gaj Mahal*, and had a full look at the unmatched fort.

'For how many years, this fort has been standing like this, unmoved by anything, big or small?' He wondered! 'Fifty years! No. For sure, not less than hundred years! Perhaps more than a century, for sure!'

With a deep sigh, he paced fast. The heavy doors of the *Gaj Mahal* creaked open and a shaft of light fell on him. Chandra Kanwar was standing in the doorway.

Later, while leaning against a velvet-cushioned headrest of a lounge chair, he shot a question.

'*Masa*, do you have any idea when this fort was built?'

'Yes! For more than a century, this fort has been standing stately, a dream fort of your great grandfather, late Maharaj Rai SinghJi. There was a wonderful architect in his court, Ah! I can't remember his name,' Chandra Kanwar struck her forehead with her fingers, a pause.

Then, she beamed, 'Yes! Yes! I got him. Karan Chand, Yes! Karan Chand, your father once mentioned. What made you to ask this question?

'Nothing serious. Just out of curiosity.'

'You…You are the only one who deserves this fort. You are the most worthy amongst all your brothers. Yes, I know, Raj got the throne only because of his seniority. So what, if you are not the eldest son? We all know the tradition that a fourth son in the line of succession cannot ascend the throne. All your brothers are weak and timid and have already succumbed to their fate; they must leave Bikaner. Sooner the better,' she uttered in an angry voice. Surat stared in her eyes.

Chandra Kanwar kept quizzing him. 'How long will you wait? Today you are twenty-four years, young, full of life. Full of vigour. You have a long way to go. Your father vacated the throne after more than five decades. Raj Singh is around forty-five. By the time he dies, you will be as old as Raj and will have no vigour to rule.' She hissed.

'*Masa!* How can I be the king? Raj *bhaisa*'s sons will be the heirs,' Surat shot back.

'You are not a small child, my son! Throne and victory belong to a capable and courageous one. The time is running fast. Do you understand, what I mean?'

Surat was taken aback, 'What do you mean, *Masa*? What can I do? He did not come in my way on his own. He has been crowned only because of our own traditions, the customary practices, all of you keep yapping about. The crown is by custom placed on the head of the eldest son. Younger brothers must lead their entire life in his servitude. Most importantly, he is so affectionate that in his presence, all my hostility melts like butter. If I ask him for the throne, I know he will willingly leave that space for my sake. And! No..., no..., I...just cannot kill him for the sake of the throne.'

'Then get yourself killed,' she replied sarcastically.

'What?' shrieked a stunned Surat.

'Yes, I have the answer of your what! Do not scream like a fool! You are not that young that you cannot see your future. You have no other option. Either you migrate to a nearby state and take refuge there or just remain content with a small piece of land in a faraway corner of Bikaner to spend the rest of your days in a languid life, indeed.'

'But...But...What do I do?'

'You must know better. You better find out yourself. You, the worthy heir of Bikaner. Just get him.' She hissed with annoyance.

Horrified Surat stared blankly. His mother stoked his hair.

'You go to your bed now. Have some rest and allow your mind and body to relax. We will talk about it tomorrow in the morning. It is quite late now, go and have a good sleep.'

✳

Surat helped his mother in getting out of the door, escorted her to her room and returned to his chamber, but he failed to get even some catnap. His eyes were apparently closed, but his mind was racing violently, juggling with so many thoughts. When a third quarter of the night was about to conclude, he was lost in deep slumber.

Chandra Kanwar was not at peace as well. She was mired in turbulent thoughts. She had always been the favoured queen of Gaj Singh and was very close to his heart. Although, he loved her company, but he never acceded to her unreasonable demands. She was sure that Raj after crossing more than forty years of his life was left with hardly any drive to rule the State and Gaj Singh was the last man to deprive his son of his right.

'Raj has no vision, no energy left in his wrinkled body, and on the other hand there is my son, full of youth and vigour and strong determination to take the State to greater heights. Under the regime of Raj Singh, Bikaner was destined to doom and gloom.' She was sure.

Chandra Kanwar could see the frustration of her son. She knew that her naive son was not capable enough to make it all by himself. She decided to make his dream a reality. After making some careful calculations, Chandra Kanwar finally devised a plan.

Next day, she called Surat, 'We must host a dinner in honour of the newly crowned king. How could you forget this simple courtesy?'

Surat stared hard inquisitively into his mother's eyes, tried to read her mind. Chandra Kanwar looked back intently.

In the innermost chambers of Kendramani fort, a conspiracy was underway to trap the ignorant prey by the mother and son duo.

✳

In the following weeks, the courtiers noticed some strange happenings in the court. Surat, the only prince, who vehemently refused to take part in the royal court proceedings for years, was now actively engaged in official matters especially the ones that involved the king alone. Surat had been getting extra friendly with the king. He was seen in the company of the king during most of the daytime. This aroused suspicion among the courtiers, but Raj did not visualise anything wrong or unusual and happily encouraged his participation.

A month had passed peacefully. There is a saying that an eerie silence precedes a tempest, the lull before the storm.

It was the morning of 25th of April. Twenty-nine days had passed after the death of Gaj Singh.

Surat entered the chamber of the king.

'Maharaj, may I have the honour to have dinner with you tonight. I hope you will not mind having food with your younger brother.'

Raj Singh accepted his invitation with a pleasant smile. Diwan Bakhtawar Singh Mohta rushed to meet Swaroop Singh Mohta, the senior minister. Somehow, he sensed something amiss in his invitation.

'Maharaj! Who else do you think must accompany you? I will make arrangements accordingly,' asked Swaroop Singh.

'Has Surat invited others officially?' asked the king, in a casual manner.

'In my knowledge, nobody has been invited,' answered the diwan.

'Then there is no need for formal arrangements. I think he has invited me in a personal capacity. As a family man.'

Maji Sahib or Maharani *Sahib* must be accompanying you.'

'I will ask, if any one of them would like to come along?'

Diwan could not divulge his doubt that was agitating his mind. In fact, he had no substantial evidence to sustain his suspicion.

Later, in the evening, just before proceeding for the dinner, Raj went to Akhe Kanwar.

'*Masa!* I know your answer; still I will ask you to join me for the dinner.'

'You know my son; I took an oath that I would never ever step on the threshold of *GajMahal.* I cannot forget the day, I went there to see your ailing father and the humiliation I faced when I was not even allowed to enter his room, leave alone meeting him. How can I go for a dinner there today! You may go!'

She, however, advised him to tread with extreme caution, albeit she was not happy about the whole thing.

Raj brushed aside all her fears and suspicions. As *Maji Sahib* and Maharani refused to accompany him, he went all alone happily.

✳

Raj crossed the threshold of *Gaj Mahal.* The sky had turned scarlet with the rays of the setting sun. Surat warmly received him at the main entrance and both of them made their way to the dining place. This was a small dining hall, not meant for large gatherings, but enough to accommodate six to seven persons. Chandra Kanwar had ensured that the dining room was properly done up.

She joined her sons in the dining room; Raj got up from his chair to touch her feet. As soon as he bent down, she gestured him half way not to do so.

'Your place is not at my feet, my most precious son. You live in my heart and soul.'

She told them about the dinner menu, especially the *kheer,* a sweet dish made of milk and rice, the delicacy she was known for.

'*Masa,* I am glad that you have prepared my favourite *kheer!* I always loved to have the *kheer* made by you,' said Raj boisterously, with child like excitement. His heart was filled with pride thinking that his ascendancy did not destroy the fabric of familial love and bonding, he always cherished. Now on, he could close the lid on all kinds of suspicions and rumours.

Chandra Kanwar herself was supervising the cooking. She tasted some of the dishes and found them perfect. She gave final instructions to the cook. 'Make sure that Maharaja Raj Singh is served first and that the largest portions are given to him.'

Raj Singh was first offered *lal maas,*mutton cooked with hot red chillies and fried in butter; the strong flavours and slightly chewy texture stimulated his taste buds. This was followed by white mutton cooked in milk, cashew, and curd that was served with the rice and *chutney*, a coarse paste of garlic, raw mangoes and berries.

Raj had quite an appetite by the liberal standards of the well-fed princes. Chandra Kanwar watched Raj tear into the tender lamb meat and reach out for more and more. Then to finish, he was offered his favourite sweet dish, specially prepared for the final moment, laced with raisins, cashew and…a paste of kusumba, poisonous wild flowers, enough to kill a person.

'*Masa*! I will come back even from heaven to have this *kheer.*'

'Stop talking nonsense, My son! You will not die before me. May goddess give you a long life and you have innumerable opportunities to eat the *kheer*!'

Raj had relished the final meal of his life, so had Chandra Kanwar – the execution of her wicked plan.

Surat with his hands folded behind the half-dead cadaver of Raj, looked lethal. As he supported Raj, to help him stand up on his legs, Raj opened his eyes, and stared directly into the eyes of Surat. Surat turned his head away and began to drag Raj out of the room.

Raj gazed at Chandra Kanwar for the last time with a strong feeling of contempt and anger, when he was being dragged like a sack, unable to move or speak, with life force parting its way slowly. In this agonising moment, he was cursing himself for not paying heed to his advisors, but now it was of no use. He was still alive, but hardly. His moment of pride, a few minutes before was lying shattered in shreds. A tear dropped from his eye. With every croaky breath, he was moving swiftly towards darkness, death. His father's words of wisdom were ringing like a whirlpool in his ears,

'Sinister designs are always served with sugar coated meal of words.'

Raj was callously placed on the back seat of the carriage parked outside, and the driver was instructed to head for *Anup Mahal*. His body twitched and shivered. Surat went back inside with a smirk on his face.

✳

Raj Singh returned to his chamber in a semi-conscious state. Two guards took him inside. His queen noticed something unusual. His mouth was a bit open. His torso was heaving. He tried to breathe in but failed. He made a last effort to breathe harder, but ended making a tattered sound.

The queen was in panic. She touched his forehead, and then put her ear close to his chest to hear the heart beat.

Sensing something very serious, she frantically called her maids. One of the maids rushed to *Maji Sahib*. Kunjaram *vaidya*, the medical practitioner was immediately summoned.

There was a deep turmoil inside him. For a moment, he was still, and lay with his eyes closed. Both hands clenched tightly, as if he was desperately trying to control himself.

Kunjaram observed the king, a couple of moments passed before he got up and turned away from the corpse of Maharaja on the bed.

He declared with a sombre face, 'There is no sign of life.'

The room was filled with shrieks and sobs.

The queen hysterically garbled, 'No! It cannot be possible!Ah! I must have accompanied him!' She fainted and fell on the corpse of her husband.

The king was found dead in mysterious circumstances. The sudden death of Raj Singh aroused suspicion; the people talked in a hush-hush tone. Everyone guessed what might have happened, but nobody dared to speak openly.

Exactly on the thirtieth day after the demise of Gaj Singh, Bikaner plunged into mourning, once again.

After the funeral rites, Pratap, the six-year-old son of Raj was placed on the throne under the regency of his uncle Surat Singh, who by now had strengthened his foothold in the court. Tradition was followed again. Coronation of the eldest son of the departed soul was done hurriedly, this time, at the behest of Surat.

✳

Sultan was shocked. He rushed back to Bikaner to confront Surat. All along his way, he was restless. It could not be a coincidence that, Raj passed away suddenly, without any visible sign of serious illness. Surat was unapproachable.

Sultan could speak with him only on the last day of his stay in Bikaner.

'Can you give me the guarantee that the child will not be harmed in any manner? You are his regent and this must be your prime duty.' Sultan asked Surat in a stern voice.

'Yes *Bhaisa*! I will do,' crisp was the reply.

'Are you prepared to take an oath of loyalty and serve the child king and Bikaner to the last day of your life?' With his piercing dark eyes, Sultan shot another question.

He then had a quick look at the innocent child, who had been thrown into the murky game of power by the irony of fate. The poor child had no inkling that the crown placed on his small head was drenched in the blood of his own father, deplored Sultan.

'I take an oath, I will be very careful. I know you might have heard some rumours. But, believe me; I am as ignorant as you are.' With a nonchalant reply, Surat turned his head.

Sultan watched him with squinted eyes. He could read what was written all over his face. He remained silent, as there was no point of arguing without any solid evidence of his direct involvement.

'Be careful Surat, your ignorance will cost you heavily. I will not spare you for your ignorance. From now onward, you must be vigilant. This is your prime duty to protect the child. If you fail, then be ready to face the music,' thundered Sultan.

'I will lay down my life for the child king,' Surat answered with a matching voice.

'I know, you have a streak of rebellion, but you are not a devil,' Sultan guffawed and patted him on his shoulder.

Although Sultan Singh did not believe him, still he thought that Surat would spare the child. 'Surat has got all the powers in his capacity of a regent for which he always aspired; why would he harm the child in the prevailing situation?' Sultan assured himself. But he did not realise that a small cloud cannot satiate the thirst of a vast desert.

Surat needed the abundance of the sky to fly high.

He was a hawk.

✳

Before leaving forUdaipur, Sultan went to say good-bye to his mother. During the conversation, Sultan was caught in a surge of emotions.

'Sometimes, I fail to comprehend the designs of Surat. I always find in his eyes, something that I cannot explain. I like to trust him, but I always fail to have faith in him *Masa*. Sometimes…sometimes…I am unable to say exactly…what is it?'

'Do not be suspicious of your younger brother. Not all the fingers are of the same size. Each finger is different and each has its own role. The middle finger is used to put a mark of reverence on the forehead.

The index finger is used to indicate, to write or to put a morsel in the mouth. All the fingers become a fist in case of a danger.' Akhe Kanwar tried to pacify the agitated mood of her son.

'My father inculcated the values of a true warrior in all of us. I remember Father used to say that the warriors are generally stabbed in the back. Who can dare attack their chest? I strongly feel Raj has died that way, stabbed in the back, and that too by his own blood.'

Akhe Kanwar nodded. 'I must have not allowed him to go for a dinner at *Gaj Mahal*. Had I put my foot down, he would have never disobeyed me.' Unable to read the writings on the wall, she was blaming herself and grieving inconsolably.

Sultan continued, 'Raj was the only one among all of us, who had nurtured a strong emotional bonding with Surat. He always had a soft corner for him, though he was warned many times. He took him as his real brother, not a step one. And see, how he was butchered by him. Trust is belied so blatantly,' moaned Sultan.

'My son, do not torture yourself anymore. Raj got what he was destined for. He ignored his most important duty as a king. His first duty was to protect himself and the state. He ignored the word of caution, about Surat and...' she paused, and then continued, 'if a king cannot protect himself, how can he safeguard his kingdom? Surat is a fighter, fighting at all times to get what he desires and Raj was not fit to rule the state. He was comfortable in a cosy corner of his home.'

'*Masa*! Would you please elaborate?'

'For a king, his duty and responsibility come first. His family, relations, brothers or sisters, sons and daughters, wives and parents, all come later. Similarly, actions of a rebellious person are always driven by his own self-interests. For him, he and his desires come first. The difference between the two is, for a king , the primary driving force must be selflessness but for a rebel selfishness.'

'In that case, how can we protect the child, the new child king of Bikaner? We have to be extra careful. Though I like to believe that Surat may not harm the child, but it is difficult to trust him. His mind is like muddy water. You can't see through it when still,' Sultan responded pensively.

'Yes, my son, our mind is like this vast desert. When it is calm, it bestows serenity. It can destroy life when agitated. I pray to the almighty, Surat goes the right way.'

Surat proved them wrong.

✳

The little angel could not melt the heart of Surat. In a hurry to eliminate the child king Pratap, he was always on some or the other scheme. But Akhe Kanwar's constant vigil frustrated his evil designs. He realised that this time, it would not be easy to get rid of the child. One day, Surat blurted out in utter desperation in front of his mother.

'*Masa*, I am getting restless. Soon, the days will turn into months and months into years. The minor will turn into a major and I will be reduced to no entity,' lamented Surat.

'Don't lose your heart. Hardly three months have passed since Raj's demise. People will never accept you as the king of Bikaner, if you kill the child king. You must tread carefully. This is not the right time to kill the new king.' She tried to instill some sense in him.

'He is not a child. To me, he is a monster. Last night, I had a terrible dream, *Masa*! I saw him seated on the throne as a huge monster and he pushed me away from the staircase to land on the last step. No *Masa*, I will not allow him to torture me like this.' Surat shouted at her.

She was taken aback at his bluntness. Chandra Kanwar was left with no option but to surrender. 'There was no way to take a U-turn. All the doors behind were closed. I had to swim with the current. I am the one , who watered this poisonous ivy to grow beyond leaps and bound,' she repented. The very next moment, her basic instincts over powered her.

'You go ahead in a systematic way. First, garner enough support of the nobles and courtiers. Second, arrange the wedding of your stepsister, who, I believe, has decided not to marry soon. I know it will be a bit difficult, but this has to be done on priority. Day and night, she is with the child like a shadow. Once she gets married, Akhe Kanwar alone won't be able to keep a tight vigil on the child. Then, it will be easier for you to fulfil your desire.' Chandra Kanwar's words were like a soothing balm on his turbulent nerves.

Surat began to bestow all kinds of gifts on the courtiers and nobles – gold and money. Still he was not sure whether they would support him, if he killed the child. A strong desire to grab the throne had turned Surat into a hard stone, devoid of emotions, but others were not like him.

Surat followed the same strategy to bump off the child that he applied to get rid of Raj Singh – first, be in the good books of Akhe Kanwar and win over her confidence. As per his well thought out plan, Surat began to persuade and pressurise *Maji Sahib* Devadi Ji to see that his stepsister was married off.

One day, sensing *Maji Sahib* in a receptive mood, he raised the issue of her wedding. '*Masa*! How long we can delay her wedding? Her in-laws have been pressurising to finalise the date.'

'But she does not want to marry soon. At least, not for some time. You know, how attached she is to his nephew Pratap?' said *Maji Sahib*.

'I understand *Masa*! But she cannot lead a spinster's life for the sake of Pratap. We are all here to look after the child. He is my nephew too. I only made him king. I am not a devil *Masa*! Trust me!'

After a lot of pestering and persuasion by Surat, she finally gave in and consented to the marriage of the princess. Within no time, her wedding was arranged. The day she left Bikaner, Surat laughed to his glory. He had crossed the biggest hurdle and was well set to chase his evil game.

✳

The fateful day was 9th October 1787. Since afternoon, Pratap was at *Gaj Mahal*. He was well looked after. Chandra Kanwar was personally paying attention to him. She cradled him in her arms, when he entered her room. Her eyes were radiating affection.

'Come, my child. Your *Dadisa* has fever today. Therefore, I asked her to send you to this place. This home is also yours,' then she called her house servant, 'Mundarika bai, take care of the little king. He is my special guest. Surat is also out of town. Therefore, he is my responsibility. Be careful.'

Surat had already left Bikaner in the early hours that day. He made a tour plan deliberately to make the courtiers and people around believe that he was away from Bikaner and would return after a couple of days.

The day was like any other day. In the afternoon, the child was taken to the same dining hall, where his father was served his last dinner.

Chandra Kanwar offered him milk, and then strangulated him on the same table, on which his father had had his last dinner.

The sun was about to set. Chandra Kanwar left her residence for making an offering at a temple, about twenty miles from the town, leaving the child king, dead, with instructions to the maids, 'Pratap is sleeping in my room. Let him sleep. Give him whatever he needs when he is awake. Take good care of him. I may return late in the evening.'

In the evening, when a maid entered the dining hall, she was thunder struck to see the lifeless body of the child king. She panicked. 'How did the child come to the dining hall? He should have been in the room of *Maji Sahib*! That is what she told me. Did he get up and come here on his own?' She ran outside shouting at the top of her voice, struggling to breathe. The frightened maid sounded the alarm bell, at *Gaj Mahal*.

Servants picked up the child in their arms and rushed to *Maji Sahib*. Weeping and wailing, the widow of Raj Singh felt as if she was thrown into a dark well. She had lost her husband and son as well within a short time.

She stepped forward and asked other women present there in a coarse voice, 'Why are you here? Can any of you bring my son back? Can any of you find out who killed my child and punish his killers? My husband, my son, both are dead. Why? Were they sick? Did they pass away in the battlefield? Can any of you answer me? Please leave me alone.'

Maji Sahib rushed towards her and held her dishevelled daughter-in-law, solitary in her grief, her arms around her wiping tears gently from her eyes. She herself was shivering.

Her constant crying engulfed the entire town into grief. It was a relentless, desolate howl. Word of the child's death shot through the city like a lightning flash.

A senseless killing of an innocent child plunged Bikaner into shock and sorrow. People began to gather in the court premises in sullen silence. Rows and rows of stone-faced people, elders and courtiers, unable to accept the fact, gathered there to express their resentment. Shell-shocked numbness bordering on disbelief descended on Bikaner. There were tears, expressions of genuine grief. Pain stricken mourners.

A terrible silence prevailed, as the sheer enormity of the tragedy gradually dawned. The impossibility became a terrible truth. Moreover, the reality of sudden, cold-blooded, death, unleashed violent shock waves. An enormous crowd collected outside the palace.

No definite news, only speculation and garbled accounts of the killing were present. 'Dreadful!' One of the courtiers said, folding his arms as if he was trying to take a grip of himself.

✳

Sultan burst like a volcano. He could never ever think that Surat could stoop so low that he would not spare even the innocent child, his own nephew. Something was dead in him and what was dead was his trust! His hope! His urge to live anymore! It was a great betrayal! This time Surat had stabbed his back! His world fell like a pack of cards.

His heart could not bear the pain, when the queen told him how she received her child as a crumpled, tender petal in the arms of a maid, cloaked in her shawl.

Surat had a strong alibi for his absence in Bikaner, but Sultan did not believe him. He invaded Bikaner in order to punish Surat for his unpardonable sin. In his endeavour, Ajab Singh openly supported Sultan. Ajab hated his real brother for killing his own innocent nephew.

Sultan and Ajab Singh assembled revolting Bhati warriors. United, they launched an attack against Surat, who however, succeeded in crushing the rebellion; they could not withstand the onslaught by the organised forces of Surat. About three thousand warriors were killed and the remaining ones retreated. Some of them surrendered, while many others took refuge in neighbouring states.

Sultan was not ready to give up so easily; again, he organised a bigger army and camped at the borders of Bikaner. He was determined to destroy Surat.

✳

Surat, too, was not very strong militarily. He had already lost many of his warriors. His revenues were depleting. Most of his nobles had joined hands with Sultan. He knew that Sultan would destroy him. He would have no choice other than to flee. Suddenly, he saw a silver lining in the dark clouds in the form of Akhe Kanwar.

He rushed to her and pleaded, 'If brothers will stand against each other and kill one another, how would the family survive? It will be a blot on the name of Rathores.'

Akhe Kanwar drew in a sharp breath. Anger and grief clouded her mind. Her piercing eyes forced Surat to cast down his eyes.

'Surat, you were behind the spree of killings of your brother and nephew, and today you are accusing Sultan and Ajab for their conduct,' she thundered.

Surat was quiet. His fists clenched tight for a while, as he had a fair idea of her reaction under the given circumstances. Seeing her hard posture, he was in the next moment at her feet, begging for mercy.

'Do you realise, Surat, one has to pay for his each deed, good or bad. Do you think you can escape from the cycle of your karmas?'

'I beg of you, you kill me! Punish me! I was blinded by my strong desire to capture the throne. Pardon me! But I tell you the truth that I have not committed this crime. Believe me; I was not present in Bikaner on the fateful day. You may ask my mother! If you do not believe her, the palace people can tell you that I was not there. How could you believe that I would kill my own nephew! I know that my brothers believe that I am mad after power, but that is not correct. I promise you, from now onwards I will follow the path, you tell me to tread on.'

She remained silent, staring angrily at him, tears rolling down her face. 'Of course, now you will follow my way of life! Why not? Your road is cleared of all obstacles,' she blasted bitterly.

Surat entreated repeatedly. Akhe Kanwar was a simple soul and she loved all her sons. She herself was distraught by the behaviour of all the sons of Gaj Singh. Unable to bear pain and agony anymore, she wrote a long letter to Sultan. This madness must end , she thought.

'My Dear Sultan,

I request you my child, please stop this bloodshed. And return to your home. Could this bloodshed revive those who have departed this land? Our prime duty is to save those who are left behind. The endless cycle of vendetta must end. Let Surat keep his desired object, the crown of Bikaner. You trust me; he will be crushed under the burden of his own deeds. He will not be spared by the divine justice. I know you have suffered a lot. We all have suffered in this headless chase of the throne. Revenge must not be the end game of our life. Do not allow it to destroy the present. No amount of bloodshed may ever return Raj or my little grandchild. Forgiving is the only way. From now on, you must work to build up a new Bikaner, where the rule of law and justice prevails. I earnestly hope you will not disappoint me.

My blessings are with you.

Your Mother.

Akhe Kanwar Devadi.'

The letter was read aloud in the presence of Sultan, Ajab Singh and other allies. Sultan always put his mother on a high pedestal. He could not ignore her words. Though he knew that Surat had used his mother as a pawn in his game of power, but he left his battle half way.

'Even after shedding his skin many times, Surat will always be a snake. And *Masa*, You will also be true to yourself, always kind, all the time trusting others, never ever doubting their intentions. But in no way, I will add more to your misery. Anyway, Surat, I know that you have stooped very low in order to win my mother's sympathy,' he thought. He put down his arms. War ceased. Sultan headed back to Udaipur the same night, not to return to Bikaner ever.

❋

Ajab Singh, left with no other option, returned to Bikaner, but he always felt threatened. Both the brothers, Surat and Ajab were not on talking terms. He had apprehension that Surat, under no circumstances would leave him alive. He had seen the true colours of his real brother. Forgive and forget were alien words for Surat, murky malice flew in his veins!

Winter had set in. The full moon of the tender night appeared on the sky. Trillions of twinkling stars, studded all over the sky had joined the moon in its shine, with their pale silvery light on sand dunes. In the centre of the sky, seven *saptrishi* stars appeared brightly and in the northern sphere, the polar star was shining all alone. Combined with their glow, Kendramani fort, amid a sandy stretch, was lit in the purity of moonlight.

Ajab felt like holding the bright moon in his hands. It was a wonderful sight. It seemed almost within his reach, so large and bright, slightly pink with a pale yellow gleam, as if one could just touch it by raising one's arms. He kept staring at the moon, completely lost in his thoughts. His wife, Padma Kanwar came behind, tiptoed and put her hand softly on his shoulder.

'What keeps you so engrossed?'

'I waited for you. Can you see that polar star? There...' he indicated, by stretching his hand in that direction, 'I am like that star, all alone. I ought to have accompanied Sultan *bhaisa*. Anyway, I will join him now, or I will go to some unknown land, but not live here anymore. Now you have to manage here all by yourself. I am not safe here. Before dawn, I will leave this place and move to a safer hideout.'

'Let me join you. Why do you leave us behind?'

'For the time being, you must stay here. You should live here tight-lipped, like a dumb person but not deaf. I do not trust Surat. He can be very wily when he wants to. So be very careful. He cares for none; he is a lethal combination of cruelty and cunningness. It will be good for us, if I leave this place. Sooner the better!'

'Are you scared of your own real brother?' questioned his wife.

'If you like to know the truth, I will say, yes! He will not harm me immediately. He paused, then blurted, 'after killing the child of Raj Singh, he will finish everyone, who he thinks, may come in his way of usurping the power. Right now, the wind is blowing against him. But at the first opportunity, he will eliminate me, my existence; because he knows that, I know the truth. I saw him sneaking into *Gaj Mahal* on the fateful day in the noon. He too had noticed me. I could see silent threat and streak of revenge in his eyes.'

His wife began sobbing, feeling helpless and unable to deal with the thought of living all by herself. She spontaneously hugged her husband, who had come closer to his wife and rested her head on his shoulder with her eyes closed tight. Both kept standing in each other's tight embrace. Tears were rolling down on their cheeks like a stream. She felt as if sand was slipping from her fingers. Ajab, engulfed into emotional turmoil, did not know how to console his wife. It was too much and too soon for her.

As they stood there in each other's embrace, Ajab felt as if someone touched his knee. They were startled to notice Fateh staring at them innocently.

'*Masa, Bapusa,* what are you doing here? Why are you crying?' Her mother crouched over her and began to sob uncontrollably, while Ajab's hand shivered over his daughter's head.

They both hugged their daughter. Ajab kissed her forehead and indicated his wife to take her inside. This was the darkest night of his life, he thought. He spent some more time there strolling then turned towards his room.

Ajab Singh left Bikaner in the garb of the dark night, leaving behind his wife and nine-year-old daughter, Fateh Kanwar.

Sultan had left Bikaner never to come back and Ajab, who hoped to return soon to take his family along, could never put his feet on his soil again.

CHAPTER 2

1800
The Dream Wedding

On a chilly January morning, in 1800, mist surrounded the Kendramani fort. People had begun to take up daily errands slowly. The sun's warmth had still not made its presence felt. Rising smoke from the courtyards indicated that the hearths were put on.

Surat Singh had completed his morning ritual. To manifest atonement of his sins, he visited without fail the shrine of his family goddess, daily. In the last three years, he had broken his regime only twice or thrice, when he was unwell. Her mother's sudden demise made him realise the futility of his past deeds. His mother was not there to enjoy the authority and pleasures of being Rajmata, which she always wished for. Within a month after his ascendance to the throne, Chandra Kanwar had died.

Once he captured the throne, established his supremacy in the royal corridors of Bikaner and nearby lesser kingdoms; his prime goal was to keep the borders of Bikaner secure.

Surat was a shrewd ruler. He was always apprehensive that Jaipur might attack Bikaner at any time because of Ajab Singh, who had taken refuge in Jaipur, but it was other way round as Ajab Singh apprehended a threat to his life from Surat.

In a bid to foster closer ties with a strong kingdom like Jaipur, Surat sent out a proposal for the marriage of Fateh with Jagat Singh, the crown prince of Jaipur.It was a well-calculated move to kill two birds with one arrow, win over his estranged brother and to eliminate forever the possibility of attack by Jaipur.

Over a period, Ajab Singh had developed a deep bonding with the Kachwahas of Jaipur. Surat made umpteen efforts to contact his brother, but Azab Singh never responded, as he was sceptical of his intentions. But at the same time, it was a fact that in the absence of Azab Singh, Surat brought up his daughter Fateh like his own child. Gradually, she became the apple of his eyes.

Chandra Kanwar tried her best to build a bridge between two of her warring sons, but Azab was not amenable to her advice. He did not visit Bikaner even when his mother died.

✻

The chief minister of Bikaner with two elders appeared in the court of Jaipur.

They were welcomed warmly in the royal court. Sawai Maharaja Pratap Singh desired to know the motive of his visit. After a display of obeisance, the minister said humbly,

'*Ghanikhamma*! Sawai Maharaj *ki jai ho*!

We are here with a message of *Sri Raj Rajeshwar Maharajadhiraj Maharaaj Shiromani* Surat Singh Ji. He is keen to strengthen cordial ties with the powerful state of Jaipur. Fateh Kanwar, the princess of Bikaner has attained the age of maturity. She is the most beautiful maiden among all the princess of our time. We are, therefore, here with the wedding proposal on behalf of our Maharaja.'

The king heard him patiently and smiled.

The minister added further, 'May I assure you Maharaj, Sri Jagat SinghJi, the crown prince of Jaipur and our princess will be a perfect match.'

'I am pleased to hear you. Pay my regards to the Maharaja of Bikaner. I never knew that he has a daughter of marriageable age.'

'The princess is the daughter of Azab Singh Ji, his younger brother. But our Maharaj brought her up like his own daughter. We will be happy if you can accept the coconut – a *shagun*, symbolising a formal affirmation to the proposal.'

'I know Azab Singh Ji. He is a man with a golden heart. He is with me for the last couple of years. Right now, he is not in the town. He is on a pilgrimage. Please be our guest. We will meet you tomorrow,' replied Pratap Singh. He directed the head of hospitality division, Thakur Devi Singh to look after the guests.

On the same day, in the afternoon session of the court, all the close and elderly knights assembled at the *durbar* hall to figure out the relevance of this matrimonial proposal. During those days, marriage was one of the primary means of translating competitive and conflicting neighbouring states into a political alliance, based on relationship. Such alliances would benefit the royalties for expansion of their social networking and maintaining political and economic equations.

There was an air of eagerness. Pratap Singh paid attention to each advice, apprehension and information. Apparently, the neighbouring state had extended a goodwill gesture by sending a marriage proposal. Kachwahas of Jaipur, too, needed such a strong and dependable ally in the times of political turmoil, the advent of the Marathas and the British.

The next morning, Pratap Singh told the ministers of Bikaner boisterously, 'We will be glad to have the princess of Bikaner, as our daughter-in-law. Please convey my regards to Maharaja Surat Singh .'

Messengers returned to Bikaner with auspicious gifts for the princess. Surat Singh twisted his moustaches in a delighted mood. Soon, Fateh, a twelve-year teenage girl, was betrothed to Jagat Singh, the crown prince of Jaipur.

✳

Fateh Kanwar woke up at the crack of pink aurora. She stretched herself a bit in her bed, turned her head left, then right; but she kept lying in her bed. It seemed that she was not in a mood to get up so early; but the chirping and singing of the birds at the windowsill made her wake up. She pulled her quilt up to her chest, covered her face with her shawl and closed her eyes for some time. Unable to sleep again, she got up and cast a look at herself in the hand mirror kept at her bedside table.

Her deep black eyes reflected her apprehensions.

She never dreamt that one day she would have to leave her home, her Bikaner. Soon, she would tie the nuptial knot with the prince of Jaipur, leave her parental abode and shift to a new land. Why must she go to some other place that too with a stranger was the question agitating her mind repeatedly? Emerged deep into her thoughts, she imagined that a fairy, holding a magic wand in her hand, would descend from the white chariot of clouds, touch her and she would become a queen by the wave of a wand. But all these magical moments must happen here. 'My prince charming should live here. In Bikaner!'

She was deeply upset over this age-old tradition. After marriage, it is the girl who leaves her parental home always. She clutched the goddess-pendant, hanging around her neck, in her folded hands and prayed:

'*Maa NaganechiJi*, I pray, please do not send me away from my home. How will I survive without my mother? I do not want to marry. Help me goddess! Pleeee...ase!'

Fateh, a twelve-year-old princess of Bikaner, was strikingly beautiful, graceful, slender, compelling, with a dark mane, a voluptuous mouth with a hint of mystery; she had all the delicate daintiness of a rose bud.

✳

Fateh Kanwar grew up listening to all kinds of fables about Bikaner and the bravery of Rathores, told and retold by her mother, grandmother, aunts and uncles.

'At one point of time, the Thar used to be an ocean. Once a huge demon with flames in his open mouth crushed all the humans and animals under his large paws and dried up the ocean. He drank the water.

'Listen Maghibai, don't give me wrong stories. I know it was not a demon. It happened because of irruption of volcano. I am no more a kid.'

Maghi, a senior most *daavari*, smiled at her affectionately. She used to tease her sometimes.

'Okay, this is a true story. The gurgling water of two rivers, Saraswati and Drishadwati used to flow right beneath, *Baijilal*, the place, where you are sleeping just now,' mocked Maghi.

Fateh Kanwar jumped on her bed, crouched, and stretched her neck to see the water flowing under her bed. Maghi laughed with amusement. Fateh made a face rolling her eyes.

Fateh always loved to listen the stories that Maghi told , before going to bed.

'In Ramayana, this place was called *Karu* jungle. That was the time when it was almost impossible to live here. This deterred people from settling here for years.' Akhe Kanwar had mentioned about this place, whilst travelling from Jodhpur.

She remembered every word she narrated –that warriors tramped this barren land for countless centuries; that they groomed splendid towns with elegant forts and amazing temples. Fateh loved the sand, scattered short trees with thin leaves and thorny bushes, the rugged patches and wild winds. She loved the harsher winter nights and drier hot summers. She loved Bikaner. She was proud of her roots.

✳

Fateh brooded over for hours in the solitude of her room. The dusky evening had set in. A maid entered the room, lit the lamps and said, '*Baijilal*, senior *Maji Sahib* Devadi Ji wishes to see you.'

Fateh entered the room of her grandmother. *Maji sahib* blessed her affectionately as she greeted her.

Akhe Kanwar looked at her face and sensed that she was preoccupied with something serious.

'I can see that something is bothering you?'

'*Dadisa*, I am completely enthralled by the tale of Bika, a rebel prince of Jodhpur, who left the comforts of his home to build his own empire in this hard land. How difficult it would have been for him?' *Maji Sahib* listened to her intently.

'Yes, but it was not Bika alone and Bikaner was not built in a day. For centuries, its thirst was quenched by the blood of warriors.' *Maji Sahib*'s wrinkled face gleamed with a recollection of the past.

She further added, 'today I will tell you, what had happened with Aurangzeb, the Mughal emperor!'

Fateh got closer to her *dadisa*.

'Aurangzeb hatched a scheme to slay Rathores of Bikaner by hook or by crook. He crafted a deceitful design to trap the then king – eliminate unprepared Rathores during a joint outdoor sport event meant for fun-rowing expedition. He sent an invitation to the king with his allies to participate in a sailing expedition in the Indus River. You know, Rajputs always love challenges. The king gladly accepted his invitation. He did not suspect anything foul. Somehow, the king learned about his wicked plan. He then devised his own plan to counter his wickedness. Rathores decided to participate in the expedition and retaliate with full force at the right time.

A loud sound of the Indus water waves striking the boats could be heard from a faraway place. The king noticed with satisfaction that Rajput warriors were seated silently in disciplined rows of boats. They were waiting for the Mughal Emperor to turn up at any moment.

The Mughal chief of the event came forward, bending half; he first greeted the king, and then informed, 'Mughal Badshah will not be able to join, as he has to attend an important errand. For him, duty is always a priority over a sport. He has deeply regretted his absence. He has wished Rathores all the best and good luck.'

The king's eyes met with his confidante and chief advisor. Both looked into each other's eyes for a moment. The message was conveyed. The king of Bikaner remained seated comfortably in his boat. He was quiet, his body tense. He clenched the oars tightly, an indication of the start of the sailing competition.'

Fateh was listening with her eyes wide open. Akhe Kanwar stopped for a while, looked at her granddaughter lovingly.

'Let me have some water.'

Fateh nodded smilingly at her. She also gulped some water. Jumped back to her bed and looked intently at her *Majisa*.

Akhe Kanwar began. 'Boats were moving ahead speedily. Surging waves. Sound of oars – *chapaak! Chapaak! Chapaak!*

Every participant was trying to outsmart the other. There was a dense forest cover on either side of the banks of the ferocious river, which was engulfed by thick fog. Reducing the visibility substantially. But none of these hurdles were strong enough to deter the spirit of the Rathore warriors. They continued rowing with full gusto, not only for winning the competition, but also for settling the score with the Mughals. As they rowed their boats to a point, where they were to be killed, Mughals launched a massive attack on Rathores, but got a shock of their life. Rathores, who were well prepared for such an eventuality, took out their hidden arms and fought back fiercely. Mughals suffered heavy casualties and were forced to retreat and run away. Their ill-conceived scheme to butcher Rathores burst like a bubble. Since then, Rathores called themselves, *Jai Jungle Dhar Badshah*–the king of the forest. And this area was named Jungladesh.'

Fateh looked into the eyes of her *dadisa* with awe.

'Wow! Those were the great days! I wish I was born during that time!'

'Centuries of struggle and strife! Since then lots of water has flown down the Ganges. No one knows the count of warriors who sacrificed their lives,' mused Akhe Kanwar.

Akhe Kanwar breathed deeply, inhaling the fragrance of flowers entering through the window of her room. She heard the voices of people who were busy in arrangements that reminded her of something important.

'Do you know why did I call you? I completely forgot. You distracted me into your stories. I have to tell you something very special. She opened a chest and took out a set of gold bangles. Intricately carved with ivory.

'Your *Dadasa* gave it to me. Now, these are yours! A special gift from your *Dadasa*! On the occasion of your wedding.' *Maji Sahib* put the bangles on her dainty wrists and hugged her affectionately.

✳

Not very far from the rumination of Fateh and Akhe Kanwar was Surat engrossed in wedding preparations. He ordered that messengers must invite all people, go to every village, and cover all the nearby friendly states.

Bikaner was in the midst of big preparations. All the gates leading to Kendramani fort were decorated with mango leaves and flags. The main area of the fort was reverberating with *naubat*, drums and *shahnai* playing sweet notes at the main entrance of the fort to welcome the guests. Vibrantly waving colourful flags adorned the gold plated domes.

Fateh had expressed her wish to get married at *Tekri*. 'This little girl lives in her own world of fantasy,' Surat mumbled affectionately and over the list of things to do in order to fulfil her wish.

Since her childhood, Fateh, fascinated by her great-great-grand father, Bika, wanted to tie her nuptial knot in the *Tekri*, where he would bless her from heaven to make her wedding a celestial occasion; a romantic fantasy she always dreamt of.

Surat stroked his thick beard softly; he turned his gaze on the *Bikaji ki tekri*, a small citadel, atop a small hillock, adjacent to the fort walls. There were lots of rooms, visible and hidden, underground chambers, and bricked up tunnels at the *tekri*.

✳

Tekri was decked up with garlands of marigold flowers. An elevated stage, decorated with flowers and colourful canopy was set up in the centre of a large courtyard.

Near the stage, there were golden-coloured canopies for the royal guests, while, for the nobles of Bikaner, there were white tents. For the people of Bikaner, different coloured canopies were set up in straight rows, extending until a human eye could see. Wherever eyes could measure, there were flowers, flags and festoons. Surat cast a contended look all around with a sense of pride.

✳

Far from Bikaner, in Jaipur, the groom's family matched the family of the bride in excitement and enthusiasm. Sawai Maharaj Pratap Singh always loved grand feasts and the pomp and show. The wedding of the crown prince Jagat Singh was an occasion of enormous significance for him.

The heavy crested gates of the palace would swing open frequently. The royal apartments, enveloped in a creamy layer with gold studs, were visible from the streets. Everything was perfect on the pink and pearly terraces of the palace. But the staff still rushed about, fussily rearranging the velvet tablecloths on the tables, setting white wickerwork chairs, and laying out silver goblets beneath the coloured umbrellas, swaying in the soft breeze.

Some sixty rooms were elaborately decorated; gold and white ornate big vases with flower strings were kept in the corners, and the floors were carpeted with intricate designs.

'Jaipur is glamorous.

It has always been affluent and enchanting,' whispered guests.

Nahargarh and Jaigarh forts were also decked with multitude of flags and garlands; no space was left unattended. Court musicians were playing haunting royal fanfare on the flute. Warrior guards, in their formal attires, leaning back against the carved elephants, sprang to attention, dusted down their scarlet and cinnamon jackets and white *churidar* and saluted whenever the gates opened for the guests.

✳

The Maharaja of Jaipur with his entourage reached Bikaner. He entered the city on an elephant, fanned by an acolyte, holding a whisk of white hair and yellow and pink turbaned two warriors seated behind him on the silver *howdah*.

On both sides of the road, *swastikas*, sacred and auspicious symbols, in different colours were hanging. Flower petals were strewn on the roads. Various auspicious signs like lotus, conch and *kalash*, round shaped big brass pots, filled with water were kept at the crossings and main gate of the fort. Mango leaves, marigold and jasmine flowers were used to decorate the streets and buildings.

At every corner of the streets, drummers and singers, in their best attires, were busy playing auspicious songs. Horses, elephants, and soldiers, all dressed up for the occasion were standing in an order on both sides of the road, starting from the main gate of the fort. Decorated palanquins covered with brocade and embroidered velvet curtains were placed on one side, while on the other side, there were *sewadaars* holding silver plates full of roses.

There was a lot of din and dust and the town seemed agog with festivity. Guests had arrived in scores from all over the neighbouring states. Several kings sent their sons as their representatives to Bikaner. People were running helter-skelter in joy and excitement around the wedding venue.

❋

Surat Singh, right in the middle of main gate of Kendramani fort was present, along with his knights, relatives, friends, to welcome the most-awaited guests.

The marriage procession was moving slowly towards the fort and as it became visible from the main gate, women began to sing welcome songs.

Maharaja Pratap Singh appeared triumphant on the day of the wedding of his son. People on both sides of the road watched this procession with awe and astonishment. They had never seen such a handsome groom, even among the royalties.

The groom in a pure white *jama* with saffron border, embellished with golden brocade looked enchanting. His *jama* specially made for the wedding had two hundred and fifty *kalis* or sections. The quality of a *jama* was judged by the number of separate pieces of cloth that have been stitched together to shape it. Maharani specially chose a saffron border because she believed that saffron was auspicious, and it would strengthen the nuptial bond between the newlyweds. Generally, for the Rajputs, saffron colour was a sign of sacrifice, a mark of their absolute obligation to fight.

On his feet were *mojris*, ethnic footwear, in bright pink stripes with golden work on the edges. A velvet shawl on one shoulder, he sat confidently on an alert and beautiful black steed. A long nine strand pearl string was adorning his broad chest, while a ruby stud was shining brightly in the middle of his pink headgear. A bright diamond studded in the sheath of the groom's sword was shining. He was radiating in his wedding attire.

The beautiful horses, part of procession, sometimes danced, sometimes jumped and neighed in a playful mood. Anklets tied to their legs were tinkling with each of their movements.

✳

The marriage procession was received at the main gate of the fort to the loud sound of the conch and drumbeats, welcoming songs and endless shower of flowers.

Prince Jagat Singh was ushered towards the toran that was placed over the portal of the main entrance. As per the custom, the groom on horseback holding a lance in his hand, proceeded to break the toran, which was defended by the damsels of the bride, who, from the parapet, assailed him with various kinds of mock arms, especially with a red powder made from the palash flowers, at the same time singing songs suitable for the occasion.

He cut the toran with his sword, young women and girls laughed and clapped; the prince, then, stepped off his steed when the maternal uncle of Fateh helped him, while Maharaja Surat Singh welcomed his entourage. He embraced Pratap Singh warmly and then greeted his relatives. Garlands of marigold and jasmine flowers were given to each of them and fragrant water was sprinkled.

Padma Kanwar, the mother of Fateh, *dadisa* Akhe Kanwar and other queens, along with female relatives, took the *aarti* of the groom. She held roli and rice pinched between her thumb and middle finger and put a tilak on his forehead, saying a blessing for prosperity and health. Meanwhile, Padma Kanwar stepped ahead and held the tip of the nose of the groom tightly. All the women laughed in glee. The outburst of bonhomie and warmth was all pervasive.

✳

Jagat Singh entered the *Tekri*. As he began to climb the steps, *Sewadaars* began to throw pious water and flowers on the prince. Priests blew conch and began to recite mantras. The *Tekri* resounded with the shouts and slogans.

'*Maharaja Surat Singh amar rahen.*' (Long live Maharaja Surat Singh)

'*Sawai Maharaj* Pratap Singh *ki jai jai.*'

'*Maharaj Kumar* Jagat Singh, *Rajkumari Baijilal chiranjivi rahen.*' (May Prince Jagat Singh and Princess live a long life)

'*Sada sukhi rahein. Bhagwan apna ashish hamesha banaye rakhe.*' (May God keep them always blessed so that they live happily always!)

Inside the chamber of the bride, Fateh was radiant, her eyes gleaming and shining with excitement. Her arms jingled with gold and ivory bangles; on her ears, she wore a pair of extremely traditional earrings. She was adorned with pearl and diamond necklaces and her fingers were loaded with ruby, emerald and diamond-studded rings. Her mother had asked the jeweller to produce the traditional bracelets and anklets, the kind her grandmother used to wear. Her hands and feet were decorated with intricate floral henna dye patterns, the night before; a turmeric *tilak* right in the centre of her brows and she was bathed with oils and rose water in the morning and then was drenched with perfumes so that she left a trail of sweet fragrance, while walking through the corridors.

She looked like a heavenly nymph in a red *bandhani lehenga*. The gold work on the *lehenga* took almost three months to be fixed. Besides, the gold and ivory jewellery caught everyone's eye, which was a hand crafted moon shaped mould, made with gold thread, polka and pearls. She, in her jewelled and heavily embroidered bridal attire was svelte and exotic in that moment of absolute quietude.

To the sounds of well-wishing songs, Fateh Kanwar, young and exuberant princess of Bikaner, made her grand appearance from the inner side of the *Tekri*, flanked by her elder maternal uncle and aunt, while twelve maids in vivid yellow and green attire went ahead, waving lucky white horsetail whisks and sprinkling fragrant water.

✳

The prince and princess were ushered to the *mandap*. Together they walked slowly upon a narrow carpet strewn with flowers, leading to an altar erected at the right side of the courtyard. They were made to sit on wooden seats. Priests chanted mantras in order to pacify the Gods so that newlyweds could lead a happy conjugal life together. Elders, one after the other, showered their blessings on them.

'There are about thirteen elaborate rituals of your wedding that you have to perform today. Every ritual has its own connotation and consequence, and cannot be done away with. Therefore, it will take hours to complete the whole ceremony. *Saptpadi* is most important amongst all. Kindly be patient.' The head priest explained to the bride and groom.

After a trail of exhaustive rituals, the fire was lit in the *havan kund*. For the *saptpadi* ceremony (Seven rounds around the holy fire of *havan kund*– the most significant wedding ritual amongst Hindus) they stood up.

The first deircle was made as they stepped over a white stone. The priest recited, 'May both of you stand as firm, be as steady as the stone kept here.' The couple walked the seven circles around the sacred fire. The next ritual was to take seven vows.

First vow. The priest recited, *Om esha ekapadi bhava iti prathaman.* It means,' The wife would offer him food and be helpful in every way.

He would cherish her and provide welfare and happiness for her and her children. The prince repeated smiling. The priest uttered for the princess. *Dhanam dhanyam pade vadet.* Means, she would be responsible for the home and all household, food and finance responsibilities. The princess promised she would comply.

The second vow. Jagat Singh sweared, *om oorje jara dastayaha* that is, together they would protect their house and children. The princess affirmed, *kutumburn rakshayishyammi sa aravindharam* that she would be by his side. She would be his courage and strength. She would rejoice in his happiness.

The third promise. *Om rayas santu joradastayaha.* It conveys that he wishes to grow wealthy and prosperous and strive for the education and healthy long life of their children. The princess gave her word, *tava bhakti as vadedvachacha* that is she would love him solely for the rest of her life, as her husband.

Fourth vow, the prince declared. *Om mayo bhavyas jaradastaya ha.* 'She has brought sacredness into his life, and has completed him. May they be blessed with noble and obedient children. The princess said, *lalayami cha pade vadet* that she would shower him with joy, from head to toe. She would strive to please him in every possible way she could.

Fifth vow, Jagat said solemnly, *om prajabhyaha santu jaradastayaha.* You are my best friend, and staunch well-wisher. You have come into my life, enriching it. God bless you.

At this point Jagat patted her palm slightly. Fateh uttered shyly, *arte arba sapade vadet.* I promise to love and cherish you as long as I live. Your happiness is my happiness, and your sorrow is my sorrow. I will trust and honour you, and will strive to fulfil all your wishes.

Sixth promise. Jagat asked, *rutubhyah shat padi bhava.* 'Now that you have taken six steps with me, you have filled my heart with immense happiness. Will you do the kindness of filling my heart with happiness like this for all times? The princess whispered, *yajna hom shashthe vacho vadet.* 'I will always be by your side.'

Seventh vow, *Om sakhi jaradastayahga.* 'We are now husband and wife, and are one. You are mine and I am yours for eternity.' The prince proclaimed and the princess willfully accepted. 'As God is my witness, I am now your wife. We will love, honour and cherish each other forever.'

Succinctly, during the long process, the bride and groom promised each other prosperity by fulfilling their respective roles in their lives. Jagat Singh vouched that he would love his wife solely looking into eyes of the princess. Fateh lowered her eyes.

Rituals and *saptpadi* lasted for six to seven hours. As they stepped aside the *havan mandap*, a flood of people – relatives, courtiers and *thikanedaars*, surrounded them. The wedding ceremony was completed peacefully.

The mother of Fateh blessed the two of them: 'May the Goddess always be with you. May she give you strength to fulfil your responsibilities. From today, you have to embark on a new path of life; now you are the crown princess of Jaipur, but for us you will always be our sweet *Baijilal*. Now you are the saviour of honour of both the families. I wish, may you have all the pleasures, comforts and happiness.'

Her heart prayed silently for her loving daughter's happiness. The bride and groom were ushered into a room to rest. *Daavaries* assisted newlyweds on to the cushions in the specially decorated chamber where they would begin their marital journey.

✳

Maharaj Surat Singh had arranged for Pratap Singh to return to Jaipur with his entourage. The bride and groom were made comfortable in a special carriage. Jagat Singh leaned against the cushions, as the women began singing ceremonial songs and showered flowers on the newlyweds.

The carriage slowly started moving away from Bikaner. *Maji Sahib*, her mother and cousin sisters had tears in their eyes. Fateh bade goodbye to them, her companions, her sisters, her playmates and her entire world where she belonged to and was all set to enter the new one. She would never ever return to her home as a doting *Baijilal* of Bikaner but as a crown princess of Jaipur. She would be a guest, a visitor for some time.

Fateh turned around to have a last look at her world through a small opening of the curtain. She saw her mother and her *kakasa* standing together and watching intensely in her direction. All were there but her father. Fateh began to cry. The tears were rolling down her cheeks incessantly. Her mother looked at Surat Singh, who was the cause of her husband's absence on such an important occasion of his life. He was the one who was instrumental in preventing Ajab Singh to perform most sacred duty of his life- *kanyadaan*. Momentarily Padma Kanwar got lost in the thoughts of her husband. 'I take an oath that I will never return to this land again, which was drenched by the blood of an innocent child. It was a blot on me and my ancestors.' He wrote to his wife later. She began crying inconsolably.

Fateh was anxious because her path led her away from her mother and home. She had all along believed that Bikaner was her permanent abode. Why then she was being uprooted and replanted at an alien place was the question she had been asking herself over and over again. Words of her mother resonated in her ears, 'from now onwards, Jaipur will be your home.' Fateh felt as if some invisible force choked her throat. She wailed uncontrollably.

✳

Three gates – Virendra pol, Udai pol and Tripolia pol to get access to the Jaipur palace, were richly decorated. All along the streets, folks had gathered to welcome their newly wedded prince and princess.

Pratap Singh with the new bride and groom entered into the palace through the Tripolia gate.

Maharani RathorniJi, mother of Jagat Singh, his two sisters Suraj Kanwar and Anand Kanwar and other women welcomed the groom and bride.

Fateh was ushered in to an oleander-pink-white room, splendidly decorated and filled with the fragrance of jasmine. Carpets of rose gold with silver embroidery were laid wall to wall. Adjoining corridors displayed inlaid ivory vases in long rows. Benares brocade covered the huge bed, garments and apparels meant for the bride were kept in brass plates on the tables. Pashmina shawls made from the silken beards of sheep and goats, fine enough to pass through a wedding ring, had come all the way from the Kashmir valley.

The full day festivities turned into a blissful evening. The heart of Fateh Kanwar was pounding with mixed feelings of excitement, nervousness and exhaustion. Now, she was the crown princess of Jaipur.

After a fortnight, Pratap Singh held an enormous public reception, in honour of his daughter-in-law. Jaipur was in the mood of jubilation.

Fateh wore a *lehenga* of a fragile fawn coloured chiffon woven of yellow, green and red silk threads and strands of pure gold. On her head, floated a veil of multi-coloured *lahariya* on golden coloured chiffon, which flashed with gold and silver strands. Twisted strands of pearls adorned her neck. Her feet had been bathed and anointed with milk and precious creams. She had put her feet into golden *mojris* with diamonds and emeralds fastened. On her toes, she wore ornately carved gold rings and on her ankles were heavy bracelets of gold with *ghungrus* that were making sweet twinkling sounds, even at the slightest jerk.

Each step of her dressing was part of a ceremony. When her hair were combed, ornaments were worn, *bajuband* fastened, *chunar* covered her head – on each step prayers were recited. Offerings to gods were made. The palace reverberated with auspicious songs. In the courtyard, women in large numbers were gathered to watch all these ceremonies.

The officials, courtiers and relatives presented the gifts and showered their blessings. There was an elaborate western banquet for the British and other guests from Europe. During the course of festivities, while variety of drinks flew like streams inside the fort, cannons were fired outside. The celebration continued almost the whole night.

✳

Early next morning, Jagat was taken to a hillside of jewels, the secret treasure of Amber. It was a tradition in the Jaipur royals, that after the wedding, the ruler's heir is taken to the fort on the hilltop, guarded by Meenas. He picks up an article for his bride from the treasure, gold urns and jars, diamonds and emeralds, beautiful artefacts, gold statues and swords encrusted with jewels. Jagat chose a parrot made of emerald with a ruby beak and two diamonds as its eyes, for his bride.

Evening had set in, weaving its magic. *Daavaries* were busy in preparing Fateh for the night.

Jagat Singh entered the room with his special gift. *Daavaries* and servants greeted the prince and the princess, tended to their needs, then bowed and left the room. Jagat and Fateh were alone in the room.

Jagat made himself comfortable on an armchair. Fateh got up from her bed and sat at the edge of the bed. They were silent. Jagat Singh looked at her. Fateh was virtually trembling. Jagat got up and walked towards his wife. He stood there holding her hand for a while. He held her arms and helped her to her feet. Fateh rose numbly, Jagat guided her into the adjoining room. He put his hands on her shoulders gently. He cupped her face in his hand and looked into her eyes.

'You are so beautiful…' he embraced her, lifted her face with his index finger. Fateh closed her eyes. Jagat kissed her eyes.

Fateh smiled demurely. Jagat smiled back.

'I will always be with you, in this new journey of your life.'

At that moment, it seemed that everything in her life was going to be smooth and enjoyable.

Little did she know what destiny held for her? So overwhelmed was she by the love showered by Jagat Singh that the idea of entry of other princesses in the life of her husband, as was the common practice in royalties in those days, did not strike her.

When Fateh Kanwar learned that Jagat would be marrying Chandan Kanwar, the daughter of Thakur Salam Singh of Pokharan, she was greatly upset. Chandan Kanwar was already betrothed to Jagat Singh and finally the wedding of Jagat, for the second time, was all set to take place, just two years after his first marriage with Fateh Kanwar.

As Jagat entered the room, he noticed Fateh Kanwar seated on the edge of her bed. Her hair had been loosened, a diamond studded *borla*, an ornament, sat on her forehead between the partings of her hair. Dressed in dark blue attire, she looked like a blue lotus in its full bloom.

She looked at her husband with a faint smile, without speaking a word. Jagat could deduce what she was going through.

'I never perceived this marriage, so soon, not in my wildest dreams. But you know, my father fixed it. I was not involved in this matrimony, believe me, yet I reassure you that I will sincerely follow my vows that I took with you. I shall always remain committed to you,' said Jagat, while trying to pacify her.

Fateh was quiet for a while, and then said, 'The people of Pokharan are happy at your union with their princess Chandan KanwaraniJi. It will make your father happy and you too, others don't really matter.'

'And what about you? You are not comfortable with my second marriage. Be honest,' Jagat cajoled her.

'Do I have any choice? Nobody asked me even once; whether I agreed or accepted the idea of your second marriage. I will have to be comfortable not only with your second queen, but any number of queens that enter in your life.' Her voice trailed.

A terrifying feeling of helplessness engulfed her. She had a premonition that her life would be more and more difficult in the times to come, in that magnificent palace of Jaipur.

Jagat instantly moved forward and pulled her into his arms.

'Trust me, my love, no one, when I say no one, I mean it, can take me away from you! I belong to you and you alone!'

Fateh was trembling like a tender leaf in a strong wind. Tears rolled down her cheeks. Jagat filled her wet face with kisses. Her fears melted in the warmth of her husband's love and assurance.

She, however, harboured deep resentment in her heart.

✳

Fateh Kanwar peered through the latticed corridors, when Jagat crossed the threshold of her palace with a new queen tugged in. When he married for the third time with Maharajkumari Sireh Kanwar sister of Man Singh, Maharaja of Jodhpur, she resigned to her fate, highly disgusted.

She was aware that her husband, the crown prince of a powerful state, could marry as many princesses as he liked and might bring a bigger number of women to the palace, without even marrying. Her own father Ajab Singh married twice, first with the princess of Jodhpur, her own mother; second, with an aunt of Maharana Ari Singh of Udaipur, her step mother.

'*Masa*! I can understand today all that you suffered in your life. Why can a man marry with as many women as he wants to? Why cannot he be punished for breaking seven wedding vows?'

The agony and sufferings of all those women, her mother, her aunts and her *dadisa*, might have undergone was quite clear to her today; her own grief got mingled into their pangs of sorrows and resentment.

Jagat Singh was biddably married many times with the princesses of neighbouring states. As all these women were not enough to satisfy his lust, under the guise of his taste for food, music, dance and painting , Jagat lured a multitude of beautiful and sophisticated dance-women to Jaipur. Whatever these women demanded, be it a gold necklace or sapphire ear rings, Jagat Singh never quibbled about the cost. He owned the best of emeralds and rubies in the entire Rajputana area. Items made of ivory, pearls and gold, coffers of diamonds and rubies, emeralds as big as peanuts and berries were rolled in the chambers of the queens. But Fateh was made of different metal. Her happiness did not lie in jewels and ornaments. Jagat was her sheer bliss.

So far so good. Fateh was still very special for Jagat, although he enjoyed the company of other wives as well.

CHAPTER 3

1800 – Jaipur
Rupan Daavari

The weather was turbulent. The wind was howling through the vast stretch of the rugged terrain of Jaipur. It was the beginning of October; not the time to rain, but untimely and incessant rain had lashed the city. Rupan had to reach the market and buy bangles, henna, rice, *sindoor, roli, chunar, dhup, agru* etc., which Fateh Kanwar had asked her to buy for the puja. She was waiting for the rain to stop for a while under the shade of a tree. She had to do her errand hurriedly. The fierce wind was not in a mood to oblige her.

The sun was about to set when she returned drenched all over, water dripping from her clothes, making a trail behind. She headed for her quarters, to change her clothes. Covered her head with a printed cotton shawl; she tied her hair with dark red thick straps beaded with small sized silver beads. Her black and yellow striped thick cotton ankle length skirt was matched with an open back black striped top, tied with black strands at the shoulders and the waist.

The same evening while Rupan was assisting Fateh for the puja, she asked Rupan, 'I have noticed you keeping silent most of the time. Though you are with me for the most part of your daytime, but I have seen you generally quiet. What happened to you Rupan? Is all well with you?'

Rupan nodded, indicating all was well. Fateh Kanwar continued, 'You give me no occasion to raise my voice. You complete the entire chore meticulously. But you have never ever shared anything with me.'

Rupan looked at her new mistress and smiled.

'No! No! Your smile is not enough! I need a reply. It seems you do not trust me. Do you have a problem? Really, I am keen to know about you. I do not know anything about you, though you are with me for a couple of months. Come on! Tell me, where do you belong to? Who all are there in your family? Do you have your family, any close friends or relatives in the town? You do not even talk about the place, where were you born and grew up. I have never seen you going out to meet your relatives. Look at you! You are pink all over! I do not want to embarrass you. Again, you are…silent. What is the matter? Is there something so private that you want to keep it a secret?' Fateh shot off a volley of questions.

Rupan smiled again. No point in evading the curiosity of Fateh anymore, she realised.

'*Ranisa*, there is nothing special about me. Nothing significant. My life is not different from hundreds of other *daavaries* in your palace.'

'Are you from Jaipur?' Fateh was insistent.

'I do not know where I was born, but I was brought up in Kishangarh, a small state near Ajaymeru. Recently, I came to Jaipur with one of my aunts in search of work. Then, fate brought me in contact of *Maji Sahib*, Rathorni Ji who very kindly assigned me a job in the palace. I do not have any close friend or a relative here. Since the day I entered this palace, it became my world. I have no contact with Kishangarh currently and honestly speaking I am not keen to have any contact there.'

Rupan was about twenty years-old, one of the slaves of Jagat Singh, who entered his palace in the beginning of 1800. Initially, she was not assigned any particular task. Later, when Maharaj Kunwar Jagat Singh got married, she was employed in the service of Fateh

Kanwar. Maharani RathorniJi had since noticed her sober demeanour; she put her in the service of the newly wedded princess. However, Fateh Kanwar came with her own band of *daavaries* from Bikaner. The prime job of Rupan was to look after the newly wedded princess of Bikaner

Rupan was seven or eight years older than the princess, Fateh Kanwar, far from her parental abode, established a deep bond with her right from day one.

Since Fateh, a teenager, missed the company of her trusted maid Maghi of Bikaner, she thought of building some sort of bond with Rupan, whereas Rupan preferred to live in her closed shell.

A couple of days passed by – Fateh's in the company of Jagat and that of Rupan's in the service of her new queen.

Fateh could not keep her thoughts away from Rupan. She sensed that Rupan was always cautious and closed. She was holding herself back. What? Her past! Her bad memories! Fateh was flooded with numerous queries.

Unable to restrain herself anymore and finding the right opportunity, Fateh raked up the issue. 'How is it, Rupan that you have never gone back, even once? Don't you miss your parents? Where are they? They also never contacted you. Is it not really strange?'

Rupan was visibly unnerved by the stream of personal queries. She got pushed into a whirlwind of self-seeking questions. She wondered why the new queen did not know that we, the *daavaries*, cross the threshold of zenana all alone, not holding the hands of our mentors, or parents or siblings? We are assigned the status of *daavari* or *khawas* or *pardayats* depending on our work and skill and our position remains the same for the rest of our life. Once we enter the zenana, doors of the outside world are closed forever. She kept silent with her head bent down.

'*Ranisa*, you are my only family,' Rupan voiced in a low tone, almost like a whisper.

Fateh kept it up. 'You are a beautiful young woman. Tall and fair. You never think of getting married with a young handsome man. *Maji Sahib* would be happy to find a good match for you. Okay, you do not worry; I will request her to find a suitable prospective groom for you. You tell me, what kind of boy are you looking for?'

Rupan chose to remain quiet.

'No, you cannot avoid this issue. You have to answer.' Fateh Kanwar was adamant like an obstinate child.

'I have so many women for company in this palace. Even otherwise, I do not need anybody's company. For getting married, one must have time and to be very frank, I do not have time. In fact, I cannot think of marriage.' Rupan's soft tone turned firm.

✻

To Fateh, Rupan appeared to be a mysterious woman; she was the woman who was assigned the duty to serve her, be with her all the time to make her comfortable when she entered Chandra Mahal as a teenaged-bride. Since then, Rupan assisted her like a loyal maid on every count. Still she seemed distant. There was always an invisible wall between both of them. She was hell bent on breaking this unseen barrier. She was not comfortable with a formal and cold relationship, not even between a maid and a queen.

One evening, when Fateh was taking a stroll in the rear-garden with her, she made an effort to gain her confidence.

'Rupan, you are like an elder sister to me. I am learning to cope with the pangs and pains of married life. I miss my mother! My home! My Bikaner! I was very young when I lost my father. He left Bikaner because of a family feud. There was no affinity or bonding among the brothers, that is what my mother told me. Vague images of my childhood days, time spent with my father; dwindle like a swing in front of my eyes. Now my father is here, but I cannot meet him frequently because I have to follow the rules of Kachwahas. I am not supposed to run and dangle in the arms of my father, because here I am a daughter-in-law. And in Bikaner when I was a daughter, my father was not with me. I trust you, that's why I am opening up, but you do not find me worthy to share your pain?' Fateh spoke slowly with her eyes fixed on her face.

Rupan resigned finally. '*Ranisa*, I would love to share my story with you, but the sad part is that I do not know my past. There is no good reason for me to remember my childhood. My parents did not give Rupan name! Those who brought me up gave it. I have a hazy memory of a mud house in a village, with sand all around. There is another memory I would like to forget forever, though it is ingrained permanently into my mind. Now it will go with my last breath.'

Rupan's tall, slender body shivered. Fateh kept her hand on her shoulder and gave her a friendly look.

✳

The noon was sultry and scorching, full of sweat and perspiration. The sun was bright and burning. Hot winds were blowing since morning. Fateh was leaning against two round pillows. She asked Rupan to give her head- massage. Fateh thought that it was the most opportune time to make Rupan comfortable.

'It's enough. Now massage my feet. Rupan pulled a small wooden chowki near her bed and began oiling one of her feet.

'I know *Ranisa* what you want to know? Today I will tell you everything.' Rupan's eyes were like red amber matching with hot blazing sun. 'That was also a similar hot summer day. The day...' she muttered under her breath.

'*I...I...was abused, physically, in my childhood, not once, not twice! Many times on countless days!*'

Fateh could not believe her ears. Horrified, she came closer to her and stretched her right ear to Rupan's lips. Rupan could not control her smile. 'Please do not torture yourself *Ranisa*. I know it is difficult to believe. Nevertheless, hard reality is enormously unbelievable than a fairy tale. I will tell you everything.'

She began in a sore voice.

'I have a hazy image of my village. Yes, but I remember very clearly that my parents were in a jubilant mood, as they had very good crops that year and the crop was about to be harvested. My family with some of neighbours and friends decided to set out on a pilgrimage. Pushkar was the chosen destination, as it was believed to be one of the most sacred lakes and a dip therein would purify our soul.'

'Yes! Yes! I have heard of this place. My *dadisa* also told me that Pushkar is a sacred place with a pious lake surrounded by a large number of temples.' Fateh nodded excitedly.

'It was the waxing moon period in October. It was the time for a big fair to be held there; a large number of people had come from faraway places. The fair continued almost for a week. They took a dip in the holy water, completed the rituals as commanded by the local priests and offered in charity things like land, gold and currency notes. My family chose to participate in the fair.

'We travelled for days, crossed the desert, covered many towns then we reached a village near Ajaymeru. Our hearts were filled with happiness. On my way, I came across many camels carrying people with their bag and baggage, food and water. In the night, we took shelter under a tree; my mother began preparing food. The men were resting. All were preparing for the journey the next morning. Camels were already loaded with the luggage and we were excited to set out on a pleasure trip. Within a couple of days, we would be at Pushkar. We hoped. Unfortunately, that journey could never see the light of day.'

She stopped, sobbed for a while and went into silence for a couple of minutes.

'Then, the dreadful night descended and turned our fortune into misery. It was a dark night. Overcast sky. There was a sudden cloudburst followed by almost six to seven days of torrential downpour. Rainwater gorged the fields and completely destroyed the crops. Once the rainstorm stopped, the water took away all our hopes with its current. We were left with nothing. It was unprecedented. People had never witnessed such a natural calamity. We decided to travel back to our village.' She seemed to wrestle with herself to open the pages of her life, which were closed so far.

She began, after a small pause, 'A few days passed peacefully. Somehow, the people garnered their spirits and began to stand up with the scratch. But the nature did not spare us even in our village. The nature turned malevolent again. It was in no mood to have mercy on us. In the evening, the sky turned red and a violent sand storm howled through the village and fields. The village lanes were choked, and water logging made the village life difficult. Uff! Those horrible days! Villagers prayed to appease the goddess, but in vain. Within no time, people began to abandon their houses, fields and their dear ones, each looking out for his own survival. The howling of starving men and women, old and young, drowned the entire village into desperation. People abandoned their own children and old family members, whose cries were silenced by hunger and thirst. Whatever small amount of silver and gold coins or jewellery they had, it was all looted by their own people. The present was gloomy and the future was bleak.'

Rupan was quiet again. She had stopped massaging Fateh's foot. Fateh also forgot the massage. She was seated on her bed with folded legs and her arms wrapped around her knees. Rupan's eyes were set far away on a cloudy patch in the sky that was visible from the open window. Fateh touched her shoulder slightly. Rupan got startled; she looked at Fateh in a weird way for a moment, and then lowered her eyes. Her voice was coarse.

'My family, in a caravan, travelled and travelled for many days in search of new fields to settle down. There was no drinking water and no food. We reached a land where there was sand all over, hot and coarse. Mornings, noon, and evenings melted into one solid time block, seamlessly dissolving into each other under a burning, brutal sky. Life was as if living on the burning ambers. The glow of fire seemed to be inching away from scalding the skin. We breathed sand, we ate sand and we slept sand. Just sand and sand. It was driving us crazy. I do not know exactly how many days we spent under that kind of scorching sun. But we continued to travel. We altered our food and other habits to cope with the situation we were faced with. Nothing seemed enough to survive. After crossing miles and miles, we found a green patch. Everyone jumped in excitement. There were a few hamlets around the grassland. We made that place our temporary abode.'

Rupan began to sob uncontrollably. Fateh tried to console her, and then let her cry. After a while, she controlled herself.

'Now I am fine *Ranisa*. I feel as if a great burden has been taken off my chest. As the saying goes, misery comes on wings and departs on foot, there seemed to be no end to our miseries. What followed next was the darkest period of my life. I was a child and I never deserved what I endured. One night, I peacefully slept with my mother, but next day, got up crying amid strangers. That was the night, which changed the course of my life forever. They gave me food. I cried and cried, wondering where my parents and all the familiar faces had disappeared? My parents did not think of abandoning me, although, they starved for days together. I was abducted in the night and was subjected to all sorts of physical violence. Thereafter, I never saw my parents. I do not know whether they are alive or not. The next day, the morning passed peacefully. Evening descended. There were scary sounds all around.' She abruptly kept quiet for a while. Breathed heavily for a minute, and then started.

'I did not know that they were nomads covering distances in a caravan. There was no permanent residence for them. They used to sleep in their temporary tents under the stars and toil under the sun to make their living. Their villages were shapeless clusters of huts. They built their huts anywhere they liked, at the outskirts of a town or in the residential area of the villages. You know *Ranisa*; they can catch any poisonous snake easily. They sell its venom. They are always on the move. At night, the men and women of the caravan gather to sing songs and dance. It used to be their daily routine.

In the night, a bearded man came to me, held my arm tightly, pulled me inside the tent, flung me on his bed and stripped my *ghaghra* off. He kept on staring at me. His hands were moving on my body – head to toe. He slowly removed his long scarf and then unbuttoned his knee length shirt. He then shed his *pyjama* and jumped on me like a leopard. I was a child and the coarse sand under me was cold and rough. I began to cry. Unmindful of my wails, he pushed me on a rough cotton quilt and began to lick my face with his wet tongue. He was biting, licking me all over and then began to tear my body until he was exhausted. When it was over, I fell into a state of deep sedation. When I woke up the next day, it was late morning. It continued for days and the days turned into months. Just imagine my plight, *Ranisa*, bonded like a slave in a remote desert, with no prospects of any help from any quarter.'

'How old were you then?'

'Twelve-year!' Rupan continued:

'One day, I got an opportunity to escape. I saw a caravan passing by, I ran and ran and joined the herd. When I escaped from the clutches of that brute, the hunter of young girls, the man who raped me for days, I met a Brahmin woman who sometime in the past got the temple of Brahma repaired. She was a staunch devotee of Lord Brahma.' The Brahmin woman saw me; she helped me, hid me in her carriage. She found me *Rupvati*, means very beautiful, so she gave me the name- Rupan.

'Who was she? Do you know her name?'

'How can I forget her name ? She was very close to the Maharani Ji of Jaipur. Later, she proved to be instrumental in changing my life as well. But as she grew old and weak, she brought me here, and now I am with you.

Yes, she was kind enough to bring me up like her own child.

She was my saviour.

She was Phundi Bai of Jaipur. A wealthy but very kind woman.'

✳

Rupan fell silent, fearing she had shared far too much about herself. Fateh Kanwar listened thoughtfully. She felt sick. So far, she had lived a well-protected life. She had no idea of the outside world beyond her four walls.

'I did not know…the world could be so ugly! So dreadful! So far, I knew men as my adorable Sultan *kakasa*. My *bapusa*. My husband Jagat. You have introduced me to a different kind of man! Phew!'

'I do not know what should I tell you? Having gone through a terrible experience, I firmly hold it is not possible for you to trust a man. But! Rupan, suppose, if you find someone now, who loves you, respects you, cares for you, will you accept his love? Will you marry him? Who knows, the person you trust now, may turn out to be an angel in future and wipe out all your sorrows.' She tried to comfort Rupan.

'*Ranisa*, I do not live in the world of fantasies. I do not think I can ever trust a man in this life. That part of human life in me died on that horrendous night. Oh! Man is a mean creature, who mostly indulges in meaningless and momentary pleasures. He is a coward and a very cunning species. I may sound prejudiced. Anyone can argue that not all men are alike. Yes! I am bitter. How so ever unreasonable I may seem, but I believe that a man is the biggest exploiter of a woman. He can never be a true partner of a woman. Men are always in a combative and competitive mode. I have learnt how to deal with such cowards.' Rupan was bitter to the core of her heart.

Fateh Kanwar was weighed down by the unfortunate childhood of Rupan. Her pain like a sharp arrow pierced the heart of Fateh Kanwar. She understood why Rupan was always busy in her duties, never indulging in any kind of fun and frolic. She enjoyed more by tending flower beds and plants in front of long corridor beside the room of Fateh in her spare time.

'Flowers are a symbol of purity, pleasure and prettiness. They bestow peace and love on us. They never hurt anyone. They never give pain to anyone. They spread contentment. You are the most beautiful flower of my garden.' One evening, while Rupan was busy in the garden Fateh came behind her tiptoed and saying so, she embraced Rupan with all his heart. Fateh tried to lift her sore spirit up. Her eyes were wet. She really cared for Rupan deep down her heart.

The two women continued to talk until late in the night. For the first time, Rupan had opened her heart in front of her new *Ranisa*. Fateh found in Rupan a person who she trusted all her life.

Gradually, their friendship turned into a strong union with each passing day. Over the years, the intimate companionship between Fateh Kanwar, a queen and Rupan, a *daavari* turned into friendship, which unfolded in spheres of everyday interaction between them.

Their bonding grew from strength to strength, as woman after woman entered in the life of Jagat Singh, which crumbled the fairy tale of Fateh.

In 1803, after the ascendance of Jagat Singh as Maharaja of Jaipur, Raskapoor, a dancer, emerged like a comet and destroyed the world of Fateh, finally. That was the time when Rupan stood by her *Ranisa* rock solid and in return won the absolute trust of Fateh Kanwar.

CHAPTER 4

1803
The Coronation

In late July, in 1803, the early morning was hot and humid. The previous night, it had rained heavily the entire night. Cloud bursts wreaked havoc, lashed the trees and flattened crops. Water had been continuously gushing downwards from the hills. The streets were full of puddles.

Pratap Singh called his queen, who was standing by his bed silently, to his side. He stretched his neck a bit and whispered, 'After my death, take care of Jaipur. Jagat is naive and too young to understand the intricacies of politics. Of course, he has many elderly, loyal and senior ministers in the court to advise him, still your role as a saviour of Jaipur begins now.'

'Why do you say so? You will recover soon,' Maharani RathorniJi said calmly.

'Do not fool yourself. My breath is numbered. You also know.'

She moved a step ahead, sat on the edge of the bed and held his hand. She remained seated there for a long time, holding his broad and cold hand in her pale palms. She felt as if her own life was slipping away from her hands.

As the sun appeared on the horizon, the son of Jaipur – Pratap Singh disappeared forever, so did the splendour of Jaipur.

Preparations began for the funeral. Maharaja's dead body was dressed in his royal robes. Down to his ancestral temple in the courtyard, amid the wailings and chanting of the people gathered there, the body of Maharaja was laid on the pyre; priests mumbled prayers, cymbals clashed in a funeral requiem.

Last rituals were made on the banks of a seasonal river a few miles down the hills of Gator, cremation ground meant for the royals. Jagat lit the pyre. Flames turned the mortal remains of Pratap Singh into ashes.

✳

It was the 3rd of August 1803. Bright sunrays penetrating the red, blue and yellow panes studded on the window frames of small-latticed windows were falling on the pink walls of the palace, weaving magic all around.

Maharani RathorniJi had consulted the astrologers.

'The auspicious time for the coronation was the first quarter of the day because it would prove to be a promising time for the new Maharaja. If all the rituals could be done timely, the new Maharaja would enjoy a very long life, success, fame, and prosperity.'

The astrologers prophesied.

Before the ceremony, Jagat was to spend a couple of hours at the Jaigarh fort for the purification ceremony. There was full assemblage within the fort premises. Jagat Singh, in his seventeenth year, fair, tall, stout and with a lively, intelligent cast of face and a somberness of demeanour was seated on a velvet cushioned wooden chowki with his arms folded in his lap, while the head priest was busy in preparation for the rituals.

The morning dawned fresh and clear. He was bathed first with cow milk, then honey and lastly with holy waters in the early hours of morning. The water was brought from the different wells, ponds, rivers etc., and was purified by chanting the *mantras* from religious texts. When the purification ceremony was over, Jagat was ushered in an adjoining room, where a new round of religious activities took place. The head priest marked his forehead with the *tilak*, a mark that entitled him to rule Jaipur. Jagat Singh went through a multitude of propitiatory rites with singular accuracy and self-possession. He looked as fresh as morning dew.

Next in the line of rituals was to make offerings to goddess Jumwai. For this occasion, Jagat Singh wore the traditional attire of his state, a garment, centuries old in its style. His golden coloured headgear of shining silk shone brightly with sprays of flowers of a turban jewel. A glittering pin in the centre of the turban was set with rubies, emeralds and pale pearls on one side, and the same stones with the addition of diamonds on the other. The stem and the sides of the jewel are enamelled in translucent green.

Pandit Sheonarayan, the senior minister tied the sword on the waist of the young Maharaja. He had the privilege of accompanying Jagat Singh to the temple. When he reached the temple, priests began to recite religious songs. The chief priest greeted him and put some sandalwood paste on his forehead; he sprinkled pure water on him with his fingers.

After the offerings and prayers to the family goddess, the senior most relative ushered the newly crowned king to the throne, which was placed on an elevated platform overlooking the court premises.

Shouts of approbation burst from the immense crowds who thronged the palace, while every ravine and hill re-echoed the sound of the canon shots from the citadel of Jaigarh.

Jagat Singh expressed his deep gratitude to his ancestors and the subjects of Jaipur.

'My great grandfather late Maharaj Sawai Jai Singh Ji's parting gift to this kingdom of Amber and to our family was this glorious Jaipur and the monumental building – Jaipur Palace, where I was born and brought up. I will always cherish my happy days.' He further added, 'I must mention that so far it has been all roses for me, and a person who had held the fort and the palace was my late father Sawai Maharaj Pratap SinghJi. Then *Maji Sahib*, it was she, who held the strings of this palace strongly, looked after the staff, managed it single-handedly. On this occasion, I would like to express my deep gratitude to my mother, my late father, and my ancestors.'

The imposing cavalcade, then, proceeded from the fort and headed for the city palace. The nobles and the courtiers well mounted their equipment, all new for the occasion and the people in their best apparel, created a spectacle that was quite thrilling.

The young Maharaja was ornamented in royal costumes according to the traditions of his creed and clan. He took the sword of his height in his hand and sat on the royal throne attached to the *shringar-chowki*. As the procession moved forward, the Brahmins recited the holy *mantras* and blessed the new Maharaja whole-heartedly. Jagat Singh afterwards proceeded with his cavalcade to all the shrines and temples in the city to make his offerings. Every avenue was crowded with well-dressed people, who shouted hearty cheers of congratulations as the procession went along, and seemed to participate in the feelings evinced towards their young prince.

As Jagat Singh dismounted at the main gate of the palace, people began to rant on slogans.

'*Jay! Jay! Sawai Maharaj Jagat Singh Ji ki jay ho!*'

'*Long live Sri Sawai Maharaja Jagat Singh Bahadur!*'

✳

The ceremony concluded with a trumpet blast; all the formalities were completed meticulously. The royal court of Jaipur was throbbing with the beats of drums. Folk singers were busy in playing their instruments, while dancers displayed their talent at the beat of drums. The palace was excited with gala celebrations.

There were parades with decked soldiers wearing their official decorations, colourful headgears, some of them mounted on horses and elephants. Grand feasts, dances, and fireworks followed them. Thousands of people from all occupations arrived at Jaipur to witness the grand event. Poor and wealthy, old and young, farmers and artisans, traders and merchants, all came from far away towns and villages. They were given silver and gold coins and grains.

Kith and kin were given precious gifts, all the royal women were given *thaans* of silk, embroidered *chunars* and *lehengas*, ornaments, garments, and *itars* (incense). Royal women were given the gifts kept on trays made of gold, while *pardayats* and *paswans* were given on silver trays. Women who were given partial rights of a queen were called *pardayats* and the keeps and maids they kept in their service, were called *paswans*.

When Jagat came to his mother, she put both her palms on his head.

'Now look after your royal legacy, protect it, and take it to the zenith.'

Maharani's eyes had turned into pools of tears of bliss.

✳

The sun was about to set. Its rays fell on the domes and ramparts of the palace to make them glow. Pandit Jayraj walked hurriedly with furrows on his forehead and a register tightly stuck under his left arm. He headed to his chamber to have a meeting with his associates –Baba Munshidas, Pandit Vishnudas, and Pandit Gunilal. In his chamber, Mangal, Faizullah, Chiman, and Fakirullah were waiting for Jayraj. They were giving final touches on the large size cut outs of Jagat Singh, which were to be placed at the entrance of the royal court.

Jayraj was the head of *Gunijankhana*, a department of scholars and accomplished artists. He himself was a renowned musician. Jayraj was assigned the duty to see the management of the grand celebration in the evening. *Pothikhana* and *Suratkhana*, two very important wings ,the home of hundreds of painters, poets, and scholars, were put under him for the event.

Jayraj kept the register on the desk and sat down on a square mattress laid on the carpet. He closed his eyes and pressed his ear lobes with his thumbs. He appeared quite stressed out.

For the last one week, he, along with his colleagues, was minutely working on the programme to make it a grand success. He knew that Jagat Singh loved a grand and gala evening, gaiety, and glitterati. For this musical evening, he invited several artists from far and wide. He travelled frequently to nearby states to contact various artists, poets, singers, and dancers.

Munshidas and Vishnudas,two of his associates, entered his office.

'What happened? Are you fine?' They expressed concern noticing his tense face.

'Yes, yes...! In fact, no...! I tell you the truth; I am worried. I had sent an invite to a dancer, a Muslim woman, from Agra. She is really a very good kathak dancer. She consented to give a performance in the royal court and promised that she would be here two days prior to the event, but today I have no clue of her, she has yet to reach Jaipur. It is already noon.' Jayraj was agitated.

'Already so many artists have arrived and they all have been practising day and night for flawless performance. If she does not turn up, it will be her loss.' Munshidas tried to pacify his agitated mind.

'No, it will be my loss. I have already declared that on this occasion, I will present a beautiful dancer who will surpass all the performances that have taken place so far, and this piece of information has reached to our Maharaja as well. I will cut a sorry figure in his eyes if she does not show up. It seems she has ditched me. Anyway, I have to brace myself to withstand the worst of my loud mouth and premature announcement. Let us finish other tasks. We are running short of time.' All of them joined their heads on the paper sheets and files spread on the desk.

✳

About six months back, Jayraj had met the dancer at *meena bazaar* of Agra. Since then, he visited her whenever he had an opportunity. He appreciated her dancing skill and she enjoyed his company. Gradually, he developed a deeper bond with her. Whenever he played the *sitar*, she could not control herself and danced ecstatically. During their meetings, she realised that Jayraj could be a ladder she can use for her own benefit.

Jayraj was aware of her clandestine ambition – somehow, to creep into the royal premises of Rajputana. *Kotha*, at *meena bazaar* was too small to accommodate her growing aspiration. He thought that the coronation of Jagat Singh could be a blessing in disguise for her. Jayraj himself sought this opportunity to come closer to her. And she instantly agreed to come to Jaipur, then, why did she not turn up today? 'Oh! I am in a deep mess,' moaned Jayraj.

As Jayraj was about to cancel her name from the list, a messenger brought the news of her arrival. Jayraj jumped from his seat in excitement. He breathed a deep sigh of relief.

Humayun, the Mughal emperor put forth the concept of *meena bazaars* or *kuhs ruz* keeping in mind the women of the harem and nobility. In order to engage, his women folk in some creative pursuits, he thought of providing an opportunity for them to display their artefacts, garments, perfumes and other fine things, at a particular place. Mughal emperor and only a few selected princes could visit the *bazaars* to buy the items. Common people were not allowed to go to such markets. Over the years, a few dancing girls began to settle in the vicinity of such *bazaars*. The special kathak dancer of Jayraj was one of them.

✳

The gala evening was to be held in *Sarvatobhadra*, the grand hall, a few yards away from Chandra Mahal. This magnificent square marble-floored hall was located between the armoury and the art gallery, meant for royal gatherings. The late king of Jaipur, Sawai Jai Singh, constructed the hall. He called various sections of the people to suggest an appropriate name for the hall. Common people gave the name *Sarbata*, while the nobility suggested *Divan-e-Khas*.Jai Singh chose *Sarvatobhadra*. Initially, it was used for consultation with ministers and hosting dinner parties for the important dignitaries. Later, *darbars* too were held on special occasions.

The walls of *Sarvatobhadra* were decorated with huge wall paintings and gold framed wall clocks. Chandeliers were lit up with thousands of candles. Persian carpets were rolled on the floors. Colourful curtains were flowing on the doors. The main marble hall was filled with intricately woven tapestries.

Queens, princesses, women of nobility had occupied their seats in the pre-allotted latticed windows. Concubines were seated in the windows on the opposite side.

The air was heavy with the fragrance of flowers and the *attar* of roses; nobles and chieftains began to gather in the hall. They were plump and thin, stout and sluggish. Their dark eyes flickered world-weary greetings. Columns of royal guards greeted them. *Sewadaars* glided amongst them with wine, gin, and whiskies, while some of them were serving a variety of soft drinks.

Gradually, all began to take their seats. They leant back, hands clasped, with the layered *jamas* covering their knees. Their calm and black brown eyes were glancing here and there.

The guards stood smartly to attention along the corridors pillared in yellowish porcelain, as Maharaja Jagat Singh, dressed in traditional brocade and turban glided into the hall with his *sewadaars* behind him.

All the guests stood up to welcome the new Maharaja. They kept their glasses filled with wine down on the side tables. Musicians too stood up, placing their instruments carefully on the quilted carpets, greeted Maharaja crouching three times, '*Ghanni Khamma* Maharaj!' Maharaja returned the greetings before taking his seat.

✳

Jayraj, the master of the cultural programme came forward and sought permission of the king to begin the programme. Maharaj raised his right hand as a sign to begin the drums and cymbals, marking the beginning of this much awaited evening.

Jayraj asked the instrumentalists to begin with classical *ragas* like *Abhogi*, followed by *Adana*, then *Bageshawri* and *Bahaar* and to conclude with *Khamaj*. The deep reverberation of various percussion and stringed instruments–*mridang, saarangi, naad, santur, chang, taanpura, dilruba,* and *rabab*–filled the hall with mesmerising melody.

First, four dancers presented a group performance. Muhammad Razaak, a *gazal* singer, enchanted the court with his melodious voice. Noori Bano, a well-known kathak dancer from Kishangarh danced for an hour. It was almost night by then.

Jayraj again came forward and said.

'Kindly permit me to present the dancer specially meant and prepared for the occasion. Her beauty can give tough competition to any celestial nymph – Uravshi or Menaka. Her sweet melodious voice can match with a cuckoo and her dancing skill can beat any Rambha.[1]'

He indicated the dancer to move forward. She came slowly like a *gajgamini*[2] and stood in the centre, bowing down her head. Dressed in a pale pink *ghaghra* and yellow and pink *chunar*, she looked exquisitely

---

[1] As per the ancient Indian texts, Urvashi, Menaka and Rambha are the celestial nymphs known for their exquisite beauty and supreme skills in dancing and singing.

[2] It is actually a description of woman in Vatsayana's definition of different types of woman -- Padmini, Mohini, Dunkini, Shrukini, Damini, Rohini etc. Gaja Gamini is one of them. Gaja Gamini is the woman who walks like an elephant. This analogy is used to describe the seductive walk of a woman. In classical Indian dance forms it is called Tribhang or the three breaks in your body.

beautiful. A thin veil covered her face. Her black hair, brushing her waist, was layered around her face. She had fine, small features and hazel eyes. Her skin was perfect with the colour of pale white pearl. Her arms were decked with bangles. Glittering stones were strewn on her ornaments. On one of her arms was tied, an ornament called *bajuband*, in the shape of two leaves. She was a ravishing beauty. Her rose petal lips shivered and the conch shaped eyes were fixed on her feet, not a word escaping her lips. She was equally skilled in her art, to match her beauty. Trained by her father, she had already earned perfection in kathak.

Maharaja motioned her to begin.

She began with a prayer, and then stunned the spectators with her entry in style, and posture she had at the beginning of her performance that followed by *chakkars* (spins). Soon she made different *tatkars* (synchronised feet-and-hand footwork) with vivid types and speeds. Practice and clarity in mnemonic syllables and spiral movements astonished each one present in the hall. *Jugalbandi*, (technical rendering of the footsteps with drum player) she presented, was of high class and spectators were amazed by the different rhythmic patterns of high speed, balancing the sound of ankle bells from minute to the higher volume.

As her performance was about to conclude, she reached the seat of Jagat Singh. He paid her all the compliments. 'You are the foremost of all the famous dancers, I salute you. O, beautiful lady! What do you want?'

'Maharaj, May I get a chance to perform again in your presence?' she said bowing.

'Yes, of course! Tomorrow, after the gala dinner for the guests, we all would derive great pleasure from your dance.'

✳

Most of the guests extended their stay for one more day as they were enjoying the hospitality of Jagat Singh.

The majority of them spent the day in hunting, while some preferred to relax in their rest rooms. A few visited *pothikhana* (library and book production department), *Suratkhana* (painting department) and *Gunijankhana* (Department of dance, music and drama).

Hundreds of people and experts like Faizullah, Mir Ali, Tan Sahib, Fakirullah, Mangal, Ramsewak, Gopal, Udai, Laksman, Saligram, Jiwan, Ghasi, Hukma, Radhakrishn, Chiman, Raju, Sitaram, Rajaram, Dayaram, and Hira recreated the court and celebrations on paper and cloth and their paintings were displayed at a painting gallery for sale. They all played an important role in the growth of *Suratkhana*. Invitees visiting the painting galleries were astonished to see the artistic treasure of Jaipur.

This was an occasion that attracted scholars from faraway places, like Ambapati, Parasram, Mahesh, Keshav, Dev Bhattacharya, Kashinath, and Vasudev from Bengal; Ramjidas from Nepal; Pran Nath, the physician, from Allahabad; Akheram Vyas, a learned Brahmin came all the way from Ratlam to attend the ceremony. They were duly rewarded whenever they produced commendable poems and stories. Kavishwar, Mandan, Padmakar, Ishwariprasad, and others from Jaipur continued to occupy prestigious seats in the court and they were even given four hundred rupees yearly out of the state budget for a long time. On the occasion of the coronation, all of them were showered with gifts, clothes, and gems.

In the *Pothikhana*, several scribes such as Umedram, Gopiram, Subharam, Tularam, Siva, and Gunamani penned down quality literary works. *Pothikhana* gradually developed into a magnificent library. It was open round the clock so that guests could visit the library at any time. A rare collection of books was displayed for the dignitaries. When the guests visited the huge library, they were shell shocked to see the collection. They spent many mornings in *Pothikhana* and were astounded to see valuable manuscripts and books. The rare collection of priceless books and paintings mesmerised them.

Late Sawai Jai Singh was a patron of arts and crafts. Art and literature were highly valued by him. He collected all kinds of manuscripts– small and big. It was said that no king had more manuscripts in his library than Jai Singh. He promoted all kinds of art forms. He himself was very interested in sports as well. All the handicraft workshops that had been thriving for long in Jaipur vibrated with activities during his rule. Many painters prospered in Jaipur and they represented a number of paintings depicting surroundings of Jaipur and beauty of women. Various groups of artists, who were the direct descendants of the experts kept alive the old traditions of art with the support of the royal court and all the three departments of dance, music and drama continued to cover new milestones during his time.

Later kings strengthened this tradition, and allowed enough space and freedom to the artists to hone their skills at their will. Unlike his father, though, Jagat Singh did not take much interest in literature, but he maintained the library with utmost care. Generally, he was particular that the manuscripts must not be issued to be taken outside the library. Indeed Jagat Singh was bestowed with rich heritage, besides the crown.

✳

The next day, the guests spent time in excitement. The night descended. The moonlight spattered its silver beam on the domes, ramparts, sprawling gardens, and corridors. At the fence, trees were silhouetted against the starry sky. Scattered clouds, fragrance of flowerbeds and cool breeze were weaving a magic all around.

The hall was illuminated by the glow of the lit lamps. The guests had gathered in the hall and taken their respective seats. Jagat was seated, attired in his best royal finery.

The chief *sewadaar* entered the hall, went straight to the chief minister, bowed, and whispered, 'Dinner is ready. Should it be served'?

The chief minister informed the king, who gave his consent. Jagat Singh got up and headed for the dining hall followed by the guests. *Maji Sahib* RathorniJi, Maharani Fateh Kanwar, other queens, princesses, and rest of the female entourage approached the female enclosure.

The aroma rousing from banqueting hall filled the nostrils of all those who were present. The servants lay down clean white cotton sheets in front of the sitting guests, before bringing pitchers of water and a basin for everyone to wash their hands. Large silver plates had been laid on the wooden tables. The servants used gold and silver serving spoons, as they distributed a dizzying array of dishes, one at a time, walking in between the guests, who were facing each other, as they sat in long straight rows on carpets, leaning against heavily embroidered velvet cushions and round shaped pillows.

First came a variety of drinks, bubbling in gold and silver glasses, followed by number of snacks – *kalmi vada*, deep fried gram flour crispies served with spicy green *chutney*, made of mint and chillies; stuffed *kachori* prepared with a filling of onions, potatoes and spices; *methi bajra poori*, steaming hot snacks served with chutney, fried potatoes and curd.

There were non-vegetarian dishes, a perfect treat for the royalties: *laal Maas*, the signature mutton dish of Rajputana cooked in red chilly gravy, hot and spicy, which gets its colour from the fiery red chillies; *mohan Maas*, kings, and queens had a special preference for, cooked with milk and mild spices, which makes it tender and juicy. The thick gravy infused with the flavours of poppy seeds, lemon and cardamom brings out the lovely flavour of the dish. For a cooler dish, there was white mutton cooked in curd, cream, and poppy seeds. Spices softly teased and seduced the appetite so that everyone was exactly high on the food. Each course had been slow cooked in clay pots; the mutton was so tender that it melted in the mouth. Then, there were royal dishes meant only for special invitees and the king and queens – fruit based dishes, partridges and quails, roasted duck and different types of fish.

Then there were vegetarian dishes, especially besan based. *Shahi gatte, or Govind gatte,* gram flour dumplings filled with generous amount of nuts and then deep fried. *Panchkuti daal,* round *baatis* dipped in *ghee* and churma,served for an appetising combination. *Ram pulao,* a rich combination of fresh steamed rice and spicy *gatte, Kersangri,* a tangy side dish, *Aam ki launji,* made of soft raw mango chunks, its sweet and sour gravy texture were added for taste buds.

The crowning glory was the aromatic and fragrant sweets covered with a thin golden net shimmering in the flickering lamps. *Gujias* with sugar syrup oozing out of the *khoya* and dry fruit. *Balushahi,* a flaky texture on the outside and sugar syrup inside; *malai ghevar, mava ghevar and plain ghevar,* disc shaped delectable sweet prepared with ghee, flour, *paneer* and sugar syrup; *mawa kachori* filled with dry fruits and *khoya,* deep fried and then dipped in sugar syrup. Hot piping *badam ka halwa* prepared with almonds and dry fruits, *suji,* sugar and *ghee,* which melts as soon as it lands on tongue. There were *churma ladoos or desi ghee ladoos* the most delicious sweets; *dil-khushal* or *mohan-thaal* a nice chewy textured sweet that leaves a grainy flavour.

Meanwhile, the head cook came by, inquiring whether the guests were satisfied with the meal. The guests smiled appreciatively at him.

The topic that dominated the dinner tables discussions was, of course, the mesmerising performance of the Muslim dancer from Agra.

Everyone present on the table raved about her, while Jagat Singh, overawed by her beauty, couldn't keep his mind on anything but her.

✳

After the dinner, he called for the dancer to appear in front of him, but in a private and discreet manner. When she was brought to him, he once again gazed at the pearl white skinned beauty and was spellbound. He got up from his seat, walked slowly towards her, sinking into the enchanting depths of her dark eyes. Jagat came to the dancer, held her face in his palms, and pressed his lips over her cheeks.

'I feel a strange pull towards you. From now onwards, you are mine. You listen carefully, you are mine,' he whispered. They looked at each other long and deep as their minds and bodies felt a strange satisfaction.

'Maharaj! Let me go! People must be waiting for you…in the hall,' she whispered.

Jagat looked at her indulgently, embraced her tightly for a moment, then freed her and left the chamber hurriedly.

Fully replenished, the guests and hosts were restlessly waiting for the king. As Jagat Singh appeared, their faces beamed.

Musicians took their place, and got ready carrying their instruments. The tabla player and Jayraj presented a fine *jugalbandi*. He was master of the instrument and was reputed to be one of the finest musicians in the state. A flute player and one artist accompanied him on the *mridangam*. Jayraj played the *sitar* and the kathak dancer performed so well that Jagat Singh was completely mesmerised.

All the men present in the hall feasted their eyes upon her beauty and her delightful dance, while Jagat Singh, all through devoured her with his eyes.

Unable to control himself anymore, he got up and walked towards her with frenzied passion. Exhilarated with the chalices of liquor he had drunk, and excited also by the uncontrollable desire of the dancing woman, he moved towards her in faltering steps.

'You are made for me. I feel…I feel…'Jagat said softly, as he tightened his arms around her.

'As if I know you for several lifetimes,' she completed his words. They felt as though their minds and bodies had found their other halves.

Oblivious to their surroundings, they continued standing in each other's arms, until *Maji Sahib* deliberately dropped a silver bowl that was kept at the small table near her.

✳

Fateh Kanwar seated in the window shivered and closed her eyes. Quietly, she left her seat, returned to her room, and fell down on her bed, crumpled up, like a little sparrow with a broken wing. She was utterly destroyed; like a rare delicate bird that was left to flutter and hover all alone in the storm. She felt as if with the suddenness of a desert sand storm that had cropped up in her life, she would be swept, shrieking and wailing.

Maji Sahib turned her face on seeing her son's disgraceful behaviour. Other women bent their faces down; their repulsion was visible on their faces.

Fateh Kanwar promised to herself, 'I may be crushed, yet I shall never ever invite pity from any quarter. I have never posed; I am not an ordinary woman. I belong to Rathores of Bikaner. I am not a fake woman. I am true to myself. So what if I am a lone fighter today.' She repeated it many times.

Fateh was devastated. Tonight, Fateh knew the true colours of her husband, the night, which changed her life forever. Tonight, it seemed somebody had cast an evil eye on her happy world. She longed for her husband's companionship, but he lay in the arms of a dancer completely oblivious of her. Her fun and laughter-filled days and nights vanished like vapour suddenly.

Tonight, Jagat had disclosed his hidden and perhaps innermost trait. Tonight, she learnt that her husband perhaps was a slave of his cardinal desires.

Jagat Singh, unmindful of the galaxy of people present in the hall, showered the dancer with pearls, diamonds, and gold coins. He prowled around her like a leopard. So enthralled was Jagat Singh that he went to the extent of naming her 'Raskapoor', instantly, right in the presence of guests and political dignitaries.

'All your wishes will be fulfilled. What is your name?'

The dancer faltered. Jagat said loudly waving his hand.

'Okay. Forget your name. From today, your name will be Raskapoor! You have won me over forever. My Raskapoor. This royal palace and my heart will be your abode from now onwards.'

The beautiful face of the dancer flushed with joy. How she dreamt of coming closer to this young handsome king, Jagat Singh! As she felt herself deeply drawn to him.

'I cannot believe…it. My dream has come true.' She said excitedly.

'I shall make all your dreams come true, My Raskapoor, essence of my life. I shall make those stars twinkle only for you. I shall make your beautiful feet dance only for me. Do you know the meaning of your name? You are an essence. Essence of camphor! Essence of my life!'

The celebrations ceased. All the guests left the hall one by one. Jagat Singh, holding the arm of the dancer, moved towards his private chamber.

Queens and other royal women had already retired. Only Jayraj remained there in the centre of the hall, standing all alone and stunned.

CHAPTER 5

1803
Reigning with Concubine

The officials and courtiers were unhappy with the behaviour of their new king. On the first day after his coronation, the throne remained unoccupied and the court, unattended. The royal court of Jaipur waited for their new Maharaja for a couple of hours and then everybody dispersed in utter embarrassment and disgust. Important state programmes and matters were left unattended, as if those were trivial issues. The second day was no different. Jagat Singh remained fully engaged with his new found interest.

Officials fulfilled their duty; informed *Maji Sahib* and requested her to intervene, as the situation was grave. There could not have been a worse day than this for *Maji Sahib*. Yet, she maintained her composure and did whatever she could.

She called her son. Jagat came in the evening in an inebriated state.

'Jagat! How was your first day in the court?'

'*Masa*, I could not attend the court as I was very tired. Why did you call me, *Masa*? All is fine?'

'I think all is not fine! I understand my son! The yoke of kingship has been put on your shoulders prematurely. Are you not ready for it?' Jagat was quiet.

' But you have no choice now. You are the only solace for me and the people of Jaipur. I am sure that you will rule the state with utmost wisdom. Your father was confident about you. He mentioned it many times that Jagat will bring glory to the Kachwaha dynasty.'

Jagat did not answer.

'If you have any issue, you are free to consult me. And you have a band of capable ministers to advise you.'

Jagat just nodded. He was still silent. He ignored his mother's pleas. He spent some time there without responding, and then went out with his head bent down.

✳

It was the morning of the third day. As the sun shone brightly on the horizon, prayers began with the *dholak, jhanjh, manjiras,* in the Govind Temple. The Maharaja came out of his room with Raskapoor by his side and headed towards the temple. Both participated in the prayers. The priests were shocked to see them. They never expected their presence in the temple in the morning. However, the head priest moved forward to greet the King.

Raskapoor took the *tanpura* kept in a corner and began to recite a *bhajan*. Everybody was surprised to see her. Her tender fingers sashayed skilfully over the strings of the *tanpura*, filling the temple premises with an ethereal piece of music, as she gave a rendition of a devotional song of Lord Krishna.

Matwalo Kanhudo mharo rang rasiyo
Rang dalyo Radha, upar bhigi chunaria sari
Ude gulal aaj ambar mein, rang ri ude phuhari
Matwalo Kanhudo mharo rang rasiyo
Radha sang holi khele dekho Kanhudo
Radha baraj baraj ke hari
Kanhudo koni maan rahyo
Phagan rang baras rahyo

Matwalo Kanhudo mharo rang rasiyo.

(My colourful lover crazy Lord Krishna,
You threw the colours on Radha and drenched her shawl.
Colours are raining and *gulals* are flying in the sky,
My colourful lover, my crazy Lord Krishna,
Krishna is playing Holi with Radha.
Radha got tired of scolding him,
Krishna did not pay heed to her words.
Colours of spring are raining,
My colourful lover, my crazy Lord Krishna.)

Meanwhile, Jagat Singh reclined serenely on the gold – embroidered cushions, admiring the newfound love of his life, from a distance. He had decided to move away from the hassles of this place with his new concubine. By the time the song concluded, he had chosen the desired place, the Jaigarh fort, to be turned into his love nest. The priest blessed and offered prasada to the Maharaj and others, including Raskapoor.

✳

One week passed. Jagat Singh did not come to the royal court, even once. He sent a message for his chief minister to take care of all the relevant matters in his absence and as he won't be available for some more time. The chief minister collected important files and rushed to get his approval on important matters but by the time he reached to his chamber, Jagat had left for Jaigarh.

Jagat and Raskapoor began enjoying ecstasy in each other's arms, cuddling and whispering in the serenity of Jaigarh – a pleasure made more passionate by the awareness that their paradise might be disturbed at any time.

Raskapoor came into his life, when he was seventeen-year, a teenage king, and married, royal representative of an illustrious

Kachwaha dynasty. She was his danseuse, his concubine, a ravishing beauty, who was, currently, his life, his source of enjoyment, his contentment, but his brainteaser as well.

The day when he was on his way to Jaigarh, *Maji Sahib* cajoled him, reasoned wittily, and persuaded him affectionately not to ignore his responsibilities anymore for pleasure... But Jagat proved to be a hard, a very hard nut to crack.

On their way to Jaigarh in a carriage, Raskapoor asked the king. 'Are you not scared even of your mother?'

'After the declaration of my love for you openly in the court, I felt as if I have unburdened my soul. No shackles! No yoke to carry. I feel as if I am a free bird now.' She put her head on his shoulder. Jagat continued, 'I am no longer of my own. My Ras, I belong to you and I will do anything to make you happy.'

Since the day, Raskapoor entered Jagat's life; the days of Fateh were never the same again.

Apparently, Raskapoor, a name meaning 'essence of camphor', was given to her by the Maharaja on that fateful evening that sucked all the essence from the body of Fateh Kanwar and filled her life with such a burning fire that was never extinguished. Raskapoor displaced her from her husband's life. She was no more in the heart and mind of Jagat Singh. She knew that her husband was bewitching, charming, but at the same time wanton and hedonist. He hardly cared for others.

✳

Jagat Singh and Raskapoor sought after each other's company through day and night, unmindful to the outside world. As ardour arose between them, they lay intertwined in each other's arms. They had discovered paradise in the solitude of Jaigarh. From a poor entertainer, who lived in a mud house, she became a powerful woman overnight; she now had a magnificent palace, luxuries, as she had never dreamt of, and a fleet of maids and servants to fulfil all her wishes. She began to act virtually like an empress.

For Jagat Singh, afternoons were his mornings. Nights were his evenings, lingering until midnight in the arms of Raskapoor, an ambitious dancer well-endowed with the instrument of pleasure.

Jagat was always overwhelmed to see her properly dressed. But today she was not her usual self when she came to him. She especially adorned herself with fragrant flowers- flowers on the forehead, around her neck and waist , on her wrists and ankles. A shawl was hanging on her shoulder to cover her well-sculpted figure. Her enormous black eyes and oval face gave her a haunting look . Her mouth, half opened, was inviting. Her long and straight tresses hung loosely over her shoulders and back, almost touching her knees. She was exotic in her sexuality.

She moved languidly towards him and looked in the eyes of Jagat, held his arms, and took him to his bed. Sitting on the carpet, she began to sing an erotic song.

Misri ko bag laga de rasia
Misri ko bag laga de rasia
Neem ki nimbodi mhane khari lage
Rasia , misri ko bag…
Thari sanwali… surat
Thari sanwali surat matwali lage
Mhane meem ki nimbodi khari lage
Rasia misri ko bag…
(Set up a garden of sweet misri, my love,
Fruits of neem tree are very sour.
Set a garden of sweet misri, my love,
Your dark face looks very intoxicating.
Fruits of neem tree are very sour.)

Jagat felt strong desire for sensual pleasure. He picked her up from the floor and began to caress her shoulders and arms softly. She brushed aside his arms and began moving around him with erotic expressions, challenging him to catch hold of her. Unable to stay away from her even for a short while, Jagat Singh almost ran behind Raskapoor, pulled her in his arms with a jerk, dropped a kiss on her forehead and when she looked up smilingly, he showered a stream of kisses on her different body parts.

They both stood there, holding each other with crossed hands, looking into eyes then they began to dance slowly in circles. There was a sleek suppleness to her movements. Each move spun sensuous curve that promised sweet pleasures as she clasped Jagat with fierce fervour.

Jagat's hands clasped her slim waist, pressing against her back in a tight embrace and spun her round and round. Her breasts were ready to burst out of her upper garment. She wanted to tear her garment off and her lithe body wanted to dance free of all restraints. The sweet fragrance, the hum of the music and her hips thrusting in tune with the rhythmic movements of the dance were all too hypnotic to keep him spell bound.

'Ah, fabulous! Superb! How dainty are these fingers! So tender like a fragile vine! What a melodious voice! Ras...Ras…ask for anything that is available in this world.'

'My Maharaj! My lord! My life! Take me to your Chandra Mahal. People talk about us, they talk about me in disdain, and they hate me for loving you. But, they are your people; I do not wish to stand in between the king and his people. Jaipur needs you right now, and I often think of letting you go, but I love you too much to do that. So, let's go and be with your people, show them what a great king you are and how strong our love is!'

'Your wish is my command! Today, I give you my words, Chandra Mahal is yours! Yes we will go back.' And he jumped into the fire raging within both of them.

✳

A couple of weeks rolled by. Raskapoor continued to enjoy special treatment in Jaigarh, though with each passing day, she was getting impatient. She was absolutely fine in Jaigarh, a majestic palace, built on the *Cheel ka teela* hills, much like a jewel on a crown, with thick walls of red sandstone, and spread over a vast range of miles in length and width. The fort was a huge palace complex, comprising *Laksmi Vilas, Lalit Mandir, Aram Mandir,* and the *VilasMandir.* But Chandra Mahal is altogether a different world! The seat of power!

Raskapoor was taking a stroll in the well-tended sprawling garden in front of *Lakshmi Vilas.* Jagat Singh had to attend a crucial meeting in the assembly hall with the courtiers, warriors, and nobles. She, in the midst of her wandering thoughts, fixed her gaze on the lights at the foothills. That was her final destination.

'Chandra Mahal, a luxurious palace, grand residence of my king, Jagat Singh.' She sighed. 'Ah! This fort is also unparalleled, beyond my dreams. I could have never imagined such a beautiful life, a few months before. If only I could get that special palace, somehow, which was meant for other queens of my lover as well. Maharaja has already given his words that he will take me there very soon.'

For Raskapoor, however, Chandra Mahal was still a distant dream. Though Jagat Singh had promised her, but he showed no inclination to leave Jaigarh in near future. Days turned into weeks.

And Raskapoor! Desperately eager to achieve her goal, to be placed in the Chandra Mahal, her dream destination. She was feeling a strange uneasiness.

'Why he is taking so long to return to Jaipur?' She wondered. 'I know I am here to satiate his desires and I will continue to do that there in the dream palace as well.'

Although Jagat had noticed unusual swings of her mood sometimes, but he did not take it seriously. Oblivious of her motive, Jagat was not in any mood to return to his normal life soon.

✳

The chief minister was anguished. The political situation of the state was slipping from bad to worse, but Jagat Singh was completely indifferent to his state-matters. The people, who did not matter much to him, began to raise their voices. Jagat Singh, however, remained unseen, unheard, and unapproachable.

'Paying attention to others judgment is not my duty. To satisfy others is not my intention here. I care for my own bliss, my own happiness. Ras is my happiness.'

After a hiatus of more than a month at Jaigarh, he, at last obliged his people. Seated on the throne, in the presence of courtiers and officials, he appeared lost and confused. He abruptly got up, left the court saying that his presence was neither required, nor important to squander his time on trivial matters...

'The chief minister can take care of all the matters. Only grave issues must come to my notice. I am not born to waste my life on dull and drab matters. I have a team of senior officials and elderly ministers for such jobs.'

This was Jagat's final *farman*(order). Same evening he returned to Jaigarh.

✳

The chief minister thought of dealing with the culprit in his own way and Jayraj was the culprit in his opinion. He then dug deep into the matter.

'Knowing the weakness of the king, why did Jayraj bring forth such a woman in front of Maharaja? Nevertheless, somehow this wretched woman must be thrown away from Jaipur. What is the motive of her arrival? Is she planted by some neighbouring state or by the Mughals? Does she have some hidden agenda? May be or maybe not. But the fact is that Maharaj himself had fallen into her trap. Is it really a trap?' Juggling with one thought after another for hours, the chief minister decided to confront Jayraj.

Jayraj was called.

'Give us the details of the Muslim dancer, you introduced on the occasion of the coronation ceremony. Who is she? Where did she come from? Why did she come to Jaipur? For money? For power? Or for something else? Is this her plan or yours? How do you know her? Is she only an artist or a prostitute? Does she have some sinister scheme? And be careful, if you try to betray Jaipur state, you will be chased through the streets of Jaipur town, to be killed like a mad dog.' The minister threw a volley of questions.

Jayraj was shocked. Though bewildered, he answered each query in a calm and composed manner.

'*Srimant*, I knew very little about her. I met her at Agra. I saw her dance performance at *Meena bazaar*. She is from a *vaishya* community, that's what she told me once. She used to sing *bhajans* in a temple to make her living. People began to like her singing for her melodious voice. She was invited to sing *bhajans* in most of the temples. When I heard of her, I thought of giving her a chance to sing at the ceremony. She preferred to dance instead of singing. I found her dance flawless. My only mistake was that I invited her for the celebrations, having least inkling about her grand design. I was swayed by her performance that was par excellence. I knew her as a talented dancer and a singer; I had absolutely no idea that she had harboured any vicious plan,' Jayraj uttered slowly.

'Are you a fool? You introduced her as a Muslim dancer. Now you are telling me that she was a *vaishya* woman!' growled the minister.

'Pardon me, sir! Of course, she behaved like a Muslim woman but she told me later…Please forgive me!' Jayraj faltered awkwardly.

Though Jayraj had anticipated some problem when he received the message and it could be something to do with the dancer, he had already guessed. He was aware of the gossips doing the rounds in the royal corridors. 'Kings and concubines, inseparable entities, were always together. This is not something that had happened for the first time. Why it is a problem now? Did she commit some crime?' he wondered.

Jayraj kept standing quietly. He had no answer. In fact, he himself did not know that her performance would eventually take such an ugly turn.

The chief minister raised his eyebrows and continued to stare at him. His gimlet eyes were fixed on his face. Jayraj stood uncomfortably, shaken and baffled. The minister indicated to him with his index finger to leave. Jayraj left the office distraught. He knew that he had landed himself in a serious problem.

❋

One fine morning, Thakur Chandra Singh, *thikanedaar* of Duni came to meet the chief minister. He was a noble and a warrior known and respected for his wisdom. *Maji Sahib* and other senior nobles used to pay heed to his counsel.

He advised the chief minister to take *Maji Sahib* into his confidence and seek her advice. Both pondered over the issue at length and then decided, as a first step, to create a rift, somehow, between Maharaja and his concubine, but their efforts bore no fruits.

Then, the chief minister and Chandra Singh held a meeting with *Maji Sahib* and brought forth the issue of Raskapoor.

'The way Maharaja Jagat Singh has been behaving since his coronation is a serious matter, *Maji Sahib Hukum!*' The minister said awkwardly, with his head bent.

Chandra Singh prophesied that the rule of Kachwahas seems fated to be destroyed by the hands of its own protector. He criticised Jagat for his behaviour that was unlike a Rajput. He was so disgusted that he could not hide his indignation.

Maji Sahib heard each word of the two of them patiently. Her face had turned red, as she was quite ashamed of her son. 'He is just like his father,' she lamented deep in her heart.

She recollected that a dancer too besotted her husband; he brought her to zenana by making her a *pardayat*, then, a singer came in his life, who ruled over his heart for some time. He even loved to bestow titles liberally to beautiful women like *rai, sukh, bai, chain, sahiba* etc., and some of them were made *pardayats*. 'My son has surpassed his father in this regard,'she deplored.

'If he can't live without her, he can follow chura paravan practice and make her his pardayat.'

Maji Sahib told the minister to convey her message to his Maharaja.

Chura paravan was a commonly accepted practice among the royals. The king used to give bangles to a woman he wished to keep with him. The *pardayats* or *paswans* were not wedded wives, but after the *chura*, they were admitted into the zenana and provided all the facilities. They were allowed to participate in the events and festivals held in the palace. The marriage of their children used to be fixed as per the tradition. They even attended condolence and funeral ceremonies. After their demise, they were cremated with due honour. Some *pardayats* enjoyed immense trust of the queens and at times, the queens on festivals and feasts invited them. Raskapoor was the latest to join the herd, but she was not happy and contended merely by becoming a *pardayat*; she had ambitions soaring high.

✳

Jagat's sojourn at Jaigarh for the last five months had begun to lose its sheen and charm. He began to miss his familiar surroundings, Chandra Mahal. At times, he felt like having a break even from the grip of his concubine.

'What has happened Maharaj? You are not your usual self. Is something bothering you? May I help you?' Raskapoor asked politely.

'SheonarayanJi, my minister, has requested me to return immediately. But how can I go leaving you here?'

'Then take me along! What is the problem?' Raskapoor suggested without wasting a minute.

'Yes, we are on the same plane, but…' Jagat stopped.

He himself thought of taking Raskapoor to Chandra Mahal. However, he knew that her entry was not going to be that easy; the potential resistance was formidable.

He asked his confidante minister to assess the response of nobility and *Maji Sahib*, if he returns to Chandra Mahal with Raskapoor. As expected, this was heavily resented by his mother, sisters, and other queens.

✳

RathorniJi opposed her son openly and her daughters-in law decided to stand by her. 'This is not the first time that my son is behaving with impunity. Kings have always been like untamed animals….' She was in anguish.

'This is not the time to be swept by sentiments for Jagat. How could a mere dancer be a queen of Jaipur? He did not even bother to come and discuss the matter with me. How could Raskapoor think of living here with us? My son had the audacity to send me the message through the minister. She could be given space in zenani deordhi, but she cannot enter Chandra Mahal! Absolutely not!' She promised to herself.

Maji Sahib called her daughters and daughters-in-law. She told them sternly that at any cost she would not allow Raskapoor to gain control over the royal household.

'I have made a firm decision. We do not employ a new person

or a stranger even as our *sewadaars*. Even for taking care of the daily requirements of *zenani deordhi*, only such persons are employed who belong to the families, which have been in the service of the palace for generations.' Her words provided great relief to Fateh. Her mother-in-law was her last anchor.

'*Masa!* Just think of the humiliation we all will face. Are we going to share our space with that dancer! I know, in the past some dancers had managed to get important positions, but they were only exceptions. They and their families had earned that trust after living many years in zenana. But no one stayed with us in Chandra Mahal! *Masa*, when I got to know the plan of *Bhaisa*, I was ashamed of myself,' added Princess Anand Kanwar. She was greatly annoyed with her brother.

'All of you don't worry. There is no question of accepting this *pattar*, who, all of a sudden, has emerged like a comet on the horizon of Jaipur.' Since then *Maji Sahib* used to spend hours in discussing pros and cons of this issue with her daughters and daughters-in-law.

✳

Ah! This lingering pain is killing me, *Maji Sahib* mused. 'As a daughter I witnessed the sufferings of my mother. After getting married, I passed through the same anguish. Now I am the mother and still this misery shows no sign of receding. The cause of my sorrow, now, is my own son. I always believed that my son, my own flesh and blood would give me solace, but why should he care for my woes? He has come into this world to fulfil his own aspirations. He is born with his own fate, his own desires. Then why did he choose my womb for his own purpose? Did I ask him at the time of conception; would you be my solace? He too did not seek my permission for making my womb his transitory abode. My wretched son finds bliss in the arms of Raskapoor. He is fully involved in fulfilling the dreams of that *pattar*. But not anymore! Yes, I am responsible to give birth to my son in this land of Kachwahas and I own the responsibility to protect the honour of Kachwahas, but I am not accountable to that Raskapoor. In no circumstances, this place belongs to her.' She brooded over for hours, cursing herself and her progeny.

While *Maji Sahib* was struggling to figure out an alibi to thwart the immoral demands of her son, other women of the royal household were quizzing themselves about the relevance of their own existence.

'Are they made only to suffer in this world? Why does a man inflict pain on a woman in his various forms, father, husband, and son and so on? Why does he have unlimited capacity to crush his own flesh and blood? Why does he care only for his desires? Why do the pains and feelings of others not matter to him?'

Maji Sahib, her daughters and her daughters-in-law–all the women were caught in the whirlwind of gloomy thoughts.

Under the influence of Raskapoor, Jagat Singh was completely disconnected from his own people and trusted courtiers.

One evening, while taking a stroll in the lawn, Raskapoor noticed that Jagat was not his usual self. He looked around forlornly. The garden was full of colourful flowers. There were rows of roses on one side and a series of seasonal flowerbeds on the other side. These flowers included marigold, hibiscus, sunflowers, and lilies. It was extremely delightful to see the delicate flowerbeds blooming. But the beautiful flowers failed to uplift the gloomy mood of Jagat Singh.

'What is bothering you my lord? Although physically you are so close to me, yet mentally you are so distant!' asked Raskapoor.

He replied her jadedly, 'Ras, why can't people leave us alone?'

'Yes, Maharaj! There is too much around us. I am the cause of all complications. Sometimes, I curse myself for dragging you in this difficult situation.'

'Never ever utter such words. You have given new meaning to my life, my existence. Believe me, I share nothing in common with people around me – the family, the relatives, courtiers, *thikanedaars,* this throne, this kingdom,' said Jagat Singh, putting his index finger across her moist lips.

'And what about your queen – Maharani Fateh KanwarJi, *Maji Sahib* RathorniJi, Sireh Kanwar Ji, other queens and your sisters? I am sure they must be cursing me day in and day out for taking you away from them. Do they also cease to exist for you? Have you forgotten them?' asked Raskapoor shrewdly.

Jagat gave her a dejected look. Momentarily, his thoughts floated towards Fateh. Her muffled cry flashed in his mind , when she placed her hands against her lips, as he glanced at the *jharokha,* unintentionally, at the coronation evening. But he was so overwhelmed by the charm of Raskapoor that no other thought, serious or light, no other experience, sweet or sour, no other event, good or bad, distracted him. Within no time, he came back to his original form, pulled Raskapoor in his arms and got lost in his own world of pleasure.

'They are my past. Today, my heart, my soul belongs to you! Only to you! My stunning seducer, now you are my life.'

Raskapoor smiled seductively at him. This was exactly what she wanted to hear from Jagat Singh. She deliberately raised this question to weigh the impact of his mother and queen on him. They were the greatest threat for her.

'Today, Jagat is in my arms, and tomorrow, who knows, he may settle on some other branch.'

She was quite perceptive to understand the fickleness of Jagat's love. His indulgence makes him plunge instantly in the ocean of love, his frailty forces him soon to come out of it. Once his thirst is satiated, then, in no time, he would sink again somewhere else into a sea of sleaze, with a blink; she, therefore, must act prudently and timely before his toxic obsession about her begins to ebb, Raskapoor said to herself.

✳

Dhuliabai, the senior most *daavari* of *Maji Sahib* conveyed the most awaited and dreaded message.

'*Ghanni Khamma, Maji Sahib*! Our Maharaja, Sawai Jagat SinghJi has returned from Jaigarh.'

The eyes of *Maji Sahib* twinkled, but only for a moment, and then turned into pool of darkness.

'Where is he? And that *pattar?*'

Maji Sahib stopped questioning her anymore. She controlled her excitement. 'Oh, what I was up to. I am promoting my maid to spy on my son! I must call the chief minister.'

She gestured Dhuliabai to leave. The Chief Minister was summoned.

'Why I was not informed that Maharaja had returned from Jaigarh. Is he already in the town?' She was annoyed.

'*Ghani Khamma, Maji Sahib*! Please forgive me! Maharaja came early in the morning today. I very much wanted to come to you, but Maharaja ordered me to arrange for their stay in the wing meant for the guests. Therefore, I got busy in making them comfortable. Pardon me. *Maji Sahib*!'

'Why did he go to *Atithi Niwas* (guest house)? He resides here, in *Sukh Niwas*!'

'*Maji Sahib*! Pardon me; probably because of...err...the dancer. She cannot get in to Chandra Mahal.'

'Enough! I am not seeking any explanation from you. Inform the Maharaja of Jaipur that *Maji Sahib* will meet him at the first available opportunity.'

Jagat Singh avoided meeting his mother. He knew that he would not be able to face her in the current circumstances. He found himself unable to handle many issues at one time. He wanted to live peacefully.

'The throne is not a seat of roses, but of thorns. It always gives pain. I am not born to suffer pains. Ah! Just give me some peace,' muttered Jagat Singh.

※

Through a well thought out strategy, Raskapoor used to recite *bhajans* early in the morning daily, in the family temple, to create a soft corner for herself amongst the royal women. Carefully, she also extended her network of goodwill among the courtiers. But nothing worked out for her.

Jagat Singh spent most of his time in either the company of some of his own officials like Sheonarayan, Jayraj and other sycophants or his newly found love – Raskapoor. His trusted officials created a mirage that all was well under his rule. With his concubine, he remained drunk and indulged in cardinal pleasures most of the time. His inability to gauge the situation, which was further worsened by the coterie of his men, had taken him far away from reality.

All the *thikanedaars*, nobles, relatives and courtiers, were concerned about the future of Jaipur, which was filled with foreboding. Only a thoughtless, imprudent ruler would be indifferent to his state. Jagat Singh, well aware of the growing antagonism, deliberately chose to ignore them.

The public was anxious about the working and behaviour of Maharaja. Sometimes, the daily journals were full of the scandals of the *zenani deordhi*, the follies of Jagat Singh, and his concubine Raskapoor.

Frequently, newspapers were filled with peppery columns on queens, who were thrown away from the love nest of the king. His strong allies having blue blood of Rathores of Jodhpur and Bhattis of Jaisalmer were deeply anguished. And Jagat Singh, oblivious of all the plights of his people, was comfortably nestled in the arms of

Raskapoor.

Apathy and adulation have always been devils. Jagat loved their company. Tensions were simmering underneath the apparently calm surface of Jaipur, but Jagat was not ready to pay heed.

✽

Pandit Sheonarayan was a shrewd man. He managed to be in the good books of the king. Due to his overbearing influence, Jagat Singh had removed some of his efficient ministers and replaced the chief minister by Sheonarayan.

Sheonarayan, who had successfully manipulated the king to get the coveted post, thought of putting an end to the growing antagonism, and for that end, he thought of a strategy to close the chaotic chapter of Raskapoor finally.

Sheonarayan knew that Jagat was quick and rash and in a burst of impulsive inanity, he would agree to act upon what pleases him most. Sheonarayan also knew what he would like to hear.

'Maharaj! May I give you an humble suggestion?'

'Huum! Shoot!'

'Maharaj, pardon me, if you do not appreciate my idea. I am suggesting issuing coins in the name of Raskapoor… I…I think … That perhaps, this one act will kill two birds with one stone. On the one hand, it will strengthen the position of Raskapoor and she will not feel threatened anymore by anyone, on the other. Maharaj, this is only a loud thought…if…you did not like it, forgive me.'

Jagat singh stared at him. Sheonarayan stood still, smacking his lips. A long silence.

'Yes! You are right. Her position will be safe once and for all and I will also be at peace. You must be duly rewarded for such a brilliant idea,' saying so, Jagat took out a ruby studded pearl necklace from his neck and put it in the hands of Sheonarayan. His eyes glimmered when he saw the necklace. His strategy worked. As he expected, Jagat Singh, without giving it a second thought, ordered to issue coins in the name of Raskapoor.

As if this was not enough, Jagat Singh dared take one more step. He declared that from then on, Raskapoor would be the queen of half of the Kachwaha kingdom. She was officially declared the queen of half of his dominion. People all around him, infuriated at his heedless acts, made an outcry. Arrogance and youth coupled with absolute power make a person entirely blind – devoid of his dharma and duty.

Furthermore, defiantly, he even asked his *thikanedaars* to treat her like a legally wedded queen and to pay due respect to her, which was, however, not acceptable to the nobility...

Incensed at their stubborn refusal to treat Raskapoor at par with his other legal queens, Jagat Singh took another appalling step. He announced that Raskapoor would appear with him publicly.

Highly agitated nobility was hell bent that in no way to accept a concubine as a queen. Non-acceptance on the part of elders, senior courtiers, and *thikanas* was visible in their hostile attitude. They kept on devising strategies to somehow destroy the dreamland of Raskapoor.

'None of us will greet her like a queen,' they declared.

Some of the young courtiers even openly voiced that Raskapoor was the culprit behind the deteriorating state of Jaipur.

'We all will always address her by her name. Now, Rajputs have been relegated to a stage that they will bow down to a concubine,' added a group of agitated knights.

'Who could have stopped such an errant king?' deplored relatives and elders.

✳

Raskapoor was on cloud nine the day that she rode on the same elephant, sitting beside Maharaja Jagat Singh in public. A sea of faces stared at them from the crowd on the streets. This brazen conduct of Jagat Singh further added fuel to the resentment of nobility and the public alike.

This action proved catalytic in the rapidly deteriorating systems in the state. It created a statewide furore. Common people as well as *thikanedaars* all were divided into two groups. Elders and loyalists of *Maji Sahib* stood together against the decisions of the king. While some of them covertly supported Jagat Singh. At this crucial moment, even the allies of Jagat Singh raised their voices against his mindless actions and refused to accept Raskapoor as their queen. Chandra Mahal had turned into seedbed of rebellion; the whole of Jaipur simmered with rage. At this juncture, perhaps Jaipur was facing the two most crucial predicaments – murky problems in the palace and the Maratha menace at the border.

✳

Nobles and senior courtiers decided to have a meeting with Maharaja to address the more grave issues hovering on the state than that of a dancing woman. Marathas are on the borders and looking for an opportunity to cross over. Jagat Singh, at last, obliged them.

They were standing around in a semicircle, while others were strolling about like wounded tigers moving around in a cage. One by one, they all began to pour over their grievances and fears.

Thakur Chandra Singh of Duni *thikana* voiced his frustration and anger accusingly.

'Due to non-indulgence of Sri Sawai Maharaj Bahadur in the governance, Jaipur has been suffering for months. Owing to constant intrusion, the Marathas, Pindaries, and Pathans are not only sitting on our borders, but are interfering in the internal politics of Jaipur from time to time. Daulat Rao Sindhia, the Maratha leader, had already made inroads into the frontiers of Rajputana with the intention to loot our state. He has sent a long list of demands saying that if we fail to fulfil his demands, he will extract money by levying our people.'

Jagat Singh was shocked. This was a revelation for him. He realised that his loyalists kept him in the dark.

'How can the plunderer Sindhia dare to challenge us? He must be given a befitting reply.' He glanced over at all present there, and then added, 'Sindhia has no authority to levy the people of Jaipur, in any form. How dare he enter our Kachwaha kingdom? Chase his people out of Jaipur. This is my order. If any of his men are found doing so, they must be imprisoned or killed instantly.'

✳

Probably, for a moment, a king in him, so long in deep slumber, finally woke up. Probably, he might have realised that all his desires could be met only if the soil of Jaipur was safe and currently its erosion was a dangerous sign.

However, this one-step of Jagat Singh could not deter the growing discontent among the masses and the nobility. His indifference pervaded all around. He was a spoiled prince and never put on the robe of a real king. He never ever wanted to know his role; that he was a protector of his people; that under his reign people must live happily; that he has a responsibility towards his state. He neither had inclination nor time to look after his kingdom. The yoke of Raj dharma was a great burden for him and his shoulders were very weak.

Obviously, his order was not implemented with full force, as he had no time to monitor the problems faced by his state. In addition, officials had turned a blind eye towards the Marathas' loot; some of them even connived to share the booty. Beneath the fine coating of his blue blood and aristocracy, his life, his zenana and royal court –all burning with rivalries and resentment were facing a gradual decay.

✳

Jagat's indulgence with Raskapoor made him myopic; beyond her, he could not see anything. Every now and then, the Marathas had been frequently raiding and plundering the villages and towns, which had resulted in draining of the resources of the people and revenues of the state. Courtiers requested Jagat Singh to take control over the deteriorating situation, depleting funds and resources.

Chandra Singh of Duni was bold and quite close to Maharaja. Once he got an opportunity to talk to the king in the absence of Raskapoor. He said without mincing words.

'You are giving too much time to your concubine,Maharaj. Her arrival in the palace has proved ominous. I am telling you, she is responsible for the doomsday of Jaipur!'

Jagat Singh was visibly annoyed.

'Mind your language, Chandra Singh. Have you forgotten whom are you talking to? You cannot blame a woman of royal status for the failures of others. This is not your prerogative.'

The annoyance of Maharaja did not deter Chandra Singh. Straightway, he put forth his point.

'Anger and infatuation must not overpower you Maharaj. If we try to conceal our follies under the carpet, they will be revealed in the worst form, one day. Truth no longer can remain hidden under the expensive garb of a lie. Truth will emerge eventually, even in tattered clothes. Dark clouds cannot cover the sun forever. Maharaj, the day she entered your life, you completely ignored the state responsibilities. Unfortunately, you do not follow the royal customs and traditions of your dynasty either. Had late Maharaj Pratap SinghJi been alive today, he would have surely choked himself to death!'

Jagat kept glaring at him. Chandra Singh stared back for some time, then took a sigh, and continued.

'Very humbly I would say that henceforth, we will not tolerate her presence either in the court or in the palace premises, even for a moment.'

'So many women reside and pass their lives in the palace. Do they all belong to a royal line? No. Then how come Raskapoor is not entitled to live with them?' Jagat Singh replied irritably

'Yes Maharaj! But none is allowed to cross the stipulated boundaries set for them. None is given the status of a queen. None is permitted to live in the Chandra Mahal meant for the king and his queens. Earlier you married thrice, but none of your queens is responsible for your disinterest in the state affairs, but Raskapoor is guilty. You treat her as if she is a nymph who has been thrown away from the heaven and you are supposed to keep her in all the luxuries, which she does not deserve at all. Why Maharaj? What is the compulsion for you to behave in this manner? Yes! She has made the king himself fall down on his knees in her subservience.'

Jagat Singh , unaffected by his words, thundered.

'No more stupid utterances! I am keeping quiet, because I take you as my close friend. It is a pity that a great man like you has fallen prey to the treacherous emotions of jealousy and envy. There's nothing more left to say.' He dismissed the meeting and left the room in a huff.

✳

A few more days passed in restrained resentment. Again, one more meeting was fixed with the king after much persuasion.

Jagat Singh, visibly annoyed entered the hall; all his *thikanedaars* and courtiers, standing quietly in a row greeted him in a traditional way. He could measure that all of them would take up the issue of Raskapoor.

Sheonarayan had already conveyed the message to him.

'They are all set to blow the same trumpet – issue of *Rani Sahib*

RaskapoorJi! Maharaj from now onwards, you focus only on state matters. It will be better to ignore the issue of *Rani SahibJi* for the time being. Don't give them any opportunity to raise this matter.'

Jagat smiled in agreement. He liked his piece of advice.

In the meeting, the other ministers and nobles maintained silence, as a mark of protest. Their silence was a clear indication of their hostility towards Raskapoor and they were in support of Duni *thikanedaar*. Unfortunately, such meetings were not bearing the desired fruit. He realised that it would be sensible to evade the issue for a while. Jagat Singh refused to discuss Raskapoor anymore.

After a few weeks Jagat Singh threw a stone in apparently calm waters of Jaipur polity. He boldly declared that Raskapoor would stay with him in Chandra Mahal. His decision added an insult to the injury of *thikanas*.

CHAPTER 6

1803…
Entry into Dream House

Renovation had already begun at a fast pace in a selected portion of Chandra Mahal. The mason department was ordered to make some alterations as per the requirements of Raskapoor in the area adjoining the first floor. Hundreds of workers under the supervision of the head of the mason department were working day and night. Preparations were in full swing for the welcome of Raskapoor as a queen of Jaipur.

An area was demarcated to be developed as her living space. The adjoining block of the palace was being converted into a separate complex for Raskapoor. Her special residence having being built by masons, who were well trained in the Mughal style. There were suites of two small rooms at both ends, a central-hall, the verandas, narrow passages and enclosed open space in between, the doorways with sculptured peacock, elephants, human figures and animals, maximum use of colour and mirrors on the walls and the ceilings were painted in bright colours. The main entrance gate with a pair of massive doors was engraved with various motifs of flowers.

There was a pond in the centre of the room. Flow pipes for cold and hot water were used to fill the pond through straight marble drains. There was a huge mirror on the north wall of the room. This room was meant to be used for bathing and dressing. The adjoining room was equally decorative. A huge bed with quilted bed covers, tables, and chairs were made. Hooks were fixed on the walls to hang the dresses, waistbands and other such items. Huge wooden boxes and intricately carved small boxes were placed in the storehouse.

Close advisors of Jagat Singh warned him many times. 'Do not commit the mistake of placing a dancer on a platform equal to your legal queens. Do not commit the mistake of lifting the dirt off the ground to adorn the crown on your head.'

Jagat Singh, adamant and blinded by his yearnings for Raskapoor, chose to ignore all the words of caution.

'Why do people unnecessarily create problems in my life? How can a person's birth decide his karma and position? Therefore, what if Ras was a dancer, today she is my queen. So what if she has come from a low background, I do not mind,' he asked Sheonarayan. He stood silently with his eyes fixed on the floor. He had no answer.

'Never pay heed to what others opine about the one, you trust the most in this world. Paying attention to others' judgment is not my duty. To satisfy others is not my intention here. I care for my own bliss, my own happiness. Ras is my happiness,' Jagat, one day, in a dark mood, defiantly, declared in the court.

'Maharaj! You mean to say that, in future, the child born of Raskapoor will be placed on the throne of Jaipur! We will never ever tolerate that. So the heir of the great Kachwaha clan will now be a son of a *paswan*! Time has come; it seems that the names of great ancestors of Kachwahas will be blackened forever. Today you are blinded by your passion, but the day is not very far, when you will repent for your deeds.'

Senior most officials, *thikanedaars, musahibs* all uttered these words in unison out of complete disgust. They left the room fuming and fretting. The chief minister was standing alone in front of Maharaja.

Jagat was, however, in no mood to succumb under any pressure. Right from his childhood, he had shown a streak of defiance; swimming against the currents of prevalent customs gave him a high. He was a rebel without a cause.

*

Maji Sahib was seething in anger. Kachwahas were proud of this palace. Since the time of her late husband, Chandra Mahal, the seven-floor-palace belonged to her and it was called Rani *Sukh Kanwar ki deordhi or Sukh Niwas.*

Standing at the terrace, she glanced around. *Sukh Niwas*, painted blue with a white lining was decorated with sophistication and an excellent taste. Walls were decorated with miniature paintings. At one corner of the open terrace, there was a temple, which she liked to call *Sukh Mandir.*

Each floor of Chandra Mahal exhibited exquisite artisanship and was given a specific title. The palace complex was like a peacock crown of Jaipur. The seventh floor was *Mukut Mandir.* The sixth floor was *Shri Niwas* and the fifth floor was *Chavi Niwas.* The fourth floor *Shobha Niwas* was used for festive celebrations. *Rang Mandir*, the third floor studded with small and large mirrors on the walls, pillars and ceilings, was meant for private meetings. The ground floor, first and second floors were meant for administrative offices, servants, and security personnel.

The pompous residential area of Chandra Mahal had breathtakingly beautiful gardens, ornamental fountains; lofty walls fortified by anti-elephant spikes enclosed the sprawling premises of the splendid Chandra Mahal. Atop the palace, important buildings and forts, adorns Sawai (one and a quarter size) flag.

The peculiar design of the flag had an interesting incident. Kachwaha kings got the title of Sawai bestowed by Aurangzeb. Emperor Aurangzeb attended the wedding of Jai Singh, the late king of Jaipur. When he shook hands with the young groom Jai Singh and wished him well on his wedding, Jai Singh used this opportunity to gain political mileage.

'Shahanshah, may I take this gesture of yours as an indication that from now onwards you will always protect my cause.'

Aurangzeb laughed boisterously. He took his comments as an honour.

'You have won over my heart! You are just not a king, you are a great king; you are a leader and so much more. Ha...ha...ha...! So from this day onwards you will be called Sawai. Yes, this is your title.'

Since then the Maharajas of Jaipur have pre-fixed their names with this title and so their flag was designed in the shape of one and a quarter. Two pieces – one of full size and the second one of quarter size of the main flag, both portions making together one flag.

Apparently, it was a paradise, though life in the Chandra Mahal had its share of complexities and intrigues. Soon, Raskapoor, the new name of a complex crisis was all set to occupy the stage that was already curtained by nefarious deeds.

Maji Sahib summoned her son. He was in no mood to comply with her order.

'Maharaj, I know you are not happy, but ignoring your mother is not good. Why do you add more to your problems? Use this opportunity to get her in your fold. Mothers are always forgiving. It always pays to be respectful and polite to your elders.' Sheonarayan tried to make him realise his mistake.

'I know what she has to tell me and that will irritate me. Anyway if you insist I will go once.' Jagat was incorrigible. Not ready to understand.

As he neared *Sukh Niwas*, he saw his mother standing at the entrance. She welcomed her son with love. 'Come... Come in,' she said curtly. She looked at Jagat and exhaled a deep sigh. Her eyes turned wet.

'Tell me *Masa*, why did you want to meet me? I need to attend something urgent. Tell me quickly.' He said in a haughty manner.

Jagat was cautious as he was preparing to face what will come next after all the love and warmth .

After a couple of minutes, *Maji Sahib* said softly, 'You are enjoying your life, it seems. Everything is just going the way you want, but why you are not happy and content? No…No… don't make that face. It is written large on your face. In your eyes. I can read it. To a mother, the happiness of her child has the utmost value in this world. When will you understand that the company of that *pattar* is the root cause of your unhappiness…?'

Jagat butted in angrily, 'Who are you talking about? She is now no more a *pattar*. She is my wife and she has a name. I expect some semblance of decency from the *Maji Sahib* of Jaipur! I think you know her name?'

'Yes, I know the name that was given by you only. Nobody knows who she is and what is her real name? I do not want to utter her dirty name.' She almost screamed. Helplessly.

Both were glaring at each other.

'I know,' she said controlling herself, somehow, 'her company gives you thrill, not happiness. Thrill is ecstatic and transient while happiness is serenity and long lasting.'

'*Masa*, she is not the cause of my grief. Let me clear this thing first. Second, this palace is full of stupid people; actually they are the roots of my grief,' he barked.

'Jagat! Do not forget to whom you are talking. I am your mother. I know everything about her. I am aware of all that is happening in your life. Why don't you understand how deceitful she is?' *Maji Sahib* snapped.

'*Masa*, please don't begin it again. If you have anything else to say, then we can talk, otherwise…' saying so Jagat got up and walked away with a dark mood.

Before he crossed the threshold of her room, he hit a chair with his foot so forcefully that it stumbled few yards. He banged the side table with his fist. A flower vase that was adding to the decor of the corner fell down and broke into pieces.

Fateh Kanwar, who was hearing this unpleasant exchange from behind the door, began to shiver.

✳

Enraged though she was by her son's mad interest in the dancer, *Maji Sahib* did not give up and continued to instil some sense into Jagat whenever she met him. Jagat, as usual, remained incorrigible.

Fateh Kanwar, far from the entire clamour, had set up her own corner of peace in the solitude of *Mukut Mandir*. It was dusk. All the birds were hovering in the cloud-laden sky, as if they were in a hurry to reach their nests, before it became dark. But for Fateh, the time behind and the time ahead was all but doomed and dismal.

Sitting under the canopy at the far end of the parapet, Fateh Kanwar kept staring without winking at the ornate gardens below, and then her gaze got fixed on the strong perimeter walls.

'How strongly are these stones joined? Not easily to be removed, years after years they are as intact as they were hundred years ago. They were built on a strong foundation. Foundation is vital for everything – for buildings, for forts, for palaces, for empires and for human relations. I committed the foolishness of building a dream-mansion on the foundation of shifting sand. It was doomed to be destroyed, eventually. When I came to this palace, I felt protected because I found the surroundings very strong. What a fool I was! Sitting on a fragile bond of marriage, I felt secure! Ah! Fragility of a royal wedding! One day a prince of a strong dominion came to marry the princess of a desert, he took her to his palatial house… and then, that's the end.'

Tears began to roll down her cheeks, drenching her neck and chest .

✳

Fateh had taken over the task of offering prayers and making preparations for the worship of Goddess Jumwai in *Mukut Mandir*. She had vacated *Chavi Niwas* the day Jagat departed for Jaigarh, holding the concubine in her arms. With her injured pride, she made *Mukut Mandir* her abode.

Fateh was like a tender rose bud, which was plucked by the cruel hands of fate and thrown into the dust to be crushed under the feet of an evil dancer. *Maji Sahib*'s heart ached whenever she saw her spending her loneliness in the company of Lord Krishna, in a small temple she made for herself in a corner, at the terrace of *Mukut Mandir*.

She had a special place for Fateh in her heart. Other princesses entered in her abode, with a conditioned mind-set that they had to accommodate with other wives of Jagat, as some of them were already there before their entry in his life. Fateh came as the first wife, at the tender age of twelve, believing that she would forever remain the only woman in her husband's life. Her home was a paradise to her, where she hoped to live united with her husband. She could not even conceive the idea of sharing the exclusive space with someone else. Her belief regarding exclusivity was so strong that, every time when a new woman entered in her territory, she felt acute pain. Her wounded body. Her desolate soul. Still, she veiled her injured pride behind the shield of her mother-in-law. Jagat's interest in cardinal pleasures strengthened solidarity between *Maji Sahib* and Fateh, albeit it was of little help to ameliorate her position.

To atone for the sins of her son, *Maji Sahib* took upon herself the responsibility of looking after her welfare seriously; she regularly enquired about her well-being on some pretext or the other. Whenever *Maji Sahib* came across her, she prayed for pardon from the almighty. Fateh exhibited high reverence towards her mother-in-law.

And Raskapoor, a charming, bright, witty and wily woman continued to rule over the heart and mind of Jagat Singh. A separate and exclusive residence for her in the palace reserved for the queen was nearing completion amid furore and anxiety.

Jagat Singh chose to ignore the dissent; instead, he succeeded in manipulating a few nobles in his favour. The final moment that filled his mother, sisters, queens and others with dread, but eagerly awaited by Raskapoor, had arrived.

*

Announcements were made at road crossings, public places, gardens, playgrounds and meeting grounds.

'Beware! Beware! All the people! Beware! *Rajrajendra Rajadhiraj Sri Sawai Maharaj Jagat Singh BahadurJi* with Raskapoor will enter Chandra Mahal as per the royal tradition. The procession of the king will proceed from Jaigarh and pass through Manik Chauk and Chaupad, then reach Chandra Mahal. Everyone must participate in the procession.'

The news of Raskapoor's entry in the palace followed by royal rituals caused great uproar statewide. People from all walks of life, for, as well as against the king's move, became very active. Both the groups held meetings after meetings.

Supporters perceived that once Raskapoor was placed in the palace, all outcries will die down finally. Raskapoor will also be part of the normal life of the kingdom. Once she was given the status of a queen, she will no more be a concubine.

Adversaries took it as a challenge for themselves. Once she is a queen, they will have to pay due respect to her and bow down in front of a petty dancer, which was not acceptable to them.

Jagat Singh made all kinds of efforts and tried to convince the adversaries, but failed to bring them around. They failed to deter the king too.

✼

The procession began to move slowly from Jaigarh. In the front, there were drummers and bugle blowers followed by a troupe of folk dancers. In a decorative bullock cart, five artists were playing *shahnai* and the flute. About hundred soldiers were marching stately. Then five warriors in their majestic outfits, holding royal insignia stepping ahead, were matching with the royal army. Soldiers mounted on the horses in their traditional attire holding swords and spears in two rows, just behind the dancers and singers, were moving slowly.

Jagat Singh wearing a green *jama* and red headgear and Raskapoor in red *lehenga* and green *chunar* were seated on a decorated chariot. Elephants, camels and cavalry flanked maharaja's chariot. Behind the chariot, there were ten warriors holding swords, seated on elephants, marching slowly in two rows.

Another chariot carrying garments, ornaments, vases, shoes, cosmetics and other valuables of Raskapoor was following the soldiers. On both sides on the streets, people had gathered in large numbers; most of them out of curiosity, to see Raskapoor, who was the fulcrum of the royal turmoil.

The procession passed through Joravar Singh pole (gate) and was about to reach silver mint. An elderly warrior holding a sword approached the king. He was allowed to reach the chariot. He bowed down in front of the king, and then spoke loudly with a grave face, so that everyone around him could hear him.

'*Annadata!* I am here to convey the message of our people. We revere you. We adore you. We put you on a high pedestal of veneration. You are our Maharaja! We would give our lives to protect you. We are ever ready to obey your command. Maharaj, kindly do not hurt our feelings and do not crush our pride. We could not bear the sight of a concubine entering the proud abode of Kachwahas.'

Both Jagat and Raskapoor appeared disturbed. The furrows were visible on the forehead of Jagat Singh momentarily, then unmoved by the emotional plea of the warrior; he brushed him aside with arrogance and gestured the procession to move on.

✳

At the main gate of the Chandra Mahal, Chandra Singh with his supporters was all set to block the entry of Raskapoor in the palace.

'Maharaj! This concubine will enter the palace on my dead body,' roared Chandra Singh.

Pandit Sheonarayan, the chief minister, came to Chandra Singh for making a truce. As a last resort, he tried to entice him by an offer.

'I have a proposal that will save all of us from this ugly situation. If the anonymous birth of Raskapoor and her Muslim identity is an obstacle, I am ready to adopt her as my daughter and thus she will attain the high caste Brahmin status. I hope, this might solve the issue. A *yagna* may also be performed to purify her soul later.'

Chandra Singh snubbed him. Sheonarayan was in a quandary. Jagat Singh was fuming. His insanity reached a point that he thought of calling the army to tackle his own people, but his cronies somehow pacified him.

'*Annadata!* Never ever, begin a war with your own people. It will not only worsen the situation, but will also not serve your purpose. You cannot turn the whole of your own kingdom into your enemy.'

Good sense prevailed. Somehow, Jagat Singh controlled himself. Sheonarayan's mind was racing like a galloping steed. Within no time, he cracked another formula.

After a couple of minutes, he was seen indulging in a heated debate with Chandra Singh and other warriors. Meanwhile, Jagat Singh's chariot turned back, moved towards the gate near Govind temple and entered Chandra Mahal uninterrupted. Inside, formal ceremony with proper rituals was on, while at the main entry gate, relatives and nobles continued to argue with the Pandit and his supporters, why Raskapoor should not be placed in the royal palace.

Bugle blew. Royal flag, indicating the entry of the king and Raskapoor in the Chandra Mahal, waved atop the palace.

Chandra Singh realised that he was cheated by the Pandit. His allies began to abuse Pandit Sheonarayan for his evil deeds.

Realising that there was no point of aggression and futile altercation at the main gate of the palace, Chandra Singh and others moved away dejectedly. Raskapoor was cocooned successfully in Chandra Mahal.

It was not the end of all the problems. Jagat was not ready to stop. He was standing on a slippery ground that pulled him steadly downwards.

He began selling off his heritage so that he could maintain her in luxury. He plundered the secret royal treasury that was kept in the Jaigarh fort in the custody of Mina tribals, whose hereditary duty was to guard the treasure from all kind of raiders, even by the Maharaja. Jagat was so intoxicated by the charms of Raskapoor, when he could get no more from the royal cache; he gave Raskapoor half of Sawai Jai Singh's prestigious library.

CHAPTER 7

December 1803
Treaty with the British

Jagat Singh was not completely devoid of political acumen; rather he was more a slave of his weaknesses. Whenever he could distract himself from Raskapoor, he took extra pains to set his royal court in order. Since the day Raskapoor was settled in Chandra Mahal, he began to appear in the court, paid attention to state affairs, partially, if not completely.

Months came and gone. Meanwhile, Jagat Singh chased the Marathas out of his territory. He was at ease, moderately free from invasions and political commotion from any corner. His state was away, so far, from exploitation by the Marathas. Mughals, too, had not intruded his terrain, although they had marred the peace of his neighbouring states. What he could not make out was that Rajputana was passing through a transient phase and Jaipur was no exception. What he did not realise was the fact that his comfort zone was not going to remain unaffected by the developments happening around.

The chief of army was busy in his office. A messenger approached him.

'What is the agenda of Amir Khan? Could you gather some important information?' The army chief asked the messenger.

'Sir! Amir Khan is a Pindari, who has come to Rajputana with a single mission– to get money. He attacks, extorts, loots and destroys whatever comes in his route.'

'And his whereabouts? Where is he camping right now?'

'He is camping at the borders of Jaipur state. He has already made inroads in our land. His bands intrude into some of the border areas from time to time, in order to extort money and valuables from the people and return to their hideouts.'

The chief of army asked him to leave with a wave of his hand. He requested for   an urgent meeting with the king and senior ministers. The council of ministers urged Jagat Singh to cut Amir Khan into pieces.

'Maharaj! It is not merely a case of common loot and dacoity from across the border; Amir has threatened our officials and demanded a portion of taxes and levies made by the state.' The head of revenue department stated.

'Yes, I have already apprehended that Amir Khan, sooner or later, could be the biggest threat to the kingdom,' Jagat Singh acknowledged the crisis. He ordered his officials to handle the situation strictly.

'This is a law and order problem and the army need not be involved unless, of course, Amir attacks our borders.'

Jagat, for the first time, got seriously involved in the security matters of his state. But under the declining administration and prevalence of rampant corruption, things slipped from under his control. The common people were having hard times. A handful of ministers and officials were rocking in wealth, while people at large were left to survive under hard conditions.

✳

Amir was shrewd enough to figure out the weakness of the Jaipur king. Intermittent intrusion by his men in his territory was the part of his well thought out strategy. He forced Jagat Singh to provide enough resources to keep his forces fighting fit. What was disturbing was that he had begun to interfere in the internal matters of the state as well. Jagat Singh could not take a strong step to drive him out of his kingdom. Rather, he meekly surrendered to his growing demands.

Marathas, who were closely monitoring the developments in Jaipur, found it an opportune time to take advantage of the prevailing circumstances.

The council of ministers advised Jagat Singh to seek an alliance with the British. He too thought of winning over the confidence of the British, somehow. However, time was running against him. The British policy of non-intervention in the fight of the Rajputs against their invaders became an obstacle in his way. At that time, the British were not strong enough politically and economically to play an active role in Jaipur polity.

Indifference of the British further created chaos in Jaipur and that indirectly helped the Marathas and Amir. They were plundering unabatedly the already pathetic Jaipur, without much difficulty, owing to the existence of a weak king and the absence of any strong counterforce. The Marathas and Pindaries reaped the maximum harvest due to the neutral stance of the British.

✳

To deal with the growing menace of the Marathas and Pindaries, the council of ministers pondered over the idea of gaining the British assistance on a long-term basis. They were sharp enough to understand that an alliance was inevitable and would be a win-win situation to both, for the Marathas who were posing a threat to the British as well as for Jaipur. Moreover, ministers had faith in the character of the British and the Company. Jagat Singh was also convinced with the idea of his nobles because he knew that the financial condition of his state was far too weak. Therefore, he readily agreed to secure their alliance somehow or the other.

Lord Wellesley, at this point, introduced the system of 'Subsidiary Alliance' with Jaipur and other Rajput states to strengthen the roots of British rule in Indian soil. Under the subsidiary alliance system, the ruler of the allying Indian state was compelled to accept the permanent stationing of the British force within his territory and to pay a subsidy for its maintenance. The alliance policy was extremely beneficial to the British, but not for Jaipur. They could now maintain a large army at the cost of Jaipur. On the contrary, Jaipur was to gain only a notional security from external threats. Nobility had the clear idea of the consequences of subsidiary alliance system.

The British gladly lapped the idea, as they were keen to root out both Amir and the Marathas, who had emerged as a comet on their horizon. To finalise the practical details of alliance, a number of meetings were held between the British and Jaipur.

✳

When the Marathas came to know about the British Treaty, they changed their colours and extended an olive branch to the king. How could they have allowed a golden goose to sit in the lap of the British? Marathas too were playing their cards to bring Jaipur in their fold. They tried to arouse religious sentiments of the Rajputs.

The Maratha leader came all the way to the Jaipur court and met the king warmly.

'Maharaj! I sincerely apologise for all the problems created by my men in the past. From now onwards, I will be your friend, a committed ally! Let us take an oath of friendship.'

'May I know the reason of this change of your heart?' Jagat questioned suspiciously.

'Maharaj we are brothers. We belong to this land. We have the same roots. We are Hindus. Maharaj! I pray, please never ever permit an outsider, from a faraway land to come and settle here. Maharaj! Kindly reflect on the grave situation, when the British will be our masters. Paying no heed to consequences may have major long-term disastrous effects for both of us. They will certainly torture our people, as they do not belong to our religion.'

'You have never shown this considerate side of yours earlier. Why did you keep it hidden inside for so long? Today, suddenly you want to be our ally because you know that I have sought an alliance with a strong power,' replied Jagat sarcastically.

※

Jagat undoubtedly lacked political acumen, but the words of the Maratha leader compelled him to think over his proposal again. For the time being, he deferred the idea of entering into the treaty.

Most importantly, because of many tales of the shabby handling of the kings and people of subordinate states by the British Residents, he stalled the process of negotiation with the British.

A private journal published by Marquis Hastings, a British official, had revealed that, mostly, instead of working like an ambassador, the British Residents had taken over the role of a dictator, and began interfering in their internal affairs, allowed unruly people against royalties in the states where any such treaty was made. The Residents disclosed the most pretentious exhibition of their side by exercising their authority brazenly.

On 24 November 1803, in the evening, Lord Lake sent his report to Lord Wellesley. In his report, he categorically pointed out that the King of Jaipur had joined hands with the Marathas.

Unfortunately, at that point, the ruling class and masses, in general, had neither any interest nor any energy to understand the gravity of the situation. Later, if the same Marathas unleashed terror on them and forced Jaipur to go by their way, the alliance might remain pending forever.

※

Though Jagat Singh deferred the idea of forming an alliance, but he was unable to hold the fort all alone for a longer period. The Marathas had retreated, but Amir Khan was continuously plundering his areas.

On the other hand, the king observed over a period that the British had successfully weakened the Marathas. The chronic internal conflicts and continuous devastation by Amir forced Jagat Singh to seal his discussion with the British to a successful conclusion.

Jagat Singh was on the point of becoming an important ally to enjoy the long-lasting alliance with the British. Even at that moment, Amir was mauling Madhurajpur, a town almost within the sound of a cannon shot of Jaipur. The unabated incursions by Amir propelled Jagat Singh to hasten the alliance with the British.

It was 12th December 1803. A solemn treaty of defensive alliance with the British Government was contracted between them. Jagat Singh signed an alliance with the British Governor General Marquis Wellesley.

The governor believed in the policy of uniting all the major principalities in a league against the invaders like Marathas and Pindaries. Anyway, Jagat Singh had a sigh of relief because he thought that this treaty would keep Jaipur safe from the Marathas and Pindaries.

The treaty, however, remained effective until Wellesley remained on the seat of Governor General; the alliance was dissolved in 1805, on the ground that the state had violated its engagements by not co-operating with the British. The Holkars, a Maratha clan ruling over the region around Indore of today, helped the Mughals against the British and at this juncture, Jaipur took a neutral stand , which did not go down well with them. Cornwallis, the successor of Wellesly, refused to respond to such approaches and followed a policy of non-intervention. He found the creation of such associations a futile exercise, hence the Treaty was broken.

The East-India Company had serious reasons for discontent. According to them, Jaipur was expected to pay an exorbitant price, as per the Treaty, for British protection: Rupees four lakhs in the second year of the Treaty; Rupees eight lakhs by the sixth year; and after that "in perpetuity" Rupees eight lakhs plus five-sixteenths of the *durbar's* annual revenues in excess of Rupees four million. Jaipur was not in a position to meet up such expensive obligations.

In this process, Jaipur's Resident made an interesting comment.

'This was the first time, since the English government was established in India that it had been known to make its faith subservient to its convenience.'

Once the treaty ceased to exist, Jaipur, like the other Rajput states began groaning under the heels of invaders. Cornwallis, though aware of the growing Maratha menace, thought it inappropriate and unwarranted to make British forces available to Jaipur.

For years, Jaipur had been ravaged mainly due to Jagat Singh's inability to handle the situation and his indifference to state matters and partly due to strong propensity of the Marathas and Pindaris for looting a weak state.

CHAPTER 8

1805
Silent Wails

Many seasons and sand storms passed over Jaipur in the coming years. Peace and prosperity continued to be a mirage for the people of Jaipur. It happened when two Kachwaha princesses, sisters of Jagat Singh tied the nuptial knots and the city and royal house were filled with joy and laughter. First, *Maharajkumari Baijilal* Anand Kanwar was getting married with Rana Bhim Singh of Jodhpur. Fateh took upon herself the responsibility to manage the celebrations and she did it dutifully. The second time was when *Maharajkumari Baijilal* Suraj Kanwar got married with Raja Man Singh of Jodhpur, all the ceremonies were held under her supervision again. The two occasions were the fleeting moments of happiness in her life.

After a month-long busy schedule, today Fateh could steal some time for her own self. She was sitting all alone in a remote corner of *Chavi Vilas*. It was the same place, where she and Jagat Singh had begun their life together, many years back.

The golden circumference of the scarlet sun was sinking swiftly into the horizon. It was difficult to judge what was depleting fast – sun or the Kachwaha rule. The birds were returning to their nests... Dusky darkness was slowly spreading its wings. Soon flickering oil lamps would be lit in all the streets, every house, at ramparts, in the palace chambers and corridors, making the night appear, as if it had umpteen dazzling eyes. Would they be able to dispel the gloom engulfing

Jaipur, Fateh thought wistfully.

✳

It was a beautifully and tastefully decorated pavilion of Chandra Mahal as befitted her status. Large rooms with high decorative ceilings, long corridors, and a spacious courtyard in front of the main entrance. It was a palace that she and Jagat Singh had lovingly turned into a cosy love nest; that was soon shattered like a pack of cards and Fateh Kanwar hid her pain and agony in the crumpled sheets of feigned ignorance. The quiet strength, ethereal allure together with spectacular manners were all bred in her since childhood. Her calm composure made her every bit of royal feminine grace that she was.

The young couple commenced their conjugal life, engrossed in adoration, admiration and affection. The two of them were like lovebirds, indivisible. They enjoyed growing up together; they were never weary of giving out love to each other. So happy were they in each other's company that whosoever noticed them, holding hands, staring into each other's eyes, laughing, giggling, believed that they were meant for each other. How wrong they were!

In this hour of her tryst with destiny, Rupan was the one who was always there to take care of her. She used to massage her feet. Give her hair an oil bath and spend time with her. Her heart ached for the young queen as tender as a flower bud that was plucked and after taking her fragrance for some time, thrown away in the hot sand. Mostly she took utmost care of her. She felt like telling Fateh, 'All men are alike, a prince or a commoner.' However, she had sealed her lips.

✳

At first, Fateh Kanwar brushed the incident of the coronation night aside, as the Maharaja's passing fancy. That night, he did not come to her, for the first time. Jagat Singh was known for his weakness for women. When he spent days in Raskapoor's company, ignoring his duties as a king, showering lavish gifts on her within a short span of two weeks, Fateh was alarmed.

'For how many years he had not visited her even for an hour,' she began to count, one, two, and three…then stopped. 'Ah! Why had he stopped coming to me? He had already married many women in the past, yet he never ignored me in this manner. Has his love flown out of the window? Or, he never loved me at all? Was I merely a toy to play? Now he has a better toy, so he is not bothered about the older one, me. Maharaj has been so infatuated by the dancing girl that…that…that he has completely neglected me. I was his first love, his legitimate queen Fateh. In the last five years, I have just turned into one of many pieces of decoration in the palace. There are so many women in the palace. I am also one of the herd. At least, they are needed for servitude. And me! I am not needed anymore! Other queens might have surrendered themselves to the circumstances. But I am made of different metal; I will not allow this to continue.' Fateh often argued with herself, to clear the cobwebs away for hours.

She recollected the days when she came to Jaipur. 'My early wedding days were like a fairy tale. I was madly in love. We were never tired of sharing with each other the daily adventures of life. My heart is heavy with the terrible burden; only a woman whose husband cheats on her can feel. He has abandoned me for a court dancer, now his Raskapoor, with whom he lives openly. Nevertheless, I am sure of one thing that he will repay for his deeds. He will suffer hundred times more than what I am suffering today. He will be humiliated thousand times more than what my humiliation is today. Divine justice is unique. That is what I dread today. One cannot build a castle of happiness on the foundation of others' sufferings and pain. His pleasure is going to be short lived and is bound to inflict hundred times more pain on him. My *dadisa* always used to tell me.' Fateh began to sob. There was no one to comfort her suffering soul.

Fateh Kanwar passed many days in extreme agony, and nights, crying her heart out. She could not reconcile to the fact that her husband did not love her any more. She was completely ignorant of the basic nature of Jagat Singh, who loved no one but himself in the entire world.

✳

One day, she interrupted him while he was passing through the corridors adjoining her chamber. He was alone. She took him to her room. For a few moments, the two of them stood like strangers, looking awkwardly at each other, without speaking a word. Jagat stood painfully close to her . Although she was boiling with rage, yet her tender heart longed that Jagat Singh would embrace her. She wished to spend few affectionate moments in his company. Jagat was after all her husband whom she adored from the age of twelve. But Jagat had no interest in her. He moved hurriedly towards the door saying he had to attend something important. Fateh rushed and closed the doors and pleaded with him to spend a few moments with her.

'No! I cannot. I have to attend an...Important...' he did not know what to say then, he blurted, 'Ras is waiting for me.'

Fateh was frozen. She thought it was his choice of words, hitting and insensitive, which caused the tight ball to spin in her stomach. Her eyes seemed to get darker. Her limbs were stiffening up. She opened the door without a smile and turned to the window. Then she turned, giving him her best glare, to caution him,

'Maharaj, ignoring your responsibility for a dancer does not behove well on your part as a ruler. Mind my words! Your kingdom will be ruined, names of great Kachhwahs will be muddied and you will be singularly blamed and this dancer, who has nothing at stake, will then return to her old abode. Think over the long term consequences of your present conduct.'

Jagat Singh glared back at her. He took her words as an insult, and walked off in a huff. Fateh was shocked at his impunity. Although, she was too young to deal with the situation, yet she was fully aware of her role as his consort. Jagat took her advice as his criticism, his insult.

He was deeply annoyed by the attitude of Fateh Kanwar. He did not like anyone who pointed out his follies, not by any of his queens, not even by his mother.

He loved to be pampered by the women.

He straightway headed to his seductress, whose charm, beauty and mannerism had made him fall at her feet.

One week had passed. Jagat and Raskapoor were lying in each other's arms, late in the evening, under the tree in full bloom. Its pink and white flowers had been scattered on a raised marble platform.

'I would like to read something I have specially penned for you,' Jagat said theatrically. Raskapoor smiled shyly. 'It's a beautiful poem. As beautiful as your love. Now listen, but don't interrupt till I finish,' he added.

Raskapoor agreed. She tried to control her laughter.

'The rain water flows to the ponds and rivers,
River flows to the ocean.
The Kachwaha king leaves behind all,
He flows to be with his love.
She is passionate, irresistible and adorable
 Made for me, she is my fate.
 Jagat is not mad, nor unreasonable.
 Only and only, he belongs to her.
Yes, I am mad when she runs into my arms.
 I burn myself inside her.
And I fly into unknown pastures.
 I fly and fly,
 holding her in my arms forever.'

Thrilled Raskapoor embraced the king tightly in her arms. In return, he showered a volley of kisses all over her face. Their entangled bodies were burning under the flowers of the blooming tree.

✳

Fateh was alarmed. 'What should I do? This concubine is a big threat not only to her existence, but also for the honour and dignity of Jaipur state as a whole. Danger is looming large on Jaipur. What to do?'

She was unable to pinpoint, but her womanly instincts were primed. 'If only there was someone in this huge palace, who could give me some relief, some assurance and a few soothing words to comfort my soul,' reflected Fateh. She asked herself – 'Is it the destiny of a princess? Why has she to suffer with so many women in her husband's life? Why? Is there anyone in the palace who can promise her that soon everything will be all right; that by remaining a dutiful wife, her desperation and hopelessness will vanish? Will everything be all right?' Nobody was there to console her. Nobody was there to calm down her turbulent mind and heart.

'Maharaj, once a doting husband has not only cheated her; he even lives in a separate palace. She knew that it was a common practice in royalties. Within a span of three years, Jagat Singh had already married thrice before Raskapoor came into his life but no one could snatch him from me . '

'I was married for political expediency, not because of love. Then, why my heart bleeds today?' she asked herself. ' Because you love him,' a meek inner voice replied.

Her thoughts wandered to that balmy summer night when she had met Jagat Singh, the crown prince of Jaipur. Striking and spirited Jagat Singh had straight away been pulled towards the beautiful and bubbly Bikaner princess. It had been love at first sight for her. His eyes swept over her charm and dignified persona. Her extraordinary beauty blinded him. Her lotus bud eyes, marble like complexion and statuesque figure made him stunned and speechless.

'Why do I not reconcile to the fact that, sometime, sooner or later, it would have surely happened, but the way Maharaja has been lured by Raskapoor is disgusting and the way he is behaving all the more shameful.' Sometimes Fateh used to curse herself, next moment she would blame Ras and Jagat.

✻

'*Masa, Masa,* where are you? Masa!' yelled Fateh with joy crossing the long corridors, calling her mother and expecting her to appear smiling and moving forward with her open arms to embrace her. Then she felt someone shaking her arm. She woke up and found Rupan looking strangely at her.

'What happened? I heard your muffled voice, that's why I am here,' Rupan told her. Fateh realised where she was and tears began to roll down her cheeks. 'Ah! It was a dream.' She got up, and kept aside her quilt.

'Rupan, you know, *Masa* was with me. She was here in this room. I could feel her.' Fateh told Rupan in a choked voice.

Rupan consoled her and said, 'Yes, she is always with you and will always be with you. A mother can never leave her child, even if she resides in another world.' Fateh got up and hugged Rupan, who caressed her head affectionately.

'*Maharanisa*! It is almost midnight. You must sleep now; I am just next to your room. Call me if you need something.'

Their idyllic marital bonds were drawing to a close fast. He had already stopped meeting her. Jagat Singh was not extraordinarily handsome, but very charming and striking as well. People expressed frustration in his absence, but in his presence, the same people yielded under his charm. He easily got the attention of people and specially women.

The one night turned into weeks and weeks became months.

Since that cursed day, she spent her days in agony; she was restless, looking around and beyond in a distracted manner. It was becoming painfully obvious that she would never be a part of her husband's life. Probably, she was the first but not the last woman in the chain of various frivolous encounters he enjoyed. But she spoke to none, did not even make a spectacle of her sorrow. She began to avoid the company of other women. Whenever she could make an excuse, she rushed away to the solitude of her chamber. Every time she heard something about Raskapoor and Jagat, her face mirrored her pain.

Her mother-in-law and Rupan were her only succour. Jagat's philandering ways brought Fateh and *Maji Sahib* closer.

Maji Sahib used to avoid the issue of her son's lascivious ways and pretended as if nothing unusual had taken place and tried hard to soothe her sufferings. Fateh too used to hide her tears keeping herself busy in her daily routine chores, bathing, changing clothes, offering prayers to Goddess Jumwai, Kachwaha's *Kuldevi,* taking a stroll aimlessly in the garden, and waiting for some miracle to happen.

✳

Days came and went. Months made entry and exit. Years passed by... Jagat Singh entered into matrimony many times, sometimes, for political reasons, at times for his personal interests. He accumulated a number of queens, in all twenty-two, but for him, Raskapoor was still his most favoured woman, though Maharaja's interest in her began to recede. She was unable to fathom his feelings. In the beginning, Jagat showered her with gifts, expensive beyond her imagination. He spent most of his time with her, but for the last many months; he made it a point lately to stay with other queens as well. Sometimes, he did not visit her for days. It did not happen all of a sudden. Cracks began to appear in their bonding soon after her entry in Chandra Mahal, she felt, but could not do anything.

'Is my paradise crumbling?' Raskapoor was wondering. 'When I was not residing in Chandra Mahal, he was with me; he fought with all the people just for one reason, to be with me. Now, as if I cease to exist to him. The distance between us is widening day by day. He is no more the same person.' Raskapoor was in the dilemma.

'What went wrong between them? Perhaps, he loves challenges. Probably, I was a challenge for him that gave him some kind of thrill. Putting me up in Chandra Mahal was a challenge to him. Once he achieved it, he lost the excitement. Did I make a mistake by getting into Chandra Mahal? She wondered.

She had understood the changing mood of her benefactor; at any time, he might throw her out she told herself.

Jagat Singh was not in Jaipur. He was camping on the borders of Udaipur with his army. Raskapoor also knew why Jagat Singh was keen to marry Krishna, a sixteen-year-old beautiful princess of Mewar.

'Krishna, a young maiden, a tender girl. Seeming to be a formidable challenge for him.'

Raskapoor was passing through a troubled phase of her life. 'How long can I stand the hostility of queens and *Maji Sahib* all alone? I snatched their Jagat from them and cared two hoots for any one of them. Now a young princess from a distant land will show me my real place,' thought Raskapoor.

✳

One day, after weighing all pros and cons, she threw the dice carefully. She sent a message to Thakur Chandra Singh of Duni, who held a strong position in the state, saying that she needed a strong support in the absence of the king.

'I am keen to meet you. I will be highly grateful, if you oblige me. Looking forward to seeing you at Chandra Mahal.'

Chandra Singh received the message. He was greatly annoyed. Why does she want to meet me in the absence of the Maharaja? Is she up for some serious game plan? Is it a trap? He refused to meet her. He did not even bother to reply her.

Raskapoor waited for his answer for long. Disappointed, she decided to go to Moti Dungri fort, the residence of Chandra Singh to meet him.

It was afternoon. Chandra Singh was busy in a family affair. A closed palanquin covered with rich silk and a net of gold ornamented with precious stones and pieces of looking glass stopped at his main door. The palanquin was meant for women of royal families.

The guard at the gate became alert. He thought, perhaps *Maji Sahib* had come. He immediately recognised the face peeking out from the palanquin.

'*Rani Sahib* RaskapoorJi is here.'

Sewadaar rushed to inform Chandra Singh that Raskapoor was waiting down stairs to meet him. On hearing her arrival at his door, Chandra Singh was furious. How could she dare come here to my residence? What does she think of herself? Somehow, he controlled himself.

'Have her seated in the *baithak*; (sitting room in the outer wing of the fort to meet outsiders) she must wait for me.' He ordered the *sewadaar*.

Chandra Singh never wanted to meet her alone, hence he sent a messenger for a senior minister to come to his house immediately. Unfortunately, the minister was not available as he had gone to Khandela, a nearby *thikana* to settle some bills.

Exasperated, he asked his servant to tell her to observe purdah.

Raskapoor covered her face with a thin veil. Chandra Singh entered the room hastily and sat on a chair placed near the door.

'What made you come here?' His tone was stern.

'Kindly allow me to pay the amount, you are supposed to pay as a penalty because of me,' beseeched Raskapoor sheepishly.

Chandra Singh got up from his seat. His eyes turned red. 'Oh, you have the audacity to remind me of the fine and you have come here to mock of my authority. How dare you insult me? Have you completely gone mad? You will pay my penalty and you have the nerve to come here and tell me such stuff! Just leave this place immediately before I commit…!' Chandra Singh thundered. He looked at her menacingly, as if he would instantly kill her with his eyes.

In a fit of fury, he left the room.

'She is definitely playing games with me. What a crafty woman!' he thought.

✳

A few months back, in a meeting, Chandra Singh pointed out Raskapoor's identity as a mere dancer. Jagat Singh knew that Chandra Singh insulted her deliberately. He imposed a fine of rupees two lakhs on him, which was mentioned by Raskapoor. She was sure that by offering such a big amount of money, she would gain his confidence.

Raskapoor was a cunning and calculative woman. She wanted to make peace with Chandra Singh because she was aware that his animosity could be very costly for her. She was also aware that Chandra Singh was not alone. Most of the nobles, queens and ministers were with him. But she failed to fathom the depth of Rajput pride. She did not know how to talk to a proud Rajput? She thought that she could lure him by offering money to him. Chandra Singh took her action as the highest degree of impudence. He was now more determined to teach her a lesson.

After about a month, Chandra Singh held a grand feast for all the *thikanedaars* and senior courtiers. Maharaja Jagat Singh was the chief guest on the occasion. *Maji Sahib* and all his queens were invited specially, but for Raskapoor.

Jagat Singh sent a crisp reply.

'I am unable to attend the feast without Raskapoor.'

His message added insult to his injury. Chandra Singh decided to avenge his humiliation.

In order to give a concrete shape to his plan, he had a secret meet with the nobles during the spring festival. The nobles, who refused to honour Raskapoor as a queen, were heavily fined. A strategy was formulated to handle Raskapoor. Impunity on the part of Jagat Singh had given rise to contempt all over. It was at this point, the nobles even thought of revolting against him. Some of them even planned to dethrone him.

CHAPTER 9

1806...
Jaipur Embroiled, Jagat Fiddled

There was nothing unusual when Jagat Singh received a proposal of marriage from Rana Bhim Singh of Mewar. Krishna, the princess of Mewar was known for her exquisite beauty in Rajputana. But the proposal was mocked of in an unusual manner, which gave rise to a situation that led to the annihilation of three kingdoms – Mewar, Marwar and Jaipur.

Polygyny among royals was a usual practice during those days. A king could marry as many times as he wished and the reasons were as varied as the number of marriages. Sometimes,it was out of political expediency and at times, it was pure lust. In addition, at many a times, physical charm or wisdom of a princess drove a prince or a king towards her, whatever the reason; all ended up in marriage.

This was the time when Bhim Singh like Jagat Singh was sailing his boat in muddy water. His borders were not secure; Marathas were constantly creating havoc. He sought a strong ally in Jaipur to counter the Maratha menace. For forging an alliance with Jaipur, Bhim Singh thought that the marriage of his daughter Krishna with Jagat Singh was the only way out, albeit, he was oblivious to Jagat Singh's infamous escapades.

Krishna was already betrothed to the Maharaja of Jodhpur, when she was a child. Unfortunately, before the wedding could be solemnised, he died in a skirmish at the border. In 1806, one day, Bhim

Singh was thunderstruck when he received the news of the sudden and untimely demise of the Maharaja of Jodhpur. Thus came the end of alliance formed with Jodhpur, as well.

Bhim Singh found a quick-fix solution by hurriedly getting Krishna engaged to Jagat Singh of Jaipur. Without giving any serious thought to the pros and cons, he instantly sent a proposal with auspicious gifts to Jaipur. Jagat Singh accepted the proposal with equal amount of eagerness. However, the matter was not as simple as it appeared.

After the demise of the Maharaja of Jodhpur, his younger brother Raja Man Singh took over the reins of Marwar. Man Singh never saw eye to eye with Jagat. Both of them never missed a chance to settle scores with each other. Jagat Singh considered the marriage proposal as a God-sent opportunity to humiliate Man Singh.

Jagat Singh sent a snide message to Man Singh.

Maharaja Man Singh Ji
Jodhpur

I have great pleasure in inviting you to the engagement ceremony of the King of Jaipur with Krishna Kumari, the princess of Mewar. Though I feel sorry for Jodhpur because the beautiful princess who was earlier betrothed to the late Maharaja of Jodhpur, will now brighten up the life of king of Jaipur with her charm and beauty. Eagerly looking forward to meeting you on this special occasion. Hope to celebrate this moment in your company.

Yours
Sawai Maharaja Jagat Singh Bahadur
Jaipur

The message was cynical, obnoxious and nasty, designed to insult Man Singh. Man Singh was furious. 'How could Bhim Singh be so imprudent? How could the princess, once betrothed to the Marwar State be married to his archrival, this shameless Jagat? His tales of impunity are known to most of the states of Rajputana. Alas! What a shame for Marwar.' Man Singh decided to teach a lesson to both, Jagat and Bhim.

Jagat Singh would have never imagined that his pettiness would result into such infamy that would never ever be cleaned by any act of his repentance and penance. A headless act ignited mammoth fire that consumed Jagat Singh, Bhim Singh, Man Singh and an innocent young princess.

Bhim Singh too would have never imagined that his one rash decision would spell the doom for his own daughter and his honour would be crushed, never to be resumed. He did not comprehend that his choice would make his daughter a pawn in his power-game, inviting the wrath of both states – Jaipur and Jodhpur. To her father, as well as her suitors, she became an instrument for achieving political gains. When other children of her age were busy in merry making, she was at the threshold of toughest challenge of her life.

✳

Man Singh declared that he would teach both Bhim Singh and Jagat Singh a lesson that they would never forget. He immediately contacted Amir Khan of Asind, a Pathan mercenary, who had his own force and was available to anyone who would pay for his services. Amir Khan was a chameleon, who always served his own interest first and accordingly planned his activities, someone who would not think twice before stabbing one in the back. Earlier, he maintained good relations with Jagat Singh and used his cavalry and artillery to cover his own gang and arms. When Man Singh bribed him with a big armoury, he took no time in deserting Jaipur and joined hands with Man Singh.

Man Singh sent Amir Khan to Udaipur with a message that the princess either be married to Man Singh, or be put to death. Amir Khan took the liberty to go one step ahead and threatened Bhim Singh with dire consequences if he refused the proposal of Man Singh. He gave a terse message to Bhim Singh, saying that he must cancel the betrothal of his daughter with the king of Jaipur.

Jagat Singh also got the message. Marriage with Krishna had turned into a distant dream, only because of his own folly. He could not swallow this humiliation and decided to avenge his injured pride; accordingly, he organised a huge force of three thousand soldiers, likes of which was not arranged since the kingdom was in its glory. He marched towards the borders of Mewar and camped near Udaipur.

Bhim Singh requested Amir Khan to find a plausible solution. See the irony of fate, a man who was nowhere on the scene had taken the centre stage in the matter of his daughter's wedding.

Amir Khan hatched a dubious strategy to kill two birds with one arrow. He came to Bhim Singh.

'RanaJi! I think, let us meet and discuss the issue with an open heart. You know we Khans are true to our words and I will watch your interest first. Though I have come here to convey the message of Man Singh, but you have won over me.' His sugar coated words made gullible Bhim Singh believe him.

✳

A meeting of the three of them, Amir Khan, Jagat Singh and Bhim Singh was fixed at a shrine of a saint of their common faith. They exchanged their turbans as a mark of solidarity and friendship.

Amid the meeting, Amir Khan took Bhim Singh aside in a corner and threw a question at him in a blatant manner.

'Suppose, if neither Jaipur nor Marwar agrees to marry the princess, how would you then save your honour?'

Bhim Singh was dumbstruck, unable to utter a word. Revealing his true character, Amir Khan then spoke up the most malicious words.

'In that scenario, you are left with only option. Your daughter must die. Her blood will save your honour.'

Bhim Singh stared blankly. He could not figure out his real motive that prompted him to utter such unkind words for his daughter and that too in his presence.

Amir Khan, as cunning as a fox was playing his game well to fool all the three – Jaipur, Jodhpur and Udaipur and for this end, he was keeping them in good humour. Shrewd as he was, he knew it well enough that without settling the triangular dispute, it would be hard to realise his own dream. Hence, he thought that the best solution was to remove the very roots of the crisis – Krishna. It was not prudent to keep all the golden goose in one basket, he thought. I must keep all the options open.

He took Rawal Ajit Chundawat, a *thikanedaar* of Bhim Singh and his close associate, into his confidence. Ajit was buttered with heavy inducements, somehow, to bring Bhim Singh around to execute the plan soon.

Ajit prevailed over Bhim Singh and convinced him about the idea that Krishna must be sacrificed at the altar of war. Otherwise, he would be left with two of the most disastrous options – either Bhim Singh must marry his daughter with Man Singh, thus forcing her into a disrespectful relationship because she was already betrothed to Jagat Singh. Alternatively, if Rana refused Man Singh's proposal, he must be prepared to ruin himself and his kingdom as both Man Singh and Jagat Singh would exert their claim on the princess.

✳

For Man Singh, it was an issue of prestige. His argument was that Krishna Kumari was the mang[3] of Jodhpur and therefore she should be betrothed to him; that the princess had been actually betrothed to the throne of Marwar not to the individual king. He made it clear that if his claim to wed princess was not honoured he would destroy Mewar.

Among the Rajputs, it was considered an insult to the family if

---

[3]Once betrothed, the girl's name is attached with the would be groom's family

a girl, once betrothed to a member of one family, was then given to another family. The girl after her betrothal was called the mang of the family. Man Singh, therefore, organised his army of about sixty thousand warriors at Merta, advanced his troops and camped at a few miles distance from Udaipur.

Daulat Rao Sindhia, a Maratha leader, entered the murky scene in order to serve his own interest and fulfil his own political ambition. Sindhia put forth altogether a different game plan. He pressurised Bhim Singh to forgo the idea of marrying his daughter to Jagat Singh. As Sindhia was denied an authority by Jagat Singh to levy his people in any form; he not only opposed the nuptial ties, but aided the claims of Man Singh. By garnering the support of Marwar, Sindhia gave a shock to Bhim Singh by raising the audacious demand.

'RanaJi, you dismiss the Jaipur embassy at Mewar. My counsel is the sooner the better. Jagat Singh will be shown his place. Maharana Ji! I have one more valuable piece of advice. I hope it would solve all your problems, once for all.'

Bhim Singh gestured him to continue. He gazed at him with piercing eyes and furrows on his forehead.

'You marry the princess with a fourth party. I mean if it suits you. You will be away from all the issues. Just once think about my proposal.'

Bhim Singh was annoyed. He rebuffed Sindhia's proposition. Sindhia swallowed the insult silently at that juncture, however, he advanced his troops, comprising of eight thousand men, camped in the valley of Udaipur, within the canon-range of the Udaipur Fort.

✳

It was 1807. The Sun was blazing brightly. A full-blown war broke out at Parbatshir, on the boundary of Mewar and Marwar. However, no one emerged the clear winner. Loyal officials of Man Singh forced him to return to Jodhpur.

Jagat Singh too, was not in a better position. His mighty mould began to crumble like a pack of cards, intrigue had set in through his ranks and the long siege of Udaipur fort had culminated in flight and indifference of his soldiers and warriors.

Jagat Singh had realised his mistake, but now it was too late. His soldiers had fallen ill. Bones of his cavalry horses were scattered all around in the battlefield. Humbled and crestfallen, he, finally, retreated from the war scene.

In Udaipur, Krishna, a tender girl, who was made the cause of chaos by the circumstances, paid the heaviest price. She was constrained to consume poison to end her life.

The tragic death of Krishna brought about an upheaval in the life of Jagat Singh. Its ominous clouds continued to hover over Jaipur for the years to come and Jagat Singh failed to wash his hands drenched in the blood of an innocent princess.

He had sleepless nights. In the lonely corner of his room, he wept uncontrollably. 'I am aware that I will survive, but how long, nobody knows! I am also aware that eventually I will overcome this phase. I will lead my life the way I would like. However, that innocent princess ended her life because of me. I am the cause of her death.' For days, this was his usual routine – questioning his existence, his follies and just repenting.

He lost interest in Raskapoor completely for the first time. For days, he did not meet her. Because of bouts of depression and guilt, he decided to quit rash and noncommittal ways.

Maji Sahib also had turbulent nights because of the reckless behaviour of her son; the way he became instrumental in pushing Krishna to end her life. She would curse her womb many times in a day for giving birth to such a wretched son.

✳

Jagat Singh returned from Udaipur empty handed. All alone, with only a handful of soldiers. For many days, he led a secluded life, even Raskapoor was not permitted to cross the threshold of his chamber. But he was one man who never learnt from his mistakes.

Knackered after a long week, he came out of his den, partially recovered from his guilt.

'The best antidote to pain and guilt is merriment,' it is said. He craved for his usual life.

The same evening, when he was with Raskapoor, she asked sheepishly, 'Maharaj, today you look so cheerful as if the full moon has appeared in the sky. For a long time, my Maharaj, you have been eclipsed by evil planets.' Jagat laughed loudly.

'We all are humans. We all commit mistakes. And because we have committed a mistake, we cannot carry its yoke, forever, till we breathe our last,' saying so, he pulled her and his lips sealed her mouth to speak further.

To him, state affairs were meant to be handled by his ministers- 'it's a very fiddly task,' mooted Jagat Singh. And he began to follow the same path that he had been treading for the last so many years.

'Ah! At times, I may not get what I aspire for. Sometimes, I will not succeed. But I cannot give up and live under the subjugation of others forever .' He bolstered himself.

Obviously, the events with which his rule was swamped were not laudable of Kachwaha dynasty – invasions, surrenders, war contributions, court manoeuvrings and confiscation of towns from his territory by the invaders. Jaipur, with its high imposing ramparts, thick stony fortifications, which were the symbol of its glory, was mauled and marauded by every predator, now and then. Trade and business houses almost collapsed, agriculture rapidly declined, partly from loot and mainly from uncertainty and indifference on the part of Jagat Singh, who was ruling his kingdom in the most unruly manner.

Jagat Singh, as usual, handled state issues in his known whimsical manner. He had time for everything, but not enough to look after his state. Occasionally, he displayed some valour, but that also became the moot point of controversy. At times, he showed interests in governance. Nevertheless, he proved himself a fool when he tried to solve court issues by using the sword or stiletto even in the precincts of the royal court.

Sometimes, he spent hours to get his life size portrait painted, but he did not have a few hours to address crucial issues. Once, he spent many days consecutively with his favourite painter Sahib Ram. When he saw the painting – his thick black piercing eyes, apparently attractive face and seemingly self-controlled forehead and his well-endowed chin, he laughed narcissistically and showered him with lots of gold coins.

✳

As if not all these problems were enough, antagonism was growing between Jains and Vaishnavs. He failed to handle the issue with sensitivity; instead, he showed indifference and made no concrete effort to create harmony between them. Though, he himself was an ardent devotee of Lord Rama, yet he preferred not to interfere in religious or sectarian conflicts of the people.'Oh! This is something to be handled by the Brahmin priests and Jain munis. I am not to be dragged in the controversy raised by them. Who am I? Let their gods descend on earth and find a solution for these thick headed. Phew!' blurted Jagat in a cynical manner, when the minister of internal affairs informed him of riots between the two communities.

Dhomu, Jain by religion, was a minister at the court of a prominent *thikana.* Jagat Singh trusted him completely and allowed him to build temples in and around Jaipur. Courtiers brought into his notice that about twenty-five or even thirty Jain temples were built around Jaipur with the support of Dhomu.

Jagat, as usual, made a bad fist to this problem as well. He ordered, 'Demolish all the Jain temples.' Soon Jain temples were razed to the ground. Only the outer walls were left intact.

This order created fissures and the State was thrown into flames of Jain–Vaishnav conflict.[4]

Jagat Singh, surrounded by a caucus of self-seeking sycophants, passed orders at their behest without giving serious thought. He began to employ any person without any check of his calibre, to look after the state affairs. One day, he made Rorji *Khawas*, who was his tailor, his *musahib*, the head of the privy councillors. Then some other day, he surprised a local trader, *baniya* by caste, to look after the court matters. After a couple of weeks, he assigned the temple priest the role of chief of internal security system. Moreover, in the same vein, he took no time in making both of them in-charge of the prison at Nahargarh fort, where criminals were kept, Thus, he put the security of his own people at the stake.

One fine morning, in the same breath, he ordered, 'All the golden plates studded at the walls and pillars of royal *yagyashala* must be removed with immediate effect. Cover the walls with ordinary and cheapest quality silver plates.'

✳

Months rolled by. *Maji Sahib* and the elders beat their chest now and then, but were helpless. Adamant and unreasonable, Jagat was the last person to pay heed to their words. Soon, they were to face another blow.

Meenas of Kalikho were assigned the task to secure royal treasures of the Jey Mindra (secret cache of Kachwahas). The royal inheritance had rapidly depleted because of Jagat Singh's headless pillage of booty. Meenas were faithful hereditary guardians of the treasure and whenever Jagat took away its portions to spend on his luxuries,

---

[4]Jagat Singh, a benevolent but gullible ruler and his scheming minister appear obviously folkloric. It may not necessarily constitute a historical fact. Many people narrate the incidents of Jain temples' conversions having taken place during the ruling periods of different kings: starting with Man Singh I (1589-1614) and up to the times of Jagat Singh.

they grieved. Several times, they held a meeting with some trusted *thikanedaars*, but their sincere efforts to save the treasure bore no fruit.

Meena leaders, finally, approached *Maji Sahib* to take some firm step.

'*Maji Sahib*, soon the family treasure will vanish in thin air. Now is the time to do or die. If we cannot perform our dharma , it is better to die. Our ancestors had taken an oath to safeguard the royal treasure . How will we face them! *Maji Sahib*, it is very painful that our Sri Sawai Maharaj is not keeping his words. Saving the treasure is not our sole responsibility. It is a joint duty of Kachwaha kings and Meenas. Sri Sawai Maharaja is squandering sacred cache on his unworthy pursuits. *Maji Sahib*, we humbly pray you, kindly do something. We entrust you with the treasure. We cannot take its responsibility anymore.'

Saying so, all of them, four in number, slit their throats with their daggers. Blood gushing from their bodies sprinkled all over, which turned the white marble floor into red.

Maji Sahib was stunned. A gutsy Rajputani was she, nevertheless, shivered like a tender tree in the tempest. She gaped in horror. Blood flowed towards her feet. She stepped back. Controlled herself somehow, she summoned the chief nazir immediately.

Hurriedly funeral arrangements were made. Dead bodies of the Meena warriors were cremated at Gaitor with honour.

This incident shook her completely. She could not bear the agony of her loyal warriors' death in this cruel way. On the contrary, Jagat was so engrossed in his own world that he had no time to comprehend the gravity of the incident. When he was informed of the suicide committed by the Meenas, he brushed it aside like a peck of dirt. All the nobles were highly aggrieved and agitated over his irresponsible and insensitive behaviour, but they were helpless.

✳

'My own blood had blackened my name that could not be atoned even by penance. What prompted my son to stoop so low? No human being in his senses could behave in this manner. I should have killed him the day he was born. Forever, from this moment onward, I shall be known as the mother of an irresponsible, an unworthy king, a debased man. His foremost duty is to save his honour, save the honour of the motherland, save the honour of his people and my stupid son only cares for his own desires and his disgusting concubine, Raskapoor! She is the root-cause of his downfall,' wailed *Maji Sahib*.

She wondered, would she ever succeed in instilling some sense in her son? She knew, why her husband asked her to take care of his kingdom and Jagat. Did he foresee his son's future? Pardon me! I failed to usher our child in the right direction.'

The queen howled for hours. Tears rolled down her face.

'Ah! My shameful son, you do not know how much pain have you inflicted upon your mother! Even the common men follow some rules, some principles. Oh! Jagat, what a fool you are!'

With the dawn, *Maji Sahib* got up, left his room behind, walked across the courtyard. The morning dawned fresh and clears after the cloudy storm of the past few days. She had made up her mind. She had chosen to tread on the same path, tramped umpteen times by her own kind in the past. She would severe all her ties with this unruly king. Surprisingly, at this point of time, perhaps, Goddess Jumwai infused some sense into Jagat.

Jagat Singh had realised that his insensitive behaviour at the death of the Meenas had left everyone in the town turned against him. But it was too late. He knew that he had committed a grave offence. Guiltily, he crossed the threshold of his mother's room to seek her forgiveness, but she did not allow him to cross the line that she had drawn for her progeny.

'This sinner does not belong to me anymore. How can a stranger dare even step into my palace?' She thundered.

For the first time, she did not welcome her son. She did not turn back, kept standing with her back on him. Jagat waited for some time, and then returned with his unsteady steps. She did not face him, but held back her tears. She did not let down her guard at that moment.

CHAPTER 10

1818
Raskapoor Caged

Seasons rolled by. Nothing changed for Jaipur. It continued its journey at the same sluggish pace. The year 1817 knocked at harried state of Jaipur. The Kachwaha kingdom had been often plundered; the Marathas and the Pindari bands extorted the people beyond limits during last couple of years.

Finally, Jagat Singh decided to take the Marathas head on in the battlefield. As the war bugle blared, Marathas and Kachwahas charged at each other. A brutal fight ensued. Though Jagat Singh's army fought fiercely, yet Jagat Singh lost the battle.

Wounded both in body and soul, he resignedly accepted the demands of the Marathas; he agreed to pay the hefty amount of money to them for the truce. As he returned after losing a crucial battle, he received yet another blow. Raskapoor was missing from the palace.

When Jagat Singh was engaged in a battle with Maratha, *Maji Sahib*, queens and nobles discussed Raskapoor and her uncontrolled authority over the king. For them, Raskapoor was the main cause of the deteriorating state of Jaipur because, they believed, under her influence Jagat had gone wayward.

Senior courtiers sought the permission of *Maji Sahib* to take appropriate action in her matter. A strategy was formulated in her presence. Jagat was far away from Jaipur and for them; this was the most opportune time to root-out the poisonous ivy – Raskapoor.

Maji Sahib was passing through a tumultuous time; seeing her son going wayward and living with the guilt of failed motherhood. She thought that now was the time to do something decisive as her last bid to save the state; she gave her consent to go ahead with the plan, but diligently.

The courtiers approached *Maji Sahib* with a fool proof scheme to eliminate Raskapoor. She called Mohanram, the chief nazir, who was in charge of the security of the palace. Nazir was the official position, denoting his capacity as emasculated security personnel of the palace. Jaipur and Bundi were the two states that had followed the practice of Mughals in the matter of safeguarding their zenanas by eunuchs. Mohanram was a eunach.

Mohanram was mainly accountable to Jagat Singh. When Raskapoor entered Chandra Mahal, the king ordered, 'Security of Raskapoor cannot be compromised at any cost. Be careful Mohan, if she is harmed, you will be liable to dire consequences.'

Over the years, Mohanram, clever as he was, had also won the trust of *Maji Sahib*. He reported the security issues directly to the king and in his absence, to her. As Jagat Singh was away from Jaipur, *Maji Sahib* held the final authority in such matters. She took him into her confidence.

'Remove this poisonous snake that has spread so much venom in our lives. Crush her fangs! Take her far away so that she can never ever return to this palace.'

Mohanram was on the horns of a dilemma. He knew that eventually, Raskapoor would be shown the doors at the first opportunity. In the absence of the king, if he failed to save her, he would pay the price. Jagat Singh was away and Mohanram had no other option, but to carry out her order. He was caught between the devil and the deep sea.

'Currently *Maji Sahib* had the upper hand; she had gotten the opportunity and I have no choice but to obey her command. It is better to please this devil now. Handle the other devil when he comes. I cannot afford to displease two devils at a time.' With a wicked smile, he set about passing the directives.

✳

It was third quarter in the night. Mohanram with a contingent of security persons entered the complex of Chandra Mahal that belonged to Raskapoor. She was in deep slumber. On hearing some sound, she woke up. Her heart was pounding fast. She got startled, heard some movement outside her chamber; she got up hurriedly, snatched her dagger from under the pillow. As she stepped out of her chamber, she noticed that some shadows , holding arms in their hands, were heading towards her room.

'Who could be they? Friends or foes! Whoever they may be, but why were they here at this odd hour?' Her mind was racing frantically from one probability to another. 'I am in grave danger!' She was sure. She decided to challenge them.

'Who is there? How dare you enter the palace? Guard! Guards!'

None came forward. Standing a few yards away from her room, yet they did not budge an inch, even after hearing her frantic calls. Raskapoor took no time to understand, the moment she was dreaded of, had arrived finally.

She was fully aware that sooner or later, someday, she would have either to leave the palace or accept the lowest position assigned to her by the queens and the elders. She knew that Maharaja's authority had been eroding gradually for some time. Moreover, he was in the battlefield at present.

'Alas! My enemy has chosen the best time to settle his score with me. Who knows, I might be thrown in dark dungeons forever. Or worse, might be killed,' she was swarmed with frightening thoughts.

The chief nazir ordered his guards to truss her up. She stood silently. Unnerved. She made no effort to escape. No attempt to resist. Raskapoor's protective paradise was completely smashed. Her love nest was shattered into shreds. As a captive, in the late night, she was carted to the Nahargarh fort, where she was thrown into a dungeon.

✳

Next day, in the morning, *Maji Sahib* called an emergency meeting with the senior courtiers.

'I have strong evidence that the chief minister has misused his office for his own vested interests. After the king returns from the battle, I personally will hand over the information to him. Well, the crux of the problem is that the king may not come back soon. By the time he will be here, Jaipur might have incurred the damage in alarming proportions. We must take action now.' She put forth her point clearly.

'*Maji Sahib*! We all are here to support you.'

'Unless we remove each and every person, who has damaged the state, we will not be able to save the sovereignty of Kachwahas. Goddess Jumwai is with us. She has given us a chance. It is up to us, either to use it for the benefit of Jaipur or waste it and repent forever.' *Maji Sahib* watched their faces one by one carefully. All nodded in unison.

'Suspend all the supporters of Raskapoor from their duties with immediate effect. Dig as deep as possible. Even a small seed may soon become a huge tree.'

The first casualty was Pandit Sheonarayan. He was stripped of his chief ministership and made captive in his own house. One by one, all the supporters of Raskapoor faced house arrest, by the evening.

✳

Defeated, crestfallen Jagat Singh had returned from the battlefield to be crushed further under the fury and frenzy of his own people. He was in no state of raising his voice, even his finger. Neither had he the capability to rebuild the kingdom, nor had he any will. He surrendered himself completely before his nobles and courtiers. Jaipur was under great debt. Finances were at an all-time low. There was no way to generate revenues. The Marathas demanded levy that was to be paid at any cost, and Jagat Singh, at this crucial time, needed the support of his allies and nobles to tackle his enemies whom he never cared for so far.

And Raskapoor! Where was she? Jagat Singh was curious and worried. His loyal courtiers informed him of what had happened in his absence. The ensuing conversation, in which the king learned the details of her imprisonment at the behest of his mother, by some of his loyal Rajput nobles during his absence from the capital, continued until midnight. Having learnt about the imprisonment of Raskapoor, Jagat as if not satisfied, approached two of her personal *daavaries* and repeatedly asked them; how she was caught and in what state she was at that time?

But, Jagat Singh did not show any keenness to bring her back into the palace. Surprisingly, he appeared distant and aloof from her. Unanticipated. Perhaps, he knew that it was not possible for him to afford her any more. The tide had turned against him. He was helpless. The changed circumstances had seemingly reduced her importance in his life a lot, though; he would have never parted with her company, if it were within his power. Probably, after a long span, almost fifteen years, constantly facing the resentment of his own people, Jagat Singh had lost the will to fight any more for Raskapoor. Perhaps, Jagat Singh had finally resigned to his fate.

Burdened under a guilt, Jagat Singh spent most of his time cursing himself for his grave misdeeds. Sometimes, he deplored the death of Krishna. His guilty conscience made him the culprit for the killing of princess Krishna of Mewar. 'Why did I write that letter to the

Jodhpur King Man Singh? Why did I stoop so low? I am a murderer of an innocent young girl for no fault of her. His pangs of conscience were killing him for his many more grave follies. And in no way he could have rectified them.

Most of the time, he would be sitting in his room, deeply lost in wild thoughts, behind the closed doors.

'Only, if only I could have reset the wheel of time. Ah! Kachwaha dynasty will end with me. I wedded so many princesses, but I do not have a single child to carry forward the name of this great lineage. I married blue-blooded women, but did I ever care to have a happy conjugal life with any one of them? What an evil seed I am! I destroyed everything. I have been the cause of suffering of many, my trusted people, *Masa*, and…and…'

Suddenly, Fateh Kanwar's face began to swing left and right like a pendulum in front of him. 'For how many months or years, I have not even seen her? Days after days were exhausted in futility and agony. Along the pace of time, my precious years were gone, fighting on all fronts, at the home turf and in the battlefields. No solace, no oasis in *Marudhara.*'

A couple of months rolled by. Rebel voices, gradually, were ebbing. Perhaps for the first time, Maharaja seriously spent time with his courtiers in generating funds to save Jaipur from the claws of the Marathas.

✳

It was a monsoon morning. The sky was overcast the whole night and as he pondered over the soul stirring issues of life, the sky parted and rain began to pour down in torrents.

With a weak body and broken spirit, Jagat Singh wearily changed his night attire, bathed in a pool of cold water and put on a simple white *jama*, plain shawl on his shoulder. He decided to lay aside his worries for the time being, and enjoy the beauty of what nature was unfolding before him.

Meanwhile, the events took a rapid turnaround in the states of Rajputana. Amir Khan and the Marathas continued to plunder the principalities that did not succumb to their demands. Kingdoms became anxious to enter into treaties of alliance with the British. Udaipur, Jodhpur, Kota and Bundi and thirteen other Rajput states entered into treaties that guaranteed them protection. The tributes due to other powers were transferred to the British Government, each being guaranteed against any attack, external or internal. Each was definitely told that independent external relations were forbidden. As they were at the last gasp of their existence, they gladly entered the British system. The Nawab of Bhopal, at this point, also signed a treaty and became a British ally.

Jaipur, for some time, persisted procrastinating the process and was the last of the Rajput states to enter the British political system. Jagat Singh knew what it meant to sign the treaty. It meant accepting the supremacy of the British. He had already been enough of cause of disgrace to his lineage. He did not intend to add more to it. On the one hand, the persistent presence of Amir Khan and the Marathas forced him to seek British alliance, on the other; issues like removal of the state flags from most of the kingdoms, with the replacement of the British flag, for instance, on the ramparts of Ajmer were a serious hindrance to the progress of the treaty. In both the situations, he was a loser.

All these factors, however, made him sign the disrespectful agreement after a long period on 2 April 1818.

The historic treaty, 'A defensive alliance, perpetual friendship, protection and subordinate cooperation,' consisting of ten articles was signed which brought Jaipur and its *thikanas* for an infinite period under the control of the British rule. The British Government was to give protection to Jaipur at the cost of an annual tribute.'

At this crucial juncture, the sole motive of Jagat was to keep the boundaries of his state intact. The first and last objective of his life was to carry on the name of his dynasty, somehow.

Hindsight had made Jagat realise what mistakes were made by him. However, all this took a heavy toll on him. He became too weak to live all by himself. He longed to be with his own people, his mother, his queens.

'For all the years went by, I did not bother to care for them. I need courage to face them,' said Jagat to himself.

With sluggish steps, sullen Jagat Singh came out of the room and headed towards *Sukh Mahal*. Finally, the much-awaited moment for *Maji Sahib* and Maharani arrived.

He put his foot at the threshold of the simply decorated room of the splendid palace. He gathered strength to cross it. He kept standing there for a while, his eyes roaming around and lo! Fateh Kanwar, the first love of Jagat Singh and his chief queen was there. After a long separation, Jagat Singh and Fateh Kanwar faced each other. Fateh Kanwar was standing in the centre of the room as if in a daze, troubled by the emotions that were rocking her.

'He is here! At my doorstep! But...! How come?'

Daavaries, who were busy in their daily chores, noticed the king. For a moment, they looked surprised to see him there, then hurriedly crouched putting their hands on their forehead.

'Ghani khamma Maharaj!' They greeted him softly and set aside one by one.

As he stood there, defeated, laden with guilt, his doting mother came forward, embraced him warmly, and showered him with blessings. She was crying uncontrollably. Jagat kept staring at his mother's glowing face, wet with rolling tears.

That was the most beautiful face on this earth. How could he remain aloof from such a divine beauty in the form of a mother? A mother's countenance, adorned with tearful kind eyes and smiling face for her child, is the most beautiful creation by God.

He sat down on the floor and like a small child; he put his head in his mother's lap, who by then sat on a wooden chowki. Something unthinkable had happened. She could not believe her eyes first. Surcharged with emotions as she was, stream of tears began to roll down her cheeks, Jagat also burst out crying like a child. The reaction of the two of them was as if they were reuniting after being separated for years by the stroke of destiny.

'Pardon me *Masa* for my follies! I allowed my heart to rule over my head. Head over heels in all kinds of wrong ways. I am the cause of your pain. I am the cause of all the miseries. But…' He said in a trembling voice.

Her tears mingled with his tears. She kept stoking his head, ruffled his hair with her fingers. She thanked the Goddess umpteen times to bring back her son, a jewel of Jaipur.

Fateh Kanwar, who had been standing behind the door, heard each word that transpired between them. She saw the blissful union of mother and son after a long time. She was engulfed in contradictory pulls. At one moment, she felt her heart bubbling over with joy, the next instant she was remorseful. At last, *Masa* had her son back, the son who was dearer to her than her own life.

❋

Jagat Singh had yet to pass through the toughest predicament of his life, how to seek forgiveness from his Maharani? Will she forgive him? He knew her fiery spirit. She was a Rathorni, the desert princess.

Maji Sahib told Fateh to welcome Jagat and mend the rough patch of her life. After countless days, months and years, she dressed herself carefully. Her simple attire was replaced by royal *lahariya lehenga* and red *chunar*, which once again transformed her into a resplendent beauty, which she actually was. *Masa* specially adorned her with the jewellery, which was lying ignored for so many years.

'Mother and son had patched up. What about me? How our relation will begin now? What does destiny hold in store for me?' Fateh's mind was flooded with so many questions.

Fateh was seated on the chair, thinking of the happy moments she had shared with her husband. Embarrassed and apologetic Jagat made his way to her. His feelings revolved only around ways in which he would make up to his queen. 'How would he deal with his queen who suffered so much of ignominy due to my irresponsible conduct? What would he do to pacify her rage?' These were the predominant questions boggling his mind. Nevertheless, Fateh was one person who always stood apart, rising to the occasion and maintaining the dignity of her position as the Maharani of Jaipur. At first, Fateh was silent like a statue. When she saw his pale face, she kept aside her wounds and welcomed Jagat warmly in a royal manner.

'My love! I feel deeply ashamed of myself. I brought about so much pain in your life. Maharani! Will you ever forgive me?' Jagat said embracing her lovingly. Fateh hid her tearful eyes.

'There is no point in raking up old wounds. I am your queen. It is my dharma to stand by you in your moment of distress. I was always there. You only closed the doors on me. My Maharaj!'

Fateh loved him and forgave him. She decided to be with him.

After a long battle that two souls fought, Fateh all alone, Jagat in the company of many women, but finally, a truce was made between the two, and tranquillity prevailed in Chandra Mahal. It seemed that perhaps the bad phase of her life had ended.

✳

Man is a slave of his habits, good or bad. Once comfortable, the wandering traits of Jagat Singh sought after fertile soil to grow up.

They were dormant, without water and soil, in the absence of a suitable environ. Fateh's simplicity and devoted love was not enough for him. His heart began to crave for the licentious charm of Raskapoor. Almost four months had passed.

'I don't understand how do people spend their precious years in such a dull manner just being duty bound?' Jagat questioned himself when he was dressing in front of a full size mirror.

Fateh heard him and answered smilingly. 'Duty is the utmost dharma of a human being.'

'Duty is binding. It makes a man slave of others. It snatches happiness and liberty of a man. It suffocates. I am a free bird and duty is a cage.'

'Maharaj! You are the king. You are free to do whatever you like. What is bothering you?'

Jagat laughed and changed the topic. Fateh too did not drag it any more as Jagat was having a mild cough and cold for the last one week. To create an ambience that did not disturb his peaceful mind was her first priority. Jagat noticed her grave expression. He picked up a small pillow that lay nearby on his bed and threw it at Fateh. She collapsed in peals of laughter.

Jagat was laughing too. 'I am certainly not the good boy. *Masa* is always sceptical of me. She does not trust me. I can read it in her eyes and in your eyes too. Am I right?'

Fateh grinned. 'Trying to understand you Maharaj!'

Jagat picked up one more pillow, and threw it at his queen. Fateh made a little effort and grabbed it, put it behind her back. 'I think, I am beginning to trust you now. Thank you for all the lessons you taught me.'

Their laughter filled the room. These light moments filled their hearts with hope and faith.

✳

On a chilly cold week of December, the town was reeling under the biting northerly winds. That year winter had set in early, Jagat Singh thought of covering himself with a velvet quilt. The closed windows kept the chilly winds away, but Raskapoor had been haunting him for the last couple of days and he was finding it very hard to throw her off his mind. He called Jayraj secretly and asked him to find out somehow the condition of Raskapoor in Nahargarh.

'It must not be known to the eyes and ears of any soul in the zenana,' he warned Jayraj.

Jayraj, had always been a very loyal official to Jagat Singh, and was ready to obey his king; he promised to maintain complete secrecy.

After a couple of days, he was standing in front of the dark cell of Raskapoor. On the pretext of learning and documenting a few classical ragas, Jayraj, obtained permission to meet her.

As it became dark at the end of the day, the torchbearer placed a flaming torch into a corner of the cell. Probably, for the first and the last time that dungeon had the privilege to listen such wonderful music. Jayraj on his sitar and Raskapoor's melodious voice created a magical world in that dungeon. It was a mesmerising treat to the other inmates.

In the last quarter of the night, Raskapoor exchanged her clothes with that of Jayraj and covered her face with one corner of the headgear. Jayraj, half-naked only in his inner garments was seated in one corner of the cell; his arms were tied around his folded knees. He was shivering badly.

Raskapoor picked up a big stone from the corridor and hit Jayraj's head with full force. He was not ready for this shock. He fell down on the floor because of the sudden blow. Gradually, he began to lose consciousness under severe cold.

Leaving him there lying unconscious, Raskapoor crossed the threshold of her cell and headed towards the boundary wall. There was a small hole in the boundary wall of the fort. She used that secret hole as her escape route. The security personnel found Jayraj in a pool of blood the following day.

✳

The next morning, Jagat Singh had caught high fever and passed the rest of the night in a state of unconsciousness. For the last couple of days, he was suffering from acute colic pain, somewhat strange pain shooting up from the lower abdomen and covering his back. He was unable to get up. With some support, he was, however, able to take a short stroll. His energy was at an all time low and his face had turned pale. The medicine practitioner could not do much to revive his condition. He suspected that Maharaj might have taken something, may be a food item or some liquor that had damaged his digestive system.

Maharaja's mind was torn by the pangs of bitter failures and frustration. Every spectacle of his life flashed before his eyes over and over again. He had played the political game for heavy stakes. He lost much more than he gained. The consequences of his fruitless aggressive policy towards his own people proved far more disastrous than what he had imagined. He failed to ride successfully through the political storm of his age; he was simply swept off by it.

Jayraj could never report back to him that Raskapoor had escaped from the cell. Jagat was seriously ill and Jayraj was wounded, lying on a cot in the corner of his room almost for a fortnight between a semi-conscious and sedated state under heavy doses of medication. He took more than a month to recover. By the time he healed up, the world had changed.

✳

It was 21 December 1818, a fateful dark moon night. The sky had been overcast the entire day, as if nature was matching with the gloom and darkness prevailing in the city. Suddenly, the sky parted and it began to rain incessantly in torrents. Generally, it was not the usual season to rain. Drops of nonstop heavy rains on the roofs sounded like many people were beating drums. It seemed as if nature had joined the people of Jaipur in the mourning. Jagat Singh breathed his last. He died at the young age of thirty- two, leaving behind the throne of Jaipur in the vale of gloom

The palace was full of shrieks and sighs. The news of Maharaja's death spread like a wild fire.

Queens and concubines, courtiers and relatives, all were completely in grief apparently and they were on the same platform as far as the mourning was concerned, yet they were busy in playing their part to secure, their positions in the palace under the new dispensation. Even at this hour of grief, they did not put their rivalries at back burner.

Daavari Rupan entered the room panting and slumped on the floor.

'Sawai Maharaj is no more, *Ranisa*! He breathed his last in the early hours of morning.'

'Just now… just now… I was there. I came to do morning chores. And… he vanished like camphor.'

In a daze, Fateh Kanwar slumped down, her head in her hands. A torrent of tears began to roll down her beautiful face and she felt as if her heart would burst. After some time, she pulled herself up and resolved to maintain her composure, but all her efforts belied her. She howled like a wounded animal. Her eyes welling up with tears continually, she fell down on her knees, covered her lovely face in her palms and began sobbing her heart out...Arid wind carried her wails into the endless expanse.

How did the day pass, she had no idea. There was no end of her sorrows. The entire night she remained seated near the bed of Jagat Singh like a statue. Maids, *sewadaars*, courtiers were running here and there with sombre faces.

❋

A female figure, clad in dark coloured tattered male attire, extremely alert, stepped in cautiously. Her destination was the king's chamber. It was about to become dawn.

Suddenly she stopped. She noticed a maid running frantically crying and howling.

'Our Maharaja! He is no more! *Anna data* left us forever!'

The figure hiding behind a bush began to tremble. Somehow, she tried to control her shrieks; she placed her palm at her half open mouth as tight as possible. For some time, she remained standing there like a statue.

'Ah! Her strong shield had left her alone to survive in this cruel world.'

She took the same route to escape that she had tramped while getting in. That was the last time; she trod on the steps of Chandra Mahal. Since then, nobody saw her, as if she had vanished in thin air.

Obviously, the mysterious figure could not be anyone else but the fugitive Raskapoor. At that moment, her life was as dark and cold as the winter night. She bid adieu and left Jaipur never to return, to explore some unknown pasture.

❋

With the arrival of dawn, strong winds fiercely began to disperse the clouds like beaten cotton puffs on the horizon. A few stars were still visible, where clouds had parted a bit. They too were about to fade into the pale glow of the morning sky.

Two shadows, fully covered from head to toe, crossed the palace corridors hurriedly and disappeared in the dense coppice, leaving the palace behind

'Oh! What a violent gush of downpour!' Muttered one of them. He by now had headed towards the residence of chief nazir. The other shadow followed him with matching pace.

Nazir was a man of considerable vigour, having the reputation of a good administrator of security affairs, although he was also known as a man, who always put his own interest first, loyalty and responsibility came later.

The shadows, all drenched, were at the door of chief nazir, Mohanram . They were his security personnel, and they had to give the breaking news to their chief; he had ensured that he must be the first person to know about the demise of the king.

The day he was waiting for, had finally knocked on his door; Jagat Singh was no more.

The next day, a condolence meeting was held in the royal court. Preparations for the funeral were on. All the ministers and kith and kin were present.

Nazir watched the surroundings cautiously. He came closer to a senior official and enquired.

'Would the queens and other women commit sati?'

The court official pretended, as if he did not understand what was happening and simply remained silent. He had no answer, though he stared at him inquisitively. He tried to decipher whether Nazir was just being curious or trying to convey some message. In fact, no such indication was received from the *zenani deordhi.*

Nazir could not hide his displeasure. With great difficulty, he could restrain himself from uttering abusive words for the queens.

Unable to hold back his frustration for long, he blurted.

'If they are not committing sati, its fine. But *Rajputanis* do commit satis. That is why I was wondering…Why? Is it not the custom of our… err… generally, they follow the tradition.'

A stern gaze by the senior ministers stopped him from saying anything more. However, none was bothered to satisfy his unwanted quest, but he did not deter. He furthered his point.

'Actually I am straightforward by nature and express my opinion or thought fearlessly. What is my stake in it? Why should I suppress my feelings when I have nothing to lose or gain? Neither I am hopeful nor am I fearful.'

Officials, courtiers eyeballed him suspiciously. They tried to measure his intention behind his unnecessary interventions. They were astonished to see his audacity.

Nazir felt as if someone had choked his throat. He began coughing as if he had some problem in breathing. Slowly, he stepped aside and left the hall.

✳

When Jagat Singh was in the throes of profound political crisis, his mighty empire was convulsing with upheavals of far-reaching nature. His successes and failures had neutralised each other; the traditional glory and greatness of his house was tottering to a fall. His kingdom presented a pathetic picture of a body without soul – a body in the grip of the process of disintegration and decay. Everywhere destructive forces were raising their heads.

The foundations of peace and stability had steadily eroded during his last ruling years; now they had to bear the stress of more violent and virulent forces, which, though simmering for a considerable time before, gained terrible momentum from the blunders of Jagat Singh, and especially after his demise.

After him, Jaipur witnessed a period of political uncertainty. Innumerable issues surfaced all of a sudden. The first and foremost was of his heir. Maharaja Jagat Singh left no legal heir for the throne. Moreover, this all-important issue made Jaipur a hotbed of unwarranted interference in its internal affairs by all kinds of people. People even forgot that Jagat Singh, good or bad, was their king and he deserved ceremonial mourning befitting a king.

CHAPTER 11

1818–1819
Fight for the Throne

Those were the days, when eunuchs used to have very close access to kings, earned their infinite trust and then unleashed unlimited powers, derived in the name of the king, even in significant court matters. Mohanram, the chief nazir, was one such eunuch, who extended his realm beyond the role prescribed for him and almost controlled all the royal matters in Jaipur, even the successor of the throne.

Chief nazir had been conspiring to capture the throne since the day Jagat Singh fell ill. He took advantage of his poor health and after weighing all pros and cons, he hatched a secret plan.

Few years ago, the Marathas attacked Nurwar, a small state of Madhya Pradesh, badly defeated Manohar Singh, the king and drove him out of his state. Since then, he had been facing severe financial hardship in his exile. Mohan Singh, the nine-year-old prince of Nurwar, was found to be best fitted in the scheme of things designed by Mohanram.

Nazir drew up a plan to plant the minor prince on the throne of Jaipur. Nazir thought that by so doing, he would be able to rule over Jaipur for many years as a regent and he would also be able to make Mohan Singh dance to his tunes.

Manohar Singh gladly lapped the proposal of nazir, as it was a God sent opportunity for him to regain his lost glory. The blood flew in his ears. Trembling with excitement, he twisted his thin moustache upwards until it stood erect.

The only catch was that the prince of Nurwar must be accepted by the zenana and the nobility of Jaipur.

Nazir was determined even to stand against the nobility, if the situation so demanded. 'Of course, it would not be easy but not impossible as well,' he assured himself.

He immediately summoned Mohan Singh to Jaipur. The Nurwar prince landed in Jaipur without any delay. There was no time to lose. At any moment, the throne would be empty. It had to be filled. The young prince was immature and too young to understand the sinister intention of nazir and to measure the implications of his conspiracy.

Perceiving his prospects to be the ruler of Jaipur, Mohan Singh was thrilled and his loyalists in Nurwar, too, dreamt to serve their own stakes through him. And Manohar could not care less of nazir's motive. He only thought that his son's ascendance would change his fate.

Thorns of murky politics, at this point, found appropriate soil in Jaipur to grow with alacrity.

Maji Sahib and some of the elders raised their eyebrows at the sudden arrival of the minor prince at Jaipur. There was no occasion for him to be in Jaipur, but considering his age, nobody doubted him.

✳

During those days, the law of primogeniture was practised in all the Rajput kingdoms. The law, in fact, was a traditional system by which a property owned by a man goes to his eldest son after his death. In princely matters, it applies to the throne. This rule was rarely set aside, if at all, only in exceptional situations. Custom and precedent would fix the right of succession, whether to the throne of Jaipur or fiefdom in a *thikana*. The eldest son, addressed as *rajkunwar, rajkumar, patkunwar* or *kumarji*, would always be the designated heir. While the younger sons were called *kumar* so and so. Seniority was in fact, a distinction that pervaded through all ranks and positions of life, in the state or in the *thikanas*. All had their *patkumars* (heir or thakur) or *patrani* (chief queen). In case the heir was a minor, his mother assumed the role of a regent queen.

The privileges of a regent queen were quite substantial in kind. During the minority period of the prince, she would be the guardian, by custom as well as by biological parenthood of her child. The title of *patrani* was bestowed based on seniority, but as soon as an heir was born, the mother would be assigned the coveted title and she was assigned the title *Maji Sahib*. The chiefs of certain *thikanas*, who with certain officials enjoyed the superior position because of established hereditary distinction assisted her in performing the role as a regent queen.

In normal circumstances, if the king dies without an heir, his close relative, brothers or cousins from special families could have ascended the throne. If there was no close male relative such as a brother or cousin with an evident genuine claim, a distant relative may be adopted. As far as possible, the adoption should be done before the king's demise, both to ensure a smooth succession and to perform the last rites of the deceased king.

In order to avoid competition and confusion, in each state one particular family, directly related to the royal clan, used to be identified as the one from which an heir was to be selected.

There were certain *thikanas* in every principality of Rajputana, in whom the right of hiership to the throne was vested. In order to restrict the number of claimants, certain succession laws were framed in all the states.

In Jaipur royalty, Jhalai branch of Rajawat clan directly descended from the sixteenth century ruler Raja Man Singh had been identified for the selection of the heir. Jhalai progeny was unanimously accepted by the nobility the most appropriate and worthy to be en-throned provided the heir had no mental or physical disability. This was an established practice for many centuries. In case of mental and physical disability, the right would pass to the Kamah branch of Rajawats. However, all these customary laws were infringed when the question of succession, following the demise of Jagat Singh, came to be decided.

✳

Nazir was getting impatient with the passing of each minute. He resolved to take control of the situation and turn it in his favour, either tactfully or by force, if needed.

He came to the courtyard holding the hand of the prince of Nurwar, where the dead body of Jagat Singh was kept and the priests were busy in preparation for the funeral rites. He had the audacity to use even the mourning time to declare that the late Maharaja Jagat Singh had already adopted Mohan Singh as his son, before his death. The prince of Nurwar also endorsed the statement of nazir .

The senior *samants* and *thakurs* were normally responsible for managing the procedure of adoption, but in the case of Jagat Singh, a eunuch became the most powerful figure at the royal court. He set aside the conventional practice of nominating an heir and swiftly completed the process for adoption of the minor son of the ousted king of Nurwar. The Nurwar king though was distantly related to the Jaipur royal clan, but, in fact, he had no legitimate claim on the throne. Nobility and *thikanas* appeared very weak, as they could not muster courage to challenge the authority of his claims. They surrendered meekly.

There was no previous consultation or even casual meeting amongst the nobles, *thikanedaars*, military chiefs, or the queens on the issue of succession; on the contrary, nazir, acting entirely of his own volition, placed young Mohan Singh, as the successor on Jagat Singh, in the 'carriage in the sun'[6] to lead the funeral procession. He also gave

[6]The carriage on which body of Jagat Singh was carried to the funeral ground.

him a second name – Maan Singh, without any further delay.

In the funeral, all the last rituals were completed hurriedly; ablution and necessary purification for the deceased were barely concluded before lighting the pyre by the adopted son.

Right inside the funeral ground, the supporters of nazir came forward and congratulated young Mohan Singh for acquiring the *gaddi*. They shamelessly began to shout slogans –

Lord of Kachwahas, jay jay!

Maharaja Sawai Maan Singh jay jay!

It seemed that the death of Jagat Singh probably was not a matter of grief; rather it was a moment of celebration for the nazir and his coterie. Transactions that followed later until the final announcement, conspicuously indicated that nazir was so anxious to fulfil his interests that, he soon began the process of getting the signatures of all the court officials attended the court, in favour of the heir planted by him.

✳

Megh Singh of Diggee *thikana* was hands in glove with nazir in all his ill-conceived motives and actions. He was equally a wily and a self-seeking person. During the early years of the reign of Jagat Singh, he used the naive king for his own benefit to the maximum. He had amassed great amount of wealth by conniving with nazir. Megh Singh belonged to the Khangarote clan, the most powerful of the twelve great *thikanas* of Jaipur. He doubled his fief by applying all kinds of means, fair and foul, without any qualms . Within no time, he assumed an important role, and became the main leader of his clan at the Jaipur court. He was in no way different from the Maratha invader in exploiting his own people. He never hesitated even in grabbing the territories of Kachwahas.

Besides Diggee *thikana*, a small segment of servants and courtiers, who were assured life time employment by nazir, also came openly in support of nazir. But this was a very small group; nazir desperately needed the support of the majority and most importantly that of *Maji Sahib*. Otherwise, there was a possibility of dethronement of his puppet at any opportune moment.

The next move for the nazir was to form a majority opinion in favour of his chosen heir.

'But how? Unless we get majority votes in support of the Nurwar prince, it will not be possible to continue with him as the minor king of Jaipur,' advised his confidantes.

Nazir gestured his hand in dismissal. 'I know! I know! Oh, that will not be a big problem. I can handle it.'

'You can handle it! Great!'

They looked at him smiling at his face but ridiculed him behind his back.

*

Nazir, pacing the room heavily, was weighing one option after the other. Suddenly, an idea flashed through his mind. 'Why not to garner the support of the British for my plan?'

'Indeed a wonderful idea! It will certainly give me an opportunity to eliminate all those who dare stand against my might and determination'. He laughed hysterically. His pale brown evil eyes gleamed.

Nazir involved the British and they easily fell in his trap on this issue. He entreated the British functionary at Delhi to send his confidential Munshi to Jaipur without any further delay. Administrators, head of departments, accountants, and secretaries hired by the British were known as Munshies.

The British agent reached Jaipur from Delhi six days after the demise of Jagat Singh. He appeared in the court and read the instructions given from Delhi.

'The British government requires a full account of ascension of Mohan Singh, mainly two reasons, for placing the minor son of the Nurwar King on the throne of Jaipur. First, his right of succession and second, by whose council the procedure was adopted?'

A few more days passed. Nazir slept on the requisition made by the British because he knew that if he gave correct answers to all the queries, his unilateral decisions would be exposed before the British.

More than a month passed by in limbo. Nazir could not produce any document to corroborate the claim of Nurwar prince on the Jaipur throne.

After fifty days of the death of Jagat Singh, on 11, January 1819, again this requisition was repeated. This time, it came with some additional queries – whether the decision to install Mohan Singh on the throne had the consent of all the queens and chiefs. If yes, then a declaration to this effect under their signatures must be forwarded without any delay.

The British too were very cautious, they were treading with utmost caution and judiciously as that was the need of the hour and was absolutely necessary to handle the delicate matter. Almost on a daily basis, nazir and Munshi had been exchanging confidential letters containing information on the queens and courtiers. With each passing day, nazir was getting edgy. Experienced and trusted messengers, Ladu, Kana, Ananda Raja and Bhima were employed to carry sealed letters bearing confidential news. They were the most reliable postal workers for carrying letters from Jaipur to the British officers at Delhi. Nazir had complete faith in them.

Finally, his evil efforts bore some fruits. If a seed is sowed, the tree will grow laden with its fruits. What kind of fruits a person gets entirely depends on the kind of seed he sows.

✳

Nazir had successfully created his own clout among the British officials placed at Jaipur royal court during all those days. Nazir became so important to them that the British government formally announced the acceptance of the nazir's choice of Prince of Nurwar as the Maharaja of Jaipur. The British were not in favour of any revolt on this issue.

On 7th, February 1819, the Court of Jaipur received two letters, one from the British agent and the other from the supreme authority in Delhi. Letters were read loudly in full court. The noubat[7] began to sound. Minor prince of Nurwar was ushered into the royal court to occupy his seat.

Nazir gave a whoop of joy at the success of his plan.

The formal recognition of Mohan Singh as the minor king of Jaipur by the British created unrest among the *thikanas*. The nomination of a prince from Nurwar under the tutelage of a eunuch was a disgrace to the Rajputs of Jaipur, and was not acceptable to them. It was a question of Rajputs' honour. At last, the Rajput pride was provoked to act decisively. They were determined that the sovereignty of the royal family must be protected at any cost.

The British had failed to gauge the strength of Rajput sentiments on this issue. Their volatile mood took a serious turn. They even thought of a revolt to throw nazir out of Jaipur in several pieces.

A letter was dispatched to the British authority in Delhi.

'We are ready to comply with the call taken by the British authority and we are ready to abide by their decision, but only after Maharani Sireh KanwarJi, sister of the Maharaja of Jodhpur gives her consent.'

This letter was an open challenge to the nazir and his supporters including Megh Singh of Diggee *thikana*.

Meanwhile, Rajawat chief of the Jhalai clan appealed to other *thikanas* as well to take up arms in his support. Within no time, the

---

[7]Auspicious sounds by the musical instruments

chiefs of Sirwar, Esurda joined him. Actually, the Rajawat chief felt slighted that his rightful claim to the throne had been entirely overlooked. Therefore, he began to mobilise his allies to seek their support for his cause. Some lesser *thikanedaars* but powerful clans of the same stock extended their wholehearted support to the claim of the Rajawat chief.

At this crucial moment, one more claimant for the throne – the son of Prithvi Singh, who was living in exile at Gwalior, came forward. He was fighting his lone battle as nobody supported him, because he lacked the qualities of a king.

Later, the British thought that it would be prudent not to indulge in internal matters of the state and stepped aside from court conspiracies. The resident felt that his resolutions are mostly met with resistance. This time, he found himself entangled in the vortex of royal intrigue, which was certainly an avoidable mess. The higher authorities, 'do not poke your nose in the internal matters of royalty', warned him.

Although courtiers and vassals were wavering amid so many conflicting views, but they remained united and resolute as far as their battle against the nazir was concerned.

✳

All this while, resentment was building up against him in *zenani deordhi*. Queens and other women in *zenani deordhi* grew restless. They somehow wanted to get rid of this eunuch, who had become their master.

Suraj Kanwar and Anand Kanwar, the sisters of Jagat Singh rushed to meet their mother.

'*Masa!* That eunuch has crossed his limits. We are amazed at his audacity. He is scheming to rule over Jaipur through proxy. Will you not stop him? This will bring disgrace not only to us, but to the whole of Rajputana.'

'Ah! A eunuch becomes the regent king of Jaipur.'

Maji Sahib always despised nazir's closeness to Jagat Singh. Once she advised Jagat not to give him a long rope. 'Keep your eyes peeled for him.' Although nazir never ever gave her any occasion to doubt his intentions, yet her womanly instinct always suspected his motives . She had a hunch that Mohanram nazir might have killed Jagat Singh. But she had no evidence, whatsoever, to fix him.

Maji Sahib had been pondering over this matter ever since the demise of her son. 'Ah! Jagat Singh spent all his vigorous life in the company of frivolous people and women of low breed, and finally, that dancing woman Ras, she came in his life to annihilate him, and perhaps to settle her score of the past life. We all have to repay in this life for our deeds of our past life. Karma! Once her debt was repaid, he passed away. Otherwise, what else could be the reason of such an abnormal infatuation, which led to such a disastrous situation? Did he ever care for his people or for that matter – Jaipur? His vagabond ways had put this great Kachwaha dynasty in such a state of peril. When he got married with Fateh Kanwar, I had great hopes. I knew that beautiful women were the weakness of my son. Moreover, Fateh Kanwar was the most beautiful woman on this earth. A celestial nymph. Her charisma is unquestionable and her love for her husband is beyond measures, her capability undeniable. Still, she was thrown away from the loving bonds of nuptials by the cruel hands of her destiny. Who could have stopped the wandering clouds when a strong wind took them along?'

Maji Sahib quite often used to curse herself for the state of peril, Jaipur was in.

'Ah! My son, can you see from that world, where have you put the pride of your ancestors, great Kachwahas! In the dirty hands of a eunuch.'

She tried her level best to control the wayward life of her son. But her all efforts ended in fiasco. Her pleas and cries were turned by his deaf ears. Her attempts to bring about change in Jagat seemed to add fuel to his uncontrollable desires and unscrupulous ways. He never paid heed to his mother.

Like father like son. *Maji Sahib* wandered in the wilds of her turbulent life. In a way, the journey of her own life was no different from that of her daughters-in-law. 'My son inherited all the traits of his father – Pratap Singh. He too was mad for a dancer, but still he knew well how and where to control his madness. Smitten by a dancer Didar Baksh, he too kept her with him until he breathed his last. Jagat went one-step ahead. He made a *pattar* his queen, perhaps the most pampered and the most powerful *pattar* in the history of the Kachwahas.'

Tears were flowing down her cheeks like a stream. Unable to go to bed, mother, daughters and daughters-in-law spent the night either pacing the floor up and down or turning sides on their beds.

The next morning, *Maji Sahib* immediately summoned the nobles and loyal courtiers. She appeared in the court, chose to sit behind the latticed partition to hide her red swollen eyes. 'I will not accept prince of Nurwar as the king of Jaipur. I will wage a war against him,' she declared. The nobility stood by her side.

✳

Nazir was greatly annoyed. He could not eat the cake that he baked and served to himself. He was not at peace. The opposition by *Maji Sahib*, the queens and kin of Jagat Singh did not go down well with him.

Nazir was as imperious as he was ambitious. Though he was in a quandary, yet he stood firm on his resolve to quash their might, despite strong protests from the nobles, queens and *thikanedaars*.

He thought of taking the help of the Maharaja of Jodhpur in making his sister, Rani Sireh Kanwar amenable to his proposal. He wrote a very courteous letter to him.

> Honourable Maan SinghJi Hukum
> Maharaja of Jodhpur
> Ghani Khamma

I, Nazir Mohanram, the servant of Jaipur, very humbly would like to bring the issue of the heir of Jaipur to your kind notice. *Hukum Sa*, Prince of Nurwar is nominated to succeed him in complete obedience to the will of our late Sri Sawai Maharaj Jagat SinghJi. I earnestly request you to let your sister, widow of late King of Jaipur, know this fact and sign the letter of consent, declaring the prince of Nurwar, the heir of Jaipur. I always need her kindness and support.

> Yours' always
> Loyal and obedient
> Mohanram
> Chief Nazir, Jaipur

Raja Maan Singh returned a prudently worded letter.

'It is difficult to comprehend why my sister's signature on the required declaration for the right of succession to the *musnad* (throne) of Jaipur, is required at this stage, which completely depended upon, and in fact, was vested in the chiefs of the twelve clans of Kachwahas. Once they approve, give their consent and sign the declaration, the queen of Jaipur , my sister, and afterwards me , would certainly sign it, if needed.'

✳

Nazir and his gang were deeply anguished. Deeply frustrated, nazir charted another course.

He attempted to build a strong alliance with the Rana of Mewar.

He sent a wedding proposal of Mohan Singh, prince of Nurwar, with his grand daughter.

The messenger presented the auspicious coconut and other gifts to him in the court. Rana was willing to accept the proposal, but the court of Mewar was not in favour of this matrimony. The elders in the court on a peculiar ground stubbed out the plot. In fact about twelve years ago, a sister of late king of Jaipur was betrothed with him. The elders opposed any betrothal again without honouring the prior betrothal. Their plea was that Rana must honour his prior commitment first that he had already made with Jaipur.

'RanaJi! First, you must tie the nuptials with the princess of Jaipur. Then consider a second one.' Rana had no option but to succumb under their pressure.

British Resident at Delhi too strongly supported the wedding proposal of Mohan, but his support did not cut any ice.

✳

In a fit of rage and utter frustration, nazir hurled abuses on his fellow eunuchs, tore his clothes and threw away his arms. Enraged, he left the palace and walked for miles. After facing failure after failure on all fronts, nazir set out on a sojourn. Perhaps, for him, that was the only way out to vent his frustration.

Moonlight was spreading lazily on the sprawling fields and hills. A bright silvery spinning ball was hidden behind the boulders of Aravalli hills. The shadow of ramparts was falling in the longitudinal ways on the fort's premises.

He glanced at Jaipur Fort, a symbol of grandeur, with its gold coated doors, its ramparts in stone, higher than the nearby hills, was located at plateau with palaces, temples, sprawling gardens with its domes and high walls. Swings and beds, marble flooring, Persian carpets, glass chandeliers, fabulous miniature paintings and sprawling lush green gardens began to dwindle in front of his eyes. The palace, temples, *chattris*, elevated, dome-shaped pavilions and *baaraadaries*, were worked with an exquisite elegance and refinement. The hard pink stone carved as if it were a soft and smooth substance.

'All the glorious buildings, gardens, luxuries are flying away, far from my reach. The rich exuberance of the decoration that displays almost superhuman skill and entitles the Jaipur fort as priceless treasure of architecture and art; the brilliant monument of Jaipur Kings' military and constructive genius, all belong to me.'

The more he looked at the fort, the more he became agitated. The devil promised to himself, 'I shall finally win, sooner or later, at any cost, even if I have to unleash all my brutality and malice. This coward race of Kachwahas, fading and failing, cannot stand against me.'

At another moment, he felt as if his long cherished dream to acquire Jaipur was slipping through his fingers like water. More he tightens his fist, more forcefully it slips through the gaps of his fingers.

CHAPTER 12

1819
The Heir Born

The golden circumference of the setting sun was sinking fast, far away into the horizon. The birds were returning to their nests. Misty twilight was steadily engulfing the trees, streets, houses and fields. Flickering oil lamps began appearing at the thresholds of the houses, and in the windows. But Fateh Kanwar did not budge an inch from her seat; she continued to sit expressionless near a latticed window all alone.

A *daavari* entered the room with an earthen lamp, but she indicated her to keep that away at a distance. She herself wanted to remain in darkness, perhaps to hide her existence from the worldly light.

The queen took a stroll for some time in the adjoining corridor, reminiscing about the past. When she got married, perhaps nobody had imagined that one day Jagat Singh would have grown into an arrogant and lustful king and he would put his own kingdom at stake for his whims and fancies. One day, she entered in this palace in bridal attire and today, in a short span of time, she is wrapped in maroon and black , symbolising her widowhood.

In the last six months, Jagat had been spending his quality time in her company quite often. She too was enjoying her days that were slowly turning into peals of laughter. At last, she seemed to regain her lost paradise.

She recalled how queens and concubines entered one after the other in her happy world and destroyed it as per their capacities, and the final blow came in the form of Raskapoor. She remembered everything, both of them promised to each other during his last days.

Sometimes, she could not believe her stars. She wondered, how could he freed himself from the clutches of Raskapoor so easily? Was her magic beginning to fade? But, how did it happen? Did he finally understand the value of family? Had the forbidden fruit lost its taste? Or did he crave for his own child? Did he realise that he needed an heir that only a legally wedded Rajput queen could have given him. A son born of a Muslim concubine would never be allowed to ascend the throne after his demise.

Fateh Kanwar heaved a sigh; she glanced wistfully at each ornament gifted by the Maharaja and at the pictures hanging on the walls of her rooms, which were painted jointly. The silver vase specially placed by him near her bed, as she loved the fragrance of fresh flowers... all flashed through her mind generating a surge of tender feelings for her husband. Her eyes moistened.

✳

Fateh gently placed her hand on her belly. She remembered the moment she had told Maharaj that she was pregnant. Jagat had covered her with rose petals. She still felt the warmth of his embrace and his kisses all over her face. She had kept each word, exchanged between the two of them, in her heart like a precious treasure.

'RathorniJi, my dearest queen, my Fateh! After a long time, no... First time in my life, you are the one, who have given me the best piece of news. Perhaps, almighty has forgiven me! He has granted the best boon, a person can ask for.' The expression of Jagat was one of pure ecstasy.

He made Fateh sit on the bed holding her arms.

'Maharaj, we are blessed.' Her face glowed. Her eyes sparkled.

'Anyone knows about it?' asked Jagat anxiously.

'No! Not so far! You have the first right to know about it.'

'Then keep it a secret.' Fateh nodded in agreement. But why? She wondered.

It was an occasion of celebration and jubilation. Was he scared of someone? Some other queen? Raskapoor? Or his faithful servant Nazir? Did he know that she would be harmed and he might lose his heir forever? Perhaps, yes! He knew the dirty politics of his palace.

Today, the one, who wanted to keep her pregnancy a secret, was no more in this world. And, Fateh had to undergo all kinds of humiliation because of the same secret. She promised to herself that she was a Rathorni and she would go all out to ensure the safety of her child. She would live only for the sake of her child.

✳

March was about to end within a week or so. Spring had set in, but nights were unusually cold at this time of the month.

Rani Sireh Kanwar rushed to *Maji Sahib*, who was about to retire. It was quite late in the night. Two quarters had passed.

'RathorniJi, this year the winter came early, but it seems in no mood to depart soon.'

Maji Sahib said deliberately. She knew that Sireh Kanwar has approached her at this odd hour with some grave concern. But she herself did not want to reveal her disquiet.

'*Ghani Khamma Masa*! I never wanted to disturb you at this odd hour and in this manner. I came to know something… Something… You must know. Probably, you already must be knowing. Nothing can remain hidden from your eyes. I thought of spending some time with Fateh *Ranisa*. When I… Actually, she is not well. You know *Masa* what I mean!' she said hesitatingly. She came very close to *Maji Sahib* and whispered in her ear.

Maji Sahib heard her patiently. She got up from her bed, covered herself with a woollen shawl, took a few steps, and then paused for a while, as if deliberating something. Then she looked straight into the eyes of Sireh Kanwar.

'I am glad to hear that she is fine. So far, all went well.' As if, she said to herself.

'May Goddess Jumwai bless her and you. *Mata Devi*! You are great. Today I will tell you that Jumwai *Mata* has saved us from humiliation… It was a timely interposition of Jumwai *Ma*. It is her eighth month. Now we have to disclose this piece of news to others. We cannot keep it under the carpet anymore.'

'Yes *Masa*! She was feeling uncomfortable since yesterday evening. She managed to bear her pain, but when Rupan came to her in the night, she could make out instantly. So far, it was not visible due to the winter months and Fateh *Ranisa* wrapped herself well in the woollens for the last four months. But now…it is visible now.'

Sireh Kanwar stopped saying further. *Maji Sahib* gestured her to keep quiet. They rushed to the chamber of Fateh, almost running.

Maji Sahib embraced her daughter-in-law and consoled her.

'Forgive me *Masa*! I could not hide it due to my pain,' Fatah said very slowly, almost like a whisper.

'Don't you worry. In fact, I was anticipating it any day. All of us together have come a long way. Let the world know that the real and rightful heir will soon come to take his seat. This one month will pass quickly. From now onwards, Fateh, you will not drink water from anyone in the palace, but from Sireh and me. Never ever, consume any medicine or eatable given to you, even the prasada. Sireh, with her trusted band of security persons, will be with you all the time. If she has to go for some errand, she may go only when I am here. No evil can touch you.'

'*Masa*, how would it be if the cook and the *daavari* who carry the food for Fateh, consumes a portion first from the food to be given to her in our presence,' Sireh Kanwar added. *Maji Sahib* patted her shoulder in appreciation.

After cautioning both of them, *Maji Sahib* gave instructions to her band of security persons.

'Under no circumstances, this information must reach to nazir Mohanram. I know it is just impossible to keep it a secret anymore from his eagle eyes. He has hundreds of eyes and thousands of ears in and around us. In case it happens, none of you will see the sun the next moment. The honour of Jaipur is at stake. Even a tiny insect must not cross the walls of *Sukh Mahal*.'

After monitoring each detail, she entered the chamber of Fateh again. She did the last bit of her duty. Fateh was spirited away through a secret door to an innermost chamber of *Sukh Mahal*, next to *Maji Sahib*'s room. She quietly glanced at the pale face of Fateh.

'This is the time when you should have the happiest time, but I have to keep you here, as if you are in the prison. Would you pardon me?' Fateh looked at her protector innocently with a faint smile.

The tearful eyes of her mother-in-law seemed like two glistening stars on her smiling face.

✳

On 24 March 1819, the news of Maharani Fateh Kanwar's pregnancy was made public.

Maharani Fateh Kanwar is pregnant.

She had entered the eighth month of pregnancy.

Nazir was instantly informed by his spies; he wondered how could it be possible to maintain secrecy for such a long time under his nose? No *daavari*, no *badaaran*, no *deordhi* official, no one noticed anything unusual? How could it be possible that *Maji Sahib* was ignorant about it? Was she? Most of the time that wretched old woman used to be with her only. Why did the superintendent of the queen's palace not give this information to me? This was his duty. Or he did not spill the beans purposefully? Did he deliberately conceal it? Oh! Yes, he did! Eight months of pregnancy is not a small thing. It is a long time. That stupid slave had turned out to be more loyal to the queen than to his superior. He would be taught a lesson. Nazir told himself.

Nazir was not yet ready to believe it. 'If I assume that my own person stabbed me in my back and did not divulge the news of the pregnancy to me on time, even then so what! The secrets of *zenani deordhi* find their own way to the public ears out of the windows. The zenana, progenitor of conspiracies, feuds, strange stories, filled with multitude of women and men within its enclosed walls had always been a vibrant and interesting place. Hushed up words, soft whispers, half-truths and half lies provide it a distinct character, we all know. In such a situation, it was utterly impossible to keep any secret for long and a secret of such magnitude, as the pregnancy of the queen that too after the demise of her husband! It was just impossible.'

After a marathon mental exercise, he assured himself that it was a false propaganda to uproot him by his opponents.

'This piece of news is a big lie. But why this news originated? If it was true, then!'

Nazir began to smack his head. 'I am a fool. What is the point in crying over the spilt milk? I am ruined. I am finished.Oh, Mohanram control yourself. This is not the best way to win the battle.'

Nazir was literally crying, howling like a wounded wolf, beating his chest, pounding the floor and splitting his hair.

'Somehow, I will not allow this snake of Jagat Singh to see the light of

the day.'

'These women, they are the cause of doom everywhere. I do not understand what magic they use to enchant these stupid kings to bring them around. Ah, I was a fool. Why did I not keep an eye on these worthless women? These widow queens are truly not worthy to be alive. Worse than earthworms! Leaches! Parasites! Just look at them, none of them committed sati; instead one of them is producing a child! Ah! I spent all my energy, all my time in placing that bastard on the throne, that puppy of Nurwar, and here these witches have played their game.' He howled for hours.

✳

Since the pregnancy was declared so late, and in order to avoid any controversy on such an important matter, *Maji Sahib* had been taking each step very cautiously. One wrong step and all is gone.

The nobles and *thikanedaars* were called for a meeting late in the evening, and all had assembled under the leadership of Rawal Berisal at the palace to discuss the issue. They had inkling about why the meeting was called.

There was restlessness concealed behind their composed countenance. All of them were in their thirties to fifties. Their faces with crimson eyes were festooned with thick grey and black beard. Cautious and aggrieved, but fearless – they were all worried for Jaipur. Rawal Berisal with a pale brown complexion and chiselled features was seated in the corner. His long and strong arms were bound in his lap. His face was a picture of discomfort.

A small assembly of nobles of Jaipur had already spent the prior night considering all aspects of the most crucial piece of news, they had received in the evening; since then they had been engrossed intensely in discussing the grave issue.

In the meeting, though all reposed faith in *Maji Sahib* and her version of the news, yet, it was unanimously decided to complete all the formal procedures.

'It would be proper to have it verified through the senior queens and the wives of the principal *thikanedaars*, so that growing suspicion could be nipped in the bud once for all. Though all of us have unwavering faith in the resolute character of Fateh Kanwar, the moot point is whether *Rani* is really pregnant or is it a symptom of some serious illness. Not a single person doubts her; neither of us suspects any hidden motive.'

After a lot of deliberation, a consensus decision was taken.

The first day of April was chosen for the verification. A council of sixteen queens, the widows of the late King and the *thakuranis* of all the major *thikanas* of the state gathered to ascertain the fact of the pregnancy, while all the *thakurs*, senior courtiers waited in the foyers located at the entrance of the Chandra Mahal.

Investigations were made. Fateh Kanwar was examined by an expert midwife. Questions were raised with squinted eyes. Fateh answered each one in a composed manner.

She said softly with tears in her eyes,

'Maharaja knew it. He asked me to keep it a secret. I do not know why? Perhaps, he was concerned about the child's safety. *Masa* was also aware of it. It was kept secret only for the child's safe arrival in this world. The only and sole heir of Jaipur.'

Fateh Kanwar, after spending so many years living almost in seclusion, suddenly, was encircled by a herd of known people and strangers. She was facing piercing eyes, blunt queries, all alone. She was not keen to satiate probing eyes, not willing to face a trial, as if she had committed some grave crime.

After a long trial was over, she wearily slumped into her bed, closed her eyes. She had a splitting headache. A midwife urgently attended her; *Maji Sahib* and other queens tried to allay her undue fears.

Finally, it was formally declared that Fateh Kanwar was pregnant beyond doubt. The legal heir of late Maharaja of Jaipur would come to acquire his rightful place after one month. Still calculations and consultations continued till the sun shone brightly in the sky.

A written declaration signed by all those who were present, avowing their unanimous belief in the pregnancy of the *Rani*, was brought forth. It categorically mentioned:

If a son is born, the nobility of Jaipur would acknowledge him as their king. They would pledge their strict adherence to him and to none else in this world

✳

When a copy of the royal message was given to nazir, he went through it with a long face. He threw it on the floor with all his might, crushed it under his shoe.

He felt as if flames of fury would smoulder his whole body. Hundreds of serpents had crawled into nazir's heart.

'These people are playing tricks with me. I will see! I will see all of them! The time was ticking by and I have not yet made any progress. And now this formal message! Ridiculous!'

In a quiet meeting with Megh Singh of Diggee, later, on the same evening, he shot a question.

'This was a piece of news that would have caused celebrations throughout the state, but why it was kept as a secret for so long? This is my only concern.'

Megh Singh chose to remain silent. He knew the reason.

To save the child from the clutches of the person just seated in front of him. There may be many more like him in the palace.

Megh Singh and nazir both were engrossed in dissecting the puzzle. Megh Singh felt pity for Jagat Singh. His last hours must have been saddened by the thought that he was leaving this world without seeing the face of his child. God granted a boon to him, but he was not given time to celebrate it.

While nazir wondered that Jagat Singh, who was indifferent to his queens all the time, could be so concerned of his unborn child in his last days that he had warned the queen not to disclose it!

'Who was the king scared of? Did he come to know the truth of my intentions?' And nazir was not wrong.

✳

Nazir was constantly up to something or the other, somehow, to damage the pregnant queen. None of his actions bore the desired outcome, all proved ineffective. She was beyond his claws.

The days came and gone. With each passing day, his sanity was wiped out by the thought of Fateh and her unborn child. 'How come, just after one month or so, a newly born infant would land on this planet to snatch away all the powers and luxuries from my hands?' He pledged that he would not allow all his efforts to go down the drain. He would never ever allow this to happen.

'Ah! I will pay these people in the same coin. I always believe in the principle of 'tit for tat'. Scheming will be answered by scheming. Fraud by fraud. I must be very alert and careful. This throne will be mine, for sure. None can stop me from taking it.' All the time, his mind was spinning schemes after schemes.

'I shall make them pay for their deeds. They will repent. They do not know me. This old woman, mother of Jagat, a wretched son, huh! What a mother? She could not do anything, when her son was alive, now in his absence, she is trying to out-smart me! Even the late king could not touch me. This Fateh was a Fateh only for name sake, victory eluded her all through her life. In the real sense, she was a loser on all fronts. A subdued, inferior woman, ignored by her husband! When did this lecherous Jagat Singh pass the nights with this woman? And the devil planted a seed in her womb! This unborn child will stand against me! One day! Never ever!'

Turning, twisting, spitting venom between his gritted teeth, resolute nazir approached the British and embarked on his operation for grabbing the throne.

In this changed scenario, the British too changed their stance. They decided to extend the support to the alliance of nazir and Mohan Singh, till the legal heir was born. Till then, Nurwar prince could continue only as an acting king of Jaipur.

He was still sure enough that *Maji Sahib* had been spreading news of fake pregnancy in connivance of Fateh Kanwar. Even if it were true, he would not allow this child to see the light of day on this earth. His opponent, *Maji Sahib*, was equally determined that the child must arrive in this world unscathed, unharmed at any cost.

✳

Maji Sahib and Sireh Kanwar were sitting at the terrace outside the room of the pregnant queen. They appeared stressed. They spent each moment with crossed fingers. Their mission would not be complete unless a male child was born.

'If it is a girl child, she will also be declared the heir! What do you say, Masa?' asked Sireh Kanwar.

'Oh, Sure! Then that would be a different fight altogether.'

Both looked at each other for some time then burst into laughter.

Zenana had been turned into a well-guarded regiment. Fateh passed her days in strict confinement under the supervision of Sireh Kanwar and *Maji Sahib*. No one was allowed to enter the chamber of Fateh Kanwar. Even the maids had to obtain due permission from *Maji*

Sahib and they could look after the queen only in her presence. Food was first to be tasted by the maid, before it was given to Fateh. No laxity! Only strict observance! Fateh was kept in good humour so that her offspring in the womb could grow healthily.

One day in the morning, Shivanand Gusai, the royal priest was reciting *shlokas* in the temple, temporarily erected for Fateh inside the enclosure a few yards from her chamber, *Maji Sahib* was seated with her hands joined at a distance of a few feet.

'*Gusaiji*, what do your planets say? Everything will be as per my wish?' She asked

'*Hujur Maji Sahib*, at this moment I can say that you have asked a question in an auspicious moment as per the *prashna kundali*. Time is in your favour. Your wish will be fulfilled.'

It was running ninth month. Any day, this palace will be filled with cries of a newly born heir of Jagat Singh.

It was 25th April1819. Since morning, Fateh was in labour pain. The midwife Singauri went through the usual checklist in her head, noting the position of the child, location of the umbilical cord. She put her hand on the abdomen feeling the baby's shoulder and eased the baby gently. Her assistant Bamani asked Fateh to push on as much as possible as her other hand slipped in round her back. Singauri's left hand moved to cup the head and neck, and then gently she lifted the mucus-covered, blood-smeared little body out of his mother.

Four months and four days after the death of Jagat Singh, Fateh gave birth to a male child. It was that time of the year when blossoming flowers in the gardens filled the palace with their fragrance. *Maji Sahib* felt as if nature had joined her in her joy. The moments of sheer emotion made her eyes wet. Her voice trembled. Her expression was one of pure delight. She was elated. She thanked the family diety with folded hands and closed her eyes.

The baby began to scream and the midwife allowed herself to smile and relax for a second before she turned back to Bamani to clamp and cut the cord. Singauri handed the child to the grandmother, allowing her a few moments to cuddle and greet him before the weighing and cleaning began. She held the child in her arms and said proudly.

This heir of my family has finally descended in my home after winning all odds. He is the saviour of our honour. Hence he will be named Jai Singh.

The day he was born, wrapped in velvet and soft cottons, he was placed on the throne. The British Governor General sent tika–a shagun, the auspicious gifts for the newly crowned infant with a *kharita*[8].

The child was showered with umpteen blessings and his arrival received an ecstatic welcome from thousands who lined the streets and around the palace complex.

The city was in a joyous commotion of expectancy. In every house, in every street, men and women and children looked on the arrival of the heir as a great and auspicious occasion in their own lives and welcomed it with enthusiasm and great hopes.

---

[8] An official declaration ,on his claim to be the ruler of Jaipur. Kharita was an official sanction or a seal on his heirship by the British. As per records of Victoria Albert Museum London, Maharaja Jagat Singh died on 21 November 1818 and Jai Singh, his son was born in April 1819. Mohan Singh named as Man Singh ruled from 22 December 1818 to 25 April 1819. Jai Singh was declared the king, placed on the throne on 25 April 1819. Man Singh returned to Nurwar.

CHAPTER 13

1819....
The Less Travelled Path

Maji Sahib was seated next to Fateh Kanwar's bed. The infant prince, now three-month-old was sleeping under the soft linens of his cradle. The life of Fateh had been revolving around her child. *Maji Sahib* spent some time with her grandchild and in between talked to Fateh on trivial matters – what to feed the child, his clothes etc., then she brought the conversation around her.

'Maharani RathorniJi, what do you think is your prime concern? asked *Maji Sahib*.

Fateh looked into the eyes of her mother-in-law. She appeared puzzled. For *Masa* she had always been Fateh. Why did she address her as Maharani RathorniJi with so much emphasis?

'To groom my child and take care of him. I must always be on guard so that nobody can harm him, 'Fateh replied thoughtfully.

'Yes! I agree that is your supreme duty. However, a person has to do many things simultaneously. So what are your other responsibilities? Now that you are the regent queen.'

Fateh remained silent.

'Of course your prime duty is to rear your child well. You must be careful that no hands can rock the cradle of the infant prince Jai Singh. But you must also know that a cradle can be rocked not by evil hands only. Even a strong wind can do this. Now is the time that you should transform yourself into a solid rock. Your name is Fateh that means victory. So, you have to prove yourself worthy of your name'. The intense eyes of *Maji Sahib* were fixed on her face.

'I cannot do anything without support, *Masa* and why me? You are the *Maji Sahib*, you alone are worthy of this role, none else. And you are the grandmother of *Kunwar* Jai. So who else could be more deserving than you?' Fateh pleaded.

'Kachwaha traditions are not to be broken. Already much damage is done in the past many years. I will be with you like a solid rock. But you prepare yourself, sooner the better. You should be a rock. No attachments, no bonding. Only follow your dharma. No wind, no storm, can destroy a solid rock. Similarly, no one can disturb a person with a peaceful mind. Be as firm as a rock and be as calm as the tranquil waters of a lake.'

'Please *Masa!* Relieve me of this burden. I am not cut out for all this,' requested Fateh with folded hands. She had seen the dark dens of power.

She moaned, 'Ah! Let me bring up my son. My treasure, my only solace! Why do you force me to venture into unknown pastures?' But she had no choice.

Her request was ignored by *Maji Sahib*. She ignored her emotional appeal. She had decided to support Fateh from the back, in view of the prevailing circumstances. Fateh needed to be strengthened.

✳

This was the turning point in the life of Fateh. Destiny had already paved the way for her to tread on the less trodden lanes. Fateh Kanwar, a simple woman, who had been living a life of seclusion and humiliation, given to her by none other than her own husband, all of a sudden, became a power centre. She never wanted to be in the helm of political affairs, but the destiny made her the regent of the infant king.

Fateh received the legacy of her husband, which was not easy to handle. She inherited the state with empty coffers and a crushing debt. Fateh Kanwar was thrown into a turbulent ocean of politics, whereas, she did not know how to swim even in a serene pond.

Life in the zenana of Jaipur, lurking beneath the veneer of apparent calm and tranquillity, was full of intrigues. The queens, *pardayats* and *paswans* all were entangled in the mire of palace intrigues. Some of them spent the whole day in marble ponds filled with rose petals, drinking wine and gin. Some played chausar, bought jewellery, flew kites; a few tamed pigeons; these were some of the activities, they indulged themselves in. And, of course, the majority of them believed in scheming. Their gimlet eyes were as dark as their manoeuvrings. They had entered the palace very young due to matrimonial alliances. They grew into stately matriarchs behind the purdah, guarded by rippling-skinned eunuchs. Crushed opium and diamonds were their aphrodisiacs. They never raised their voices, they were virtually languid, yet it was difficult to escape from their venom. Fateh had also seen the thorny side of royal life. She had retired in her own small world, free of royal intrigues and problems of the state.

'I have to wake Fateh up. She cannot survive for long by living in a cocoon. She is not realising that the existence of the State and her own is in peril.'

Fears of *Maji Sahib* were based on solid grounds; the elements of disorder, though subdued, were not crushed completely, and she also dreaded nazir Mohanram and Megh Singh of Diggee, who had proved big thorns in the feet of her late son throughout his life.

'This Megh Singh had usurped so much land and accumulated wealth from Jagat. Nazir benefitted maximum by using my son's weaknesses as a ladder. I think they will strike again. These two are not the exceptions, if you open the lid you will find many worms crawling in the pot. Fateh now is the time for you to hold the baton. Sooner the better,' mumbled *Maji Sahib*.

✳

Fateh Kanwar, as guardian of her son's rights, had begun her life from the scratch in an extremely hostile situation. She, however, embarked upon her journey with small steps. She stepped slowly into her new role not because of her personal choice or her capabilities, but because of the need of the hour.

For Fateh, a duty bound woman, the responsibility as a mother, obligation to the family and duty to protect her people in the role of a caretaker ruler were far more important than that to be a powerful queen.

When *Maji Sahib* was carving out a ruler in her daughter-in-law, nazir and his gang were working on all possible options to oust her from their way. They were ready to eliminate her at the first opportunity. They were beaten by those whom they least expected.

'Instead of committing *sati* this woman has assumed power and begun ruling over us as regent queen. Her rule will continue up to the age of the maturity of her son and what will we do during all these years.' He with his gang had been doing brainstorming every day to solve this problem

Maji Sahib was also dictating and directing the new Regent daily without fail.

The first, most important decision of the Regent Queen was to discharge nazir from the post of Mukhtiar[9] and appointing Rawal Berisal of Samod *Thikana* in his place.

✳

Nazir had already anticipated that he would be axed any time. He rushed to David Ochterlony, the British Resident for the Rajputana states, for his rescue.

The Resident assured him of all help. He expressed his desire to have a meeting with the queen.

---

[9]A person given authority to manage state affairs

Fateh was not ready to have any meeting with a British official. She agreed only on one condition that her mother-in-law would be present at the meeting. *Maji Sahib* agreed.

The meeting was held in the hall meant for public meetings. Both Fateh and *Maji Sahib* were seated side-by-side behind heavy velvet curtains.

'I personally find your decision unjust and biased against nazir Mohanram. I beg to differ with your decision and I urge you that nazir should be allowed to remain in the office and be given a chance to serve the state. It would be a win-win situation for both of you. I mean, this decision will relieve you of undue burden and nazir will be all the more happy.'

Fateh looked at her mother-in-law for support. Her presence helped in building confidence of Fateh. *Maji Sahib* patted her hand. She had prepared her daughter-in-law well for this meeting. Fateh was hesitant.

'Speak…speak! It's now or never.' *Maji Sahib* exhorted her. Fateh mustered courage and blurted.

'Mr Resident, I have strong evidence against him. First, during my pregnancy, nazir had gone to the extent of harming my child in the womb. He used black magic. We have proof. Mr Resident you may not be aware of it, but this practice is quite in vogue in most parts of the country.' She stopped speaking abruptly. Her breath was heavy.

Maji Sahib stroked lightly at her back. Ochterlony waited to hear more. The queen began:

'Second, he was found guilty of conspiring against my husband, late Maharaja Jagat Singh. *Maji Sahib* will give her testimony in this matter if you like. And the last, based on secret reports, I have reason to believe that he is working against the interest of the State and my child. I cannot put the security of my child and my State at stake. He has to go.'

Seeing the adamant attitude of the queen, the Resident consented to her proposition. Left with no other choice, he extended an olive branch to her and also displayed an affable attitude towards Rawal Berisal.

✳

Ochterlony's real intention behind his gracious manners, later, became clear. His main motive was to sow the seeds of suspicion in the mind of Fateh Kanwar and create a rift between her and *Maji Sahib*. Their solidarity was a threat not only to nazir and his clout, but to his interests as well. He wanted to weaken their bond.

After a couple of weeks the resident again requested the queen to have a meeting with the Regent Queen. Ochterlony , a seasoned and crafty player, played his cards well . This time, in order to instill confidence in Fateh, *Maji Sahib* asked her to meet him on her own.

'I am your strong backup. Use me whenever you need me. You must know that I will not be here forever. You have to learn to handle such things on your own. This is your priority. Your prime job. Let's see, what that fair monkey offers you this time? Always try to see beyond the wall.'

'I will do! May I take anyone with me?'

'Of course! Why not? Remember one more thing! You don't take up this role for me, not for yourself, not for anyone on this earth, but only for dharma.'

She added after a pause, 'who do you consider best suited for this job? Remember, these are policy matters. Strict secrecy and extreme loyalty are basic prerequisites for this job. '

A subtle warning. 'I am considering grooming Rupan. What do you think *Masa?*'

'Completely your discretion. Now from this moment, you need to be careful. Do not trust blindly anyone. Not even me! Remember, if you have to strangulate a person, first you must go very close to him. And your nearest and closest person can strangulate you. Before plunging into a pond, one must have a fair idea of its depth. Rupan must pass many acid tests before she wins your trust and proves her worth.'

Unable to understand the subtle advice of *Maji Sahib*, naive Fateh Kanwar took Rupan along with her.

'The Regent Queen! Her highness, this is my humble request to you that you must not concede your position so easily.' Ochterlony conveyed his message in a low tone when *Maji sahib* was not present in the meeting.

'Why? What prompted you to speak so? Did anyone ever mention it to you that something is brewing against me? Is anyone else is conspiring to be the ruler? If anyone is keen for any such eventuality, you must reveal his name,' Fateh Kanwar stated sternly. Furrows appeared on her forehead.

'I am afraid; lest you should compromise with your authority and sovereignty. You are merely a pawn in the hands of others. Think over your decision again. You may face grave consequences,' Ochterlony cautioned her.

'Don't talk such eyewash. How dare you utter such words in my presence? You should never forget that you are in front of a Rajput woman. You have the audacity to tell me that I am a fool! That I am devoid of any political acumen! That I would commit a mistake if I trust my *Maji Sahib*, with whom I have spent so many years of my life! Who had always stood with me in my thick and thin? I know that you are pointing a needle of suspicion towards my own mother.'

The queen snubbed him. Ochterlony felt slighted; he had no option, but to remain quiet. She had defeated his detrimental designs. She did not fall into the trap laid by him. She further asserted.

'I shall never ever question the supremacy of *Maji Sahib*. My son and I will always remain trustworthy and dutiful to her. I hope, I am loud and clear. Mr Resident! I am grateful to you for your concern. You do not stress yourself. I am capable of handling it.'

Ochterlony paid his greetings with a smirk and left the palace disappointed, while Fateh ran to *Maji Sahib* and narrated the details of the meeting enthusiastically.

'*Masa*, I never knew that I could give him left and right. *Masa*, I wish you were there to see his long face...ha...ha...!'

Maji sahib looked at her daughter-in-law, her face was glowing with new found confidence.

Fateh was an intelligent woman. She could figure out that the whole exercise of Ochterlony to act as her sympathiser was dubious with malicious intention. In fact, by creating a rift between them, ultimately he would be the winner. Conflict between them ultimately would pave the way for him to easily enter into the internal matters of Jaipur and eventually usurp the powers. The end game of the British! She strongly repulsed his hidden intention to create a contention between them.

'Who else can understand better than me, how a small crack can bring a building crashing down. So is the case with life!'

The two meetings with the Resident inspired the queen to take keen interest in the day-to-day administration of the State. Her trusted *daavari* Rupan stood by her shoulder to shoulder. With each step, Fateh gained more confidence.

Time-to-time, the queen began to write letters to the British Resident in Delhi, indicating the deplorable conditions prevailing in the State. She gradually learned how to raise questions, if she got any information about negligence on the part of the British officers. She tried her maximum to defend the welfare and safety of Jaipur. She began to reflect her mettle in governance as well as in trading matters.

Whereas, Rupan began to tighten her grip on the *Jamakharcha Bahis* that were the accounts of purchases made in various heads like, saddles, bridles, scabbards of swords, covers of books, cloth, bed sheets and shoes made of leather.

They both began to learn the rules of the game. Fateh was moving forward with small steps, slowly but steadily, while Rupan was taking big leaps quickly.

✳

Many seasons rolled by.

It was the hot month of June. *Maji Sahib* had been bedridden for long, owing to her deteriorating health. Fateh Kanwar spent most of her time indoors because of the blazing sun. Looking after her ailing mother-in-law was her utmost duty. She, therefore, authorised Rupan to manage routine matters of the court on her own. She directed her to bring only important matters to her notice.

This was the turning point in the life of Rupan. In the close company of Fateh, she had tasted power. She loved this newfound authority. Power and authority corrupt humans and Rupan was no exception. *Maji sahib*, due to her prolonged illness was not in a position to check the affairs of the palace and court matters. Fateh was more busy in bringing up her son, taking care of *Maji Sahib* and resolving the internal matters of the zenana.

Rupan began to take decisions on her own, even without consulting Fateh Kanwar. Gradually, she stopped bringing even important matters to her knowledge. Then, to top it all, she started cooking up tales to cover up her actions. She took only trivial matters to her, which Fateh dismissed then and there. At times, Fateh got annoyed for getting her involved in insignificant matters.

'Why the hell you come to me to solve this petty issue? Can't you handle even a small household burglary case? What is the security force meant for? Sometimes, you disappoint me, Rupan!'

✳

In the night, Fateh Kanwar headed hurriedly towards the chamber of *Maji Sahib* in order to consult her privately before making a final decision on certain important issues... She looked around and spent a few moments standing outside the chamber.

The vast sprawling sand dunes were enjoying the shinning silvery light of the moon. *Saptarishi,* the Seven Stars pointing north were blazing with their incandescent light in the centre of the sky. Combined with their glow, Chandra Mahal was lit in a purity of moon rays.

'All around , abounding beauty. However, I don't see the beauty anywhere! No beauty is able to lift me up. I am feeling a strange heaviness! I am sinking!'

When she entered the inner quarters, she found Rupan and others very pale, beside *Maji Sahib,* who was lying on the bed. In a whisper, Rupan informed her, '*Maji Sahib* is no more.' Fateh Kanwar was shaken with anguish at the cruelty of fate, over her sudden death.

Shocked seniors and elders inside the inner corridors of Chandra Mahal tried to console the queen. The first decision that she made was to keep the tragic development a secret, at least for one day, until the daughters of *Maji Sahib* reached Jaipur. A messenger was dispatched , with clear instructions not to divulge the information to anybody else and to return immediately.

The pyre was lit by Prince Jai Singh, her grandson. He took his grandmother's ashes and performed the last rituals for the departed soul.

Fateh Kanwar remembered the last words of *Maji Sahib,* her strength, her mentor, her *guru,* that she would always be with her through her life journey.

'As you know, you are working with all kinds of people, good and bad, to build Jaipur. We tend to be short-sighted when dealing with them. We think that we can solve any problem as we have the power. Let us fly over Jaipur, to understand people and their psyche. Some are behind the four walls, in their huts and houses and others behind the mighty gates of the palaces and forts. Each person describes life, society, human values in a different way. Nazir sees it in capturing the throne, while for a *daavari*, it lies in serving us. And for you it is in building and nurturing the state, where each person is safe and secure and can pursue his goals. Rajputs and specially Rajput women must stand for a noble cause. What we believe in must be our dharma and the rest be left to the Goddess. She takes care of everything. And most important...' She paused, and then said wistfully, 'At times you will have to take hard decisions. At that moment, no relation, no emotion must come in your way. Remember, a thorn is removed by a thorn only.'

These were the last words of *Maji Sahib*, when she spent some time with her in the afternoon.

✳

Time flew away swiftly. Summer gave way to rains. It was the end of the month of August. There was an air of festivity in Jaipur. Rainy season brings many festivals to make the city agog with festive fervour.

The festivals of *Teej* and *Rakshabandhan* are occasions for celebration, with siblings, with the family and near and dear ones. This was the most important occasion to receive and honour the daughters of the Kachwaha royalty as well as of the *thikanedaars* and Fateh Kanwar was very particular that they were treated with due respect and were given a large amount of money and gifts.

Generally, Chandra Mahal since the time of *Maji Sahib*, was the hub of festivities, king's birthday, marriages, child birth were celebrated with grandeur. The festivities and celebrations kept the queens, *paswans*, *pardayats* and others occupied. Besides, it was also a centre for various political and religious rituals. *Maji Sahib* celebrated each occasion in different and unique way. It was also a centre for making and re-emphasising political alliances through exchange of gifts and bestowing grants. Rajputs of different clans generally resolved their hostilities through the gifts of daughters in marriages and by formation of alliances, when they participated in such festivities. In the company of her mother-in-law, Fateh had learnt how to observe formalities and courtesies.

As has been the usual practice, sisters-in-law used to visit Jaipur to join the family festivities. This time Anand Kanwar *Baiji* with her two children would spend some time with her sisters-in-law. Special arrangements were made for her stay at *Pritam Niwas*.

✳

Rupan came to the queen with a decorated silver plate filled with sweets, rice, gifts, *roli*, red colour powder used to put a mark on the forehead, and *rakhi*, a thread tied by the sister on the wrist of her brother, as a symbol of love, sibling bonding, and to get an assurance of her protection from her brother.

Fateh was surprised to see the scale of festive preparations. In fact, she was in no mood of celebration because of the death of *Masa*. She thought of having the celebration at a cut down scale just for the sake of custom, without any pomp and show.

'Why Rupan? You seem to be quite happy today. Anything special? Do you expect any of your lost brothers today? Why have you brought all these things? I am glad that you are taking extra pains for *Baiji* Anand Kanwar, still…' inquired Fateh.

'*Ranisa*! This plate is for Thakur Shyam SinghJi, who considers you his own sister, rather more than his real sister. He is in Jaipur. He is eagerly waiting for an invite from you to tie the *rakhi* at his wrist. As a *rakhiband* brother, he will always protect you from all the dangers. Now, you really need such a devoted brother. Otherwise, who else is here to safeguard your interest?'

Fateh smiled and nodded. She continued staring at the floor pensively. Though she always trusted Rupan, but she did not like her enthusiasm for an outsider Shyam Singh.

'Anyway, in future you must ask me before giving words to any one on my behalf, 'Fateh told her curtly.

The next moment, she felt bad for being rude to her. Rupan had a bizarre look on her face.

'Rupan, I always pay attention to the advice you give me. If you consider Shyam SinghJi worthy enough to be my brother, send him the message.'

Rupan could not have been happier. She expressed her gratitude with glee. As she was about to depart, Fateh interrupted her.

'Make arrangements in the complex, which is meant for outside visitors. And yes, also no goof up in preparations for Anand *baisa*. She would be visiting almost after two years. Arrange for her comfortable stay near my chamber. She will be here by afternoon.'

Rupan left hurriedly lest Fateh should change her mind. Rupan was instrumental in helping Shyam Singh of Bissau *Thikana* to win over the confidence and complete trust of the queen.

And Fateh did not think that there could be any scheming behind this rakhi ceremony... Still...!

✳

Fateh had always been close to Anand *Baisa*. She thought of spending her days in the company of her sister-in-law. She had too much to share with her. She needed her advice on many issues.

In two large size silver plates, gifts for Anand Kanwar were displayed; *thans* of four gaz each from *Kirkiri Khana* had already been collected. This time Fateh had planned to gift her sister-in-law two *odhnis*, two *sarees*, two *kurtis* and two *lehengas* in *lahriya*, all with intricate *zari* work.

It was a tradition that daughters and sisters of the reigning king must be treated as the highest recipients of gifts and honours. They must always be presented gifts of higher values in comparison to the daughters of the other *thikanas*.

Fateh was careful that both her sisters-in-law must be given money or gifts in equal measure. Whatever was given to one sister, a similar amount of money and gifts must be given to the other sister. She tried to calculate the gifts given to Suraj Kanwar *baisa* when she last visited on the occasion of *Rakshabandhan*. Late *Maji Sahib* and Jagat Singh gave her a large amount of money. Fateh herself monitored all the arrangements. This time, Fateh Kanwar increased the number of *mohars* from twenty to twenty-eight and rupees from two hundred to two hundred and eighty to be given as gifts.

✳

Pritam Niwas and *Sabha Niwas* were the complexes for receiving the dignitaries of state. The entries to these complexes were selective in nature depending on the political status of the visitor.

Shyam Singh entered the outer wing of *Sabha Niwas* accompanied by a priest and a eunuch nazir. Shyam Singh was welcomed by Fateh with a curtain between them. The priest tied the rakhi, on behalf of the queen, on the wrist of Shyam Singh.

Fateh exchanged a few words with him; her words were sensible and forcible.

'I rely absolutely on this new bond. My blessings for you on this occasion.' She dismissed him with a few words.

'Do not forget that from now onward, Prince Jai Singh is also part of your responsibility, because of the relationship, you made a few moments back. You must keep his welfare in your plans and actions,' she added after a pause.

'I promise you, I will protect you and your child with my life. I served late Maharaja Sawai Jagat SinghJi Bahadur with utmost sincerity and will continue to serve you faithfully. Jaipur will know that it has a loyal friend in me forever,'Shyam Singh responded.

'I am happy to know it. In addition, over the period I will make sure that you make progress in our State. Your interest will always be taken care of and you will never be disappointed in the rewards that will follow,' assured the queen.

Shyam Singh bowed in gratitude for the opportunity to create a special bond for that he was obliged. He turned towards Rupan and handed over a small wooden box in her hands.

'Kindly accept a small gift from this brother. I earnestly hope that you will treasure it as much as I have treasured your late husband, Sri Sawai Maharaja's kindness.'

Fateh was not surprised by the gift; she already expected something like this on his part.

'There was no need for this gift. Of course, you are my *rakhiband* brother. Nevertheless, I need only your support. It would not be appropriate to accept any personal gift from you. If you insist, it must go to the treasury of the State.'

Shyam Singh showed no sign of being slighted.

'I am a well-respected *thikanedaar* and now your guest, today, and just a couple of moments before; I have made a new bond with you. Yes, I have brought this gift for you. I, as a brother have only this gift to offer you on this occasion today. As a sister would you turn me down?'

Fateh Kanwar gave in and accepted the gift. She signalled to Rupan, who presented Shyam Singh with gifts in return: two *thaans* of cotton and one *thaan* of silk.

Shyam Singh accepted the gift, bowed in gratitude and took her leave.

When Fateh retired into her room, Shyam Singh gave a bribe of five hundred rupees to Rupan for her successful execution of his plan.

✳

The whole day was spent in various rituals. Fateh was very tired. She headed back to her quarters to have a good sleep. Rupan followed her. Fateh turned her head slightly and smiled.

'It's good, you are here. I really need a good head massage.'

Rupan rushed to get almond oil, and returned within no time. She opened her braid, combed hair and began oiling her hair. As the two women sat silently, Rupan retained her composed appearance despite the storm in her mind.

Fateh asked Rupan, 'What do you think about Shyam Singh? Can we trust him? Would he prove to be a strong ally of Jaipur in future?'

Rupan shivered a bit. She dreaded this topic. She had deceived her queen. For the first time she connived with a wrong man to serve her own interest. To get some money.

'I think, he is err…trustworthy, a nobleman but not without his weaknesses. To me he is a …good ally, but not with a political acumen,' Rupan answered with sombre face.

'What do you mean? And what weaknesses you are hinting at?'

'He seems to be a kind-hearted man, a good human being. He is an emotional being, becomes too attached, too soon. This is his strong point as well as weak point. May be, I generally do not believe male folk. We must verify first whether should he be trusted or not before assigning him some important charge.'

'Oh, so you have a lot of information about him. Good Rupan.

One must always be vigilant. I agree with you. You just tell JuntharamJi to have an eye on Shyam Singh. I am still wondering what is his end game behind this achieved brotherhood?' said Fateh in a pensive tone and closed the discussion.

They spent some more time together enjoying night. The full moon was covered under the blanket of clouds. Millions of stars, studded each and every corner of the sky, were buried under the thick heavy clouds.

CHAPTER 14

1820
Caught in the Cobweb

Why did Rupan deceive Fateh when she trusted her the most? Fateh never broke the bond that she built with Rupan during her earlier days, when she came to Jaipur and Rupan was placed in her service. However, Rupan betrayed her when she actually needed the most strength from her. When her strongest anchor, her *Majisa* had left this mortal world, what made Rupan ditch her? Perhaps, Rupan tasted power; too much power. Perhaps, greed overpowered her and turned her ungrateful to Fateh, who catapulted her position phenomenally.

In the solitude of her room, Rupan was torn into two worlds. One that needed her in the same fold, she was for the past many years, serving the queen with total submission, while the other constantly lured her to lead a better and secure life. 'Today she is with me, a solid support base, but what about tomorrow, when she will not be here.'

What would be the best option? She weighed the pros and cons of both, choices. 'If I continue to lead my whole life in the servitude of Fateh it can give me a secure life, but only for a short period, until the queen is alive. Yes, she cares for me. She treats me like her elder sister. She gives me due regard, but what about the period after her! Who can give me the guarantee that I will be given the same treatment after her! In a palace, no guarantee can withstand on its slippery ground. Promises are made to be broken. If I choose the second option, I will certainly be deceiving the person, who trusts me the most in this world

– my adorable mentor, Fateh! But this choice guarantees a luxurious life forever.'

Nevertheless, it was not easy for her to decide which path to follow. She brooded over the two options for days together. Undecided Rupan continued to flow with the current, until an event gave her a jolt; she realised that she must do something.

✳

Years passed by. Prince Jai Singh had completed twelve years. So far, he did not cross the threshold of the zenana. Fateh Kanwar kept a strict vigil on her son day and night. She virtually became the shadow of her son.

One day, the people of Jaipur assembled around the royal court premises and made a strange demand.

'We want to meet our Prince; soon he would be the king of Jaipur. So far we have not seen him even once. We do not know how he looks. After a couple of years, he will be crowned. We want to ensure that the prince we meet today is the same person when he is crowned.'

Fateh Kanwar wondered, what made the people make such a peculiar demand? It was not a sudden development. The idea had been gathering momentum for months, for sure.

Jai Singh appeared in the balcony with his mother. People greeted him exhibiting great enthusiasm.

The same day Fateh called the royal painter and entrusted him the task of making portraits of the prince that were to be placed at crucial points in the royal court and the town.

Rupan, who was indecisive so far, finally made up her mind to go for the second option considering her long-term security, no matter even if it was at the cost of betraying Fateh. She immediately sensed the potential threat to her existence.

'After some years Jai Singh will come and grab his crown. What will I do then? In no way I would like to part with my powers! And, why should I do it? I have put in lot of pains and labour to achieve it! Nobody has served it to me on a platter!' Insecurity engulfed her. Rupan was all set to change her course.

She had already taken the first step. She accepted the bribe from Thakur Shyam Singh and allowed his entry into the palace without verifying his antecedents and motive. Then, she also tried to be in the good books of Juntharam.

Juntharam was initially appointed as a *kamdaar*, to manage the state affairs. His grandfather Mohandas used to work as a diwan during the time of Late Maharaja Jai Singh.

Fateh noticed his efficiency and brought him to the knowledge of her mother-in-law during the initial stage of her regency. Late *Maji Sahib* also found him a hardworking man. Fateh promoted him from a mere *kamdaar* to a revenue official, and soon after to the position of the chief minister of the state. The queen needed a good team, which could carry forward her work efficiently.

His oblong saintly face always helped him in earning the trust of the people easily. His middle-aged physique with muscular arms did not go well with his smooth, healthy skin and flawless fair complexion. He was a bit obese, potbellied, so he waddled slowly in his brown *jaipuri* footwear, like a duckling. He usually wore pale coloured *kurtas* with a white *dhoti* and a gold-bordered white shawl. But behind this garb was hidden a sharp, callous mind that was committed to his own cause alone – money, trade and propagation of Jainism. He was sure that he would play long innings in the royal court of Jaipur.

✳

May begins with unprecedented warm days. Sultry and scorching. There was no rest or respite. The sun was bright and burning. Like a burning fireball. The fields around the palace were dry and parched.

The hot winds were blowing unabated day and night.

Rupan grumbled, 'This weather will make me sick. Ah, this sweat and perspiration.'

With a grouchy face, Rupan set down to write a letter to Juntharam. Fateh Kanwar instructed her to keep Juntharam in the loop.

She mentioned merely the lists of the amounts and products of offerings sent to the temples by the order of the queen.

Juntharam responded in similar vain. Gradually, the letters exchanged personal messages asking about the health and happiness of each other, fondly remembering previous meetings, expressing gratitude for receiving a 'favour letter' (*kripa patra*) and conveying information about the pilgrimages they undertook together.

Rupan had developed a friendly bonding with Juntharam. She frequently consulted Juntharam on various administrative matters, and at a later period, when she gained significant voice in decision-making of the state, she took great efforts in promoting his son Bakshi, to the chief military officer in the army. This one obligation made Juntharam her accomplice forever. At times, Juntharam also remained the travel companion of Rupan in her pilgrimage journeys to religious centres around and nearby places of Jaipur.

Generally, during those days in a royal family or in a common household, religious activities such as pilgrimage journeys, created an opportunity for women and men to travel together. This was the time when they interacted with each other and built strong bonds during the journey. After the pilgrimage, some of them maintained their ties, while others discontinued. But Rupan and Juntharam maintained their friendship even after such journeys were over. It was during the journeys when the two of them found that their togetherness might prove to be a game changer for their benefit.

That was the time, when Rupan wielded so much influence over the queen that she could even decide the fate of ministers. That was the time when all kinds of rumours travelled all around – in and beyond the royal corridors.

Prominent *thikanas* believed that Juntharam had overpowered the queen by black magic, while the British got the information from their spies that most of the time, the queen was drugged by Rupan and the inebriated queen would sign wherever Rupan asked her to.

Fateh ruled over the state from behind the veil. Rupan was the eyes and ears of Fateh, which she used to maximise her own benefit. Fateh a god-fearing woman always trusted Rupan.

✳

Rupan stood by the window in her room, built at the far end of the official wing of her personal residence.

Undoubtedly, Rupan was very sharp. Her position, initially, as a *daavari* accorded her a low status, but in due course of time, she acquired immense wealth and authority. No one had the courage to say so to her face, but she knew what she was called behind her back: 'a bitch, a devil.' But she couldn't be careless, as she had suffered enough abuse in her childhood to inure her to slur and shame.

Rupan with the help of Juntharam squandered revenues of the state with reckless extravagance. She would send money out of the palace through Juntharam.

Although Fateh had been receiving all sorts of information through her sources, but initially she refused to believe them. The state was impoverished. She did not believe anybody and kept all of them at a distance as mere rumourmongers.

The British were puzzled and trying to figure out the genesis of the problem at their end.

What was the role of the regent queen? Did she lack the competence to run a state efficiently? People were also wondering whether the

British were merely the mute spectators or they had also become party to her detractors by extending support from behind the curtain.

✳

Diwan Juntharam woke up to the chirping of birds. He spread his arms thrice, set in lotus *asana* and joined his palms. His eyes were closed and his lips uttered *mantras*. He remained seated in his bed for a while in this position. He threw off his heavy quilt after some time and got up. It was bitterly cold and Juntharam wrapped himself with a dark grey woollen shawl. He picked up a round pale yellow headgear, placed on his bedside stool, with both hands and fixed it gently on his head. The sun's pale rays provided sufficient visibility of the ground between the courtyard and the bathing area.

Juntharam's home was a large old *haveli* situated at Puranaghat. It was a grand and well-preserved *haveli* with a *trine-sikhara* (three tapering spires) and a round dome. There was an inscription in the centre above the locked main entrance.

Sanghi Ajit Das, son of Sanghi Mohan Das, ki haveli-1657.

He first built a temple of Vimalnath, then the *haveli* in the adjoining temple premises. Its spires and domes adorned with golden pinnacles were visible from far away.

Juntharam glanced at the names of his ancestors reflectively and the year when it was built. For how many years, this home of my ancestors has been standing erect weathering rain, dust, sun and wind. He touched one of the pillars softly.

The right wing of the *haveli* had a separate entrance into the private residence for his family with a *chaityalay* (a home shrine) that belonged to Juntharam. Small marble bas-reliefs of Jinas above the main entrance led into the inner courtyard; similar images were installed above the door to the altar room. A huge square marble platform in the middle of the altar room held images of Jinas enthroned. Sometime, in 1820, when he had a strong foothold in the royal court, Juntharam installed a *vijaya –yantra*, a symbol of his achievements, in the temple.

Jhuntharam took over the control of his ancestor's temple by virtue of being a descendant, and began to manage all its affairs actively. Thereby, *Sanghi*, a leader of a *sangha*, an honorary title of *sangha*, the Digambara Jain community representative, was conferred on him. He earned this title more by manipulation and less by spending money sanctioned for organising collective pilgrimages. However, he had succeeded in earning the reputation of a pious man in his community.

Juntharam had emerged as a comet on the political horizon of Jaipur. He was in the good books of the queen. She believed Juntharam and had full faith in his abilities. For her, Juntharam was a *sanghi*, who could never harm even an insect on earth. On the contrary, Juntharam was capable of killing a giant without a hitch. He was very shrewd. His true self was well hidden behind the garb of a mellow and timid persona. He knew how to turn the flow of water in his favour.

✳

Juntharam clad in a beige kurta and a white dhoti with a printed jacket entered the outer wing of the chamber of the queen. He kept the registers on the table very neatly, and then bowed facing the curtain.

'*Ghani Khamma Ranisa hukum!*' Saying so, he turned towards Rupan, handed over some registers to her and waited to get back the registers duly signed by the queen.

Fateh Kanwar had summoned Juntharam after having received too many complaints from the elders and nobility.

'Why are our *thikanas* turning against us, JuntharamJi? They are our allies. Our friends! I hope you have not antagonised them in any manner?' she inquired.

He immediately came closer to the curtain. Standing there with folded hands, he pleaded.

'I have not done anything wrong! Trust me *Rani Sahib*. I know very well that they are our people. Actually, it was the Nathawats who had led the coup. *Rani Sahib*, you know that the treasury is depleted. You know *Maji Sahib*. Our late Maharaja…'

'Juntharam!' The queen raised her voice…

'I am sorry to take the name of our late Maharaja, but our coffers were empty even during his time. I just requested the Nathawats to reduce the number of cavalry. That's all. I had no choice. I had to cut the expenses of *thikanas* and I was not selective in this process. The same rule applied to all. If some *thikanas* did not like it, they could have approached me. It is the Nathawats, who began to oppose our move, and others joined the league.'

'Anyway, we cannot annoy the Nathawats, SanghiJi! They have always been strong supporters of Jaipur. We cannot lose them. Make peace with them. Somehow.'

Rupan saw a steely look on the face of queen. She stepped aside slowly and moved towards the other side of the curtain. She indicated Juntharam to be quiet.

'Control yourself. And control your tone,' she almost whispered in his ear.

'I think you people have gone mad. And yes! Before taking any decision, you must seek my permission.' Fateh guessed what was conspiring between them.

Fateh Kanwar issued a stern warning, and at the same time consciously made an effort to maintain her calm.

Juntharam felt as if *Rani*'s piercing eyes were penetrating through him. He took some time to control himself.

'It is the brute British, *Rani Sahib*. *Gora sahibs* have taken them into their fold. I am not wrong. We will recover our position soon,'

Juntharam tried to shift the blame on the British.

'Why are you telling me all these stories? Why didn't you approach me earlier? This is a fact SanghiJi that you had spent more time on your Jinas and less on your job. Do you have any idea how difficult it is for me to build support for you? Everyone is blaming you for this fiasco.' She could not restrain her annoyance.

'*Ranisa* believe me, the Nathawats have turned against you at the behest of the British. I am not cooking up tales.'

Rupan who was the mute spectator in the conversation so far, butted in.

'*Ranisa,* he seems right on this issue. I think we should believe him and give him a chance to sort it out amicably.'

'I profusely apologise for the inconvenience caused to you. But I assure you that all the differences with the Nathawats will be sorted.' Juntharam crouched to pay her respect and stepped back to leave.

Fateh Kanwar had all the reason to believe him as in the past, several times, British Residents in Jaipur together with the partisan Rajput nobility attempted to circumscribe her power. She was also aware that many influential Rajputs considered both Juntharam and Rupan, as an uncontrolled growing clout that was not going down well among them. She, however, did not know that *thikanas* perceived her as a person of doubtful integrity. Fateh liked to trust her people. She was kind hearted and intelligent. But she was not well versed with the manoeuvres of power corridors. Simple as she was, she was unable to foresee the likely fallout of her decisions. Rupan and Juntharam could make out in no time that it was easy for them to manoeuvre her. In due course, they weaved a web that she could not disentangle in her lifetime.

✳

Juntharam vigorously used each opportunity to weaken the *thikanas*. He, first, brought the queen around to his design by harping on to summon some sections of infantry and cavalry to the capital under the pretext of curbing their demands of arrears of pay. And he did succeeded in making a dent on the thought process of Fateh Kanwar. She, without realising the implications of her decision, gave him the authority to take actions independently. This one wrong move of Fateh Kanwar made him all-powerful. Then on, he wreaked havoc.

His first casualty was the *thikanedaars* of Ranthambore. Juntharam passed an order without wasting any time in the name of the queen.

'Disband your troops as soon as possible. The state is passing through a financial crisis, which, of course, is likely to be overcome soon. Once the problem is resolved, the number of soldiers will be increased.'

Similar advisories were sent to others. Not happy with the royal *farmans,*the *thikanas* tried to seek a meeting with the queen, but she unmindfully turned down their request summarily.

Fateh was highly tense. This was not her forte. She brought Juntharam in her inner corridor of advisors, believing that he had the magic wand to fix the complex issues. Juntharam was quite capable of resolving the ticklish problems, but the same were a sine-qua-non for his own survival. For Fateh, political intricacies were more a trauma and less a challenge. The *thikanas* virtually revolted against the queen, as they felt the queen had added insult to their injury by refusing to listen to their grievances. The common men took to the streets to support the *thikanas*. Anarchy prevailed in the state. For two months, all the shops in Jaipur remained closed and business operations came to a standstill.

Undeterred Juntharam worked on a strategy very cleverly to curb the revolt as well as manage the declining law and order situation in the capital. His strategies, however, could not bear the desired results. The rebel Rajputs were in no mood to surrender.

The queen was closely watching the situation, but through the eyes and ears of those who were the genesis of the problem. With each passing day, the situation turned from bad to worse.

Finding no better option, the queen finally summoned the Shekhawat *thikanas* to Jaipur.

'All of you have always stood by Jaipur. You are our strong allies. Jaipur always considers your contribution in reverence. We must iron out the creases and stand together in any eventuality.' Fateh addressed the assembly of *thikanas* in a kind voice, from behind the curtain.

'How can we believe you? How can we support you, when on the one hand we get a very humiliating strongly worded letter from you and on the other, you are trying to tell us that by extending an olive branch you are forgiving us. As if, we are at fault. Unless, *Rani Sahib* addresses our grievances, no further negotiation is possible. ' An elderly *thikanedaar* replied in an agitated tone twisting his moustaches.

They all got up and walked out from the meeting. These attempts further deteriorated the situation, which ultimately brought Jaipur on the verge of an armed conflict.

✳

The British Resident in Jaipur, who, so far, was indifferent to the internal issues of Jaipur, had to call in a brigade of Company soldiers from Nasirabad for the security of his own people. His soldiers were guarding him and his office round the clock vigilantly.

Meanwhile, Juntharam was having meetings with the queen almost on a daily basis in which Rupan was an important participant. Unfortunately, their meetings bore no fruits.

As Juntharam failed to control the worsening situation, he executed his second plan. ' Why not to make Berisal, a scapegoat? That is a better idea to save my own skin. All along, I was confident to handle the situation. I never anticipated, it would blow out of proportion to the extent of a rebellion. Anyway, I cannot allow the situation to slip out of my grip, or else, it will damage my cause in the end,' he brooded.

Without wasting any time, he tried to create suspicion in the mind of the queen, regarding the role of Berisal and the British Resident . So far, he had never failed to get what he wished for –by any means.

Fateh Kanwar noticed that Juntharam was unusually quiet, while she was signing the letters. Generally, he would be telling her all kinds of tales.

'What is troubling you? Today you look very upset,' she asked.

And the clever Juntharam began, 'What greater cause for sorrow I need to have? When grief comes to you, how can I remain unconcerned? Berisal RawalJi is covertly helping the Nathawats. *Ranisa!* You know very well, why? Berisal is a Nathawat. In no way he will go against his clan brothers. He has also joined hands with the British official, Captain Steward. They both are working hand in glove against you. Berisal is not only instigating, but also providing finances to the Nathawats, at the behest of the British. A flood of misfortunes is rising to swallow you *Ranisa!* A large calamity is all set to befall you and the crown prince.'

'Don't forget Juntharam who you are talking to! You better control yourself! No evil can harm our *Ranisa!*' Rupan obstructed him from saying anything further, in a stern voice.

'Do you have any evidence to support your point? If you have any, tomorrow present it in the court,' ordered Fateh Kanwar.

'*Ranisa*, I will come to you now with evidence only. But you just think over only on two facts. First, why is Berisal spending long hours in the office of the Resident. Second, has Berisal made any effort to make a truce between you and the rebels?'

Meeting dispersed. Fateh Kanwar, who had looked upon Berisal as her very strong supporter was enmeshed in Juntharam's arguments and became helpless.

Apparently, Fateh did not believe him, yet, Juntharam had succeeded in sowing the seeds of suspicion.

✳

It was the waxing moon period; hence, the moon would appear late. Stray stars were twinkling. Fateh bowed before the Goddess and slowly crossed the boundary of the temple premise and entered into her chamber. She was pacing the hall frantically.

The palace was engulfed in silence, though lamps –big and small, lighted the long galleries and rooms.

She stopped taking a stroll and with a stern face moved towards her chair.

Rupan came to her with a glass of water. 'Something is bothering you *Rani Sahib*?'

'Indeed, I am troubled. You tell me what I should do! Should I believe Juntharam? Tell me. You are clever and know the way out.' Fateh clung to Rupan. In her opinion, at that moment, Rupan appeared to be the most reliable and worldly-wise person.

'This is strange, *Ranisa*! Pardon me; it is not suitable for me to tell you who to believe or who not to! Don't get impatient. Don't get scared. Just wait and watch! Be calm. Yes, Berisal was an upright person. But people do change with the time. When others change, we need to change ourselves as well.'

Fateh immersed in deep thoughts for a while, and then asked Rupan, 'The first thing in the morning, you go to the British Resident and fix a meeting with me.'

'Suppose, if the Resident does not pay heed to what I tell him!' Propped one more question. And Rupan made a prompt reply.

'Yes, indeed, it is a possibility. He may try to get around you. Do not yield. He may offer many alternatives. Accept none of them. You insist only on what you think is right.'

So far Fateh could manage to impose her decisions on the British. Whenever the British made decisions on appointing new officers, she opposed them and had her own men appointed. 'And now this Berisal! He has perhaps forgotten that it was I who recommended his name for the post of *Mukhtiar*. He was committed and loyal then. But now, he is working against me'.

'Oh, Berisal! You are a black sheep. I trusted you most, made you *Mukhtiar*, and you stabbed me in my back. This world is full of malicious games and treachery. *Masa*, you should be here to handle such complex problems. Why did you leave me alone?' moaned the queen.

✳

The next day, in the morning the Resident and Fateh Kanwar met at *Sarvatobhadra*. She put forth all her issues and tried to persuade him to appoint a new minister and to relieve Berisal from his duties. The Resident out rightly did not refuse any of her proposals. At the same time, he did not give her any assurance.

'I will refer this matter to the Governor General.' He evaded the issue; bowed courteously and left the chamber.

'It's not easy to remove Berisal. The Resident is a hard nut to crack.' Later, Fateh confided in Rupan.

'Don't worry. Make it difficult for him to continue. Victory embraces only those who do not accept defeat,' Rupan counselled.

They both knew that the Governor General would not approve her proposal to remove Berisal with immediate effect.

✳

The next day, there was unusual calm in the court. An order was circulated amongst all officials.

'Rupan is appointed *Raj Badaaran*, in-charge of finances.'

The British had given Fateh Kanwar a free hand to run the administration. She gave Rupan this position with a *khillut*, a dress of honour, arms, money and ornaments.

Rupan took the *khillut* from her hands, touched it to her forehead and said in a sweet voice, 'I have no words to express my gratitude, my kind hearted and gentle *Ranisa*. I am honoured. I am truly lucky to have a protector and a benefactor like you. You have changed my destiny.' She was overwhelmed with excitement. It came like a boon for her.

Fateh smiled serenely at her.

'It means a lot to me. I don't know how I will repay this debt.' Rupan was standing with her folded hands.

'No need to say it in so many words. First, you have earned it. You deserve it. Second, I always took you as my sister. A very close and trusted friend. So no thanks! On this occasion, I will say only one thing. Use this authority for the good of the people of Jaipur. And I am sure you will never opt for a different way.'

'I will take your leave now,' saying so, Rupan crouched in front of the queen three times. As she walked away from her, Fateh felt lightness in her being. Positive thoughts coursed through her mind. Whereas, Rupan walked with exhilaration thanking the goddess profusely for giving her what she aspired for.

With one stroke, her status changed. From merely a Rupan *daavari*, she became Rupanrai, a very important person. She got what she longed for so long.

Badaarans were appointed to look after the zenana administration;

generally, they were not allowed to marry. They were responsible for treasury and jewels, and were expected to look after the newly wedded queens in the absence of other senior women. Their words carried weight in the internal matters of zenana. *Badaaran* was a key position. Sometimes, *badaarans* even nominated their successors.

✳

As if this was not enough, after a couple of months, Fateh Kanwar elevated Rupan from *Rajbadaaran* to *Mukhtiar*. From an inconsequential woman , overnight, she had turned into an authority, a very powerful person. Earlier her job was to pay heed to the orders Fateh gave her. Whenever, Fateh went out of her room for worship, she used to carry the *kalash*, a brass pot filled with pious water for offering to the Goddess, on her head. Sometimes, Fateh decided to wear a new *chura*, a set of ivory bangles, and then Rupan had to make all the arrangements. She used to perform many household chores and was busy day and night. She, who used to be an unseen, unheard and an insignificant person in the *deordhi*, had emerged as a much sought after person in administrative matters. Now she moved around the town with her head held high to mark her new status.

Rawal Berisal Nathawat, of Samod *Thikana*, who was accountable to manage the state affairs, found himself in an awkward position, as his popularity and standing in the inner court that was at an all-time high, among the Rajput nobility, had suddenly nose-dived. Having seen Rupan controlling jewels and finances, he virtually became mad. He had earned the reputation of an efficient administrator, and it was unbearable for him that a *daavari*, and a trader Juntharam, were trusted more than him. Why was he not considered worthy enough to manage the state affairs? He was boiling in rage.

Berisal was sure that the queen had designed a secret plot against the revolting *thikanas*. The queen did not even bother to share her strategy with him. He had been branded as an antagonist and incompetent person. Clearly, *Ranisa* did not trust him. It was her coterie behind the rumours that were circulating against him.

'I have served her with utmost loyalty and now she does not count on me anymore. Those terrible Rupan and Juntharam will run their hands through the gold and line their pockets freely. They will have the pleasure of sticking the royal revenue.' He beat his chest in disappointment. He resigned from the post of *Mukhtiar* and left Jaipur, in a state of utter disgust.

Jaipur, now, had two women to carve its future, its destiny.

A woman working for her own future!

A woman reigning to build the future of her son and her State!

✳

With power comes authority. With authority coupled with willingness to do good, makes a person a noble being. With authority, also comes greed and treason. Authority generated greed and insecurity in Rupan. She had transformed into a new person– full of vigour to fulfil her dreams. She was surprised to meet herself in this reincarnation.

Rupan built up her own strong faction, consisting mainly of Juntharam, the most infamous character then in Jaipur and Shyam Singh, the most notorious *jagirdaar* and herself.

Her clout constituted of younger servants, who were appointed mostly by her. As she was older than the new recruits joining at the fringe positions of the zenana, she could exercise her authority over them without any qualms. Indeed, she was deemed competent and reliable to supervise the administration of substantial financial matters independently. She had her own *risala* (retinue of soldiers). Administration was run from the zenana and Rupan communicated all orders to the court .

She began amassing wealth by indulging in unlawful activities. Means were not important, money was to her.

She built her own independent house with beautiful rooms, *chattries* and balconies that was named *Roop Niwas*. It was enclosed from all sides by an exquisite symmetrical garden, appropriately smaller when compared to the queen's, her conscious choice.

Her residence adequately reflected her status. Needless to say, it brought her immense power and influence. Rupan, a clever woman, always acted with utmost caution. Before starting the construction of her house, she obtained due permission of the queen, so that people may not make an issue out of it.

'*Rani Sahib*, I have seen a small piece of land, at the outskirts of the town. I am thinking of buying it for constructing a small house of my own.'

'Rupan, why do you need a separate house for you? You know it well that lifelong you will be with me !'

'Excuse me, *Rani Sahib*, who can predict the future? This would be only as security for my lean days.'

' Oh! I can see, my Rupan bai has turned into a philosopher! No issues. Then, why a small one, make a nice house.' Fateh chided her affectionately.

Rupan was on cloud nine as the queen fell in her trap and granted what she had dreamt of.

The British, always suspicious of the activities of Rupan, had many complaints about Rupan, but they failed to gather evidence to sound their suspicion. The reports, on the contrary, supported the notion of her capability and cleverness in handling the court matters.

✳

The Resident submitted to the Governor General, a report of the income and expenditure of the state, which indicated that the revenue had decreased drastically – almost from thirty-four lakh rupees to twenty-two lakh rupees. He raised the issue that it was difficult to settle the tribute due with such a small amount; hence, he must be given greater authority over revenue matters of Jaipur.

Fateh Kanwar rejected his submission openly and ignored the report, dubbing it false and the one prepared with vested interest. She then forwarded a proposal to appoint Juntharam and Amarchand Diwan as in-charge of the revenue, which was not appreciated by the Governor General. Her proposal was instantly rejected. Instead, she was asked to appoint Berisal as the head of the revenue department.

Finally, under the pressure of the British, she had no other option but to entrust the revenue department to Captain Stewart and Rawal Berisal jointly. Rawal Berisal, who had left Jaipur never to return, was reinstated with due honour. Fateh and her loyalists had to swallow their defeat. Their scheming had bitten the dust.

Left with no other alternative, Fateh at the behest of her coterie was hell bent, somehow, to curtail the authority of Stewart. She brought around Thakur Megh Singh of Diggee *Thikana* to her plan with the help of her *rakhiband* brother Shyam Singh. Megh Singh gladly accepted the proposition on one condition – he will help the queen only if he is made in-charge of finances. The queen agreed as she was determined to remove Berisal at any cost again from his post.

Again, a conspiracy was hatched to remove Berisal on one pretext or the other. Finally, she succeeded in appointing Megh Singh as her minister for the revenue in place of Berisal.

Stewart and Governor General were greatly annoyed at her decision and pressured her to remove   Megh Singh immediately. Governor General raised a question that how two persons could be appointed for one post and how could the queen of Jaipur appoint a person on such a senior post without taking the Resident into confidence?

Moreover, on the one side, was the British Resident, and on

the other side was the Regent Queen with her favoured advisors – Juntharam, Shyam Singh and Rupan. Now Megh Singh had joined the powerful trio.

Fateh was in no mood to compromise. She was certain on one issue – the British could not interfere in the internal matters of Jaipur. Who should be given what position was not their business. The sole responsibility of the British was to protect the boundaries of Jaipur from invaders and for this alliance; they were being paid a hefty amount to manage their logistics.

✳

Political agent, Lieutenant Colonel Roper was given the charge of handling the case of Berisal. Roper tried to turn the tide in favour of him. Only after much persuasion, meetings after meetings , allegations and counter allegations, Fateh was coerced to allow Berisal to continue until a new person was appointed.

Rawal Berisal was reappointed, which did not go down well with the queen and then began the period of tussle between Fateh and Berisal. She began to send notes almost on a daily basis, complaining to the Resident against the malpractices Berisal was involved in.She took the appointment of Berisal as undue interference of the British in her internal affairs.

Charles Metcalfe, the acting Governor General of India took a call. He felt that it would not be prudent to interfere in the internal official matters of Jaipur unless it affected the interests of the British. He advised his agents in Jaipur that the queen had the right to appoint her own ministers and they must not interfere in the internal matters of the royal court.

'Let the queen appoint her officials. Let her keep Jhuntharam. For us, Company's interests are important, not that of Juntharam or Berisal. The British Resident in Jaipur must help the queen in curbing the riots and unlawful activities.' Metcalf issued the clear directive.

Although the British were in favour of appointing Berisal , yet they could not help him in any manner, due to the hardened attitude of Fateh Kanwar.

The British Resident in Jaipur was left with no choice. He consented to help the queen in suppressing the *thikanas*, who were acting against the queen.

This incident proved to be a watershed that provided a strong foothold to Juntharam in the administration of Jaipur.

✳

Juntharam began to spread his wings. His ambitions and means knew no bounds. He derived maximum benefit from Metcalfe's advisory. Some Rajputs and the leading traders in this changed scenario came closer to him in order to serve their own interests.

One by one, Juntharam installed his own people at key positions. His elder brother Hukum Chand, his nephew Fateh Lal, his relative Amar Chand and many more of his relatives, trusted friends – all Jains, were given top most influential posts in the royal court. Hidayatullah Khan was the only non-Jain person, who was part of the clout. Their wretched activities flourished under the rule of Fateh Kanwar.

Juntharam started to use the Jain temple as the centre of proliferation of his religion to accumulate wealth and to gain political mileage. Fateh Kanwar, though never supported any of the sects or religions in political matters, but at the same time, she remained oblivious of what was happening around.

At this point, Rupan, the most dependable person of the queen, her principal adviser, so far Jhuntharam's tacit supporter, now joined his clout openly. At such a crucial time when Fateh needed her allegiance the most, she switched her loyalty to Juntharam and proved to be a snake on her sleeves.

Fateh was completely under the influence of Rupan. Fateh took her as her best friend, but she had turned out to be her worst foe in the garb of a friend.

Rupan and Juntharam gradually became the *de facto* rulers of the kingdom, for about fifteen years.

CHAPTER 15

1824-1833
Trail of Killings

Bishop Haber landed in Jaipur in the beginning of the year, 1824. As he approached the city, he marvelled at the beauty of the rough and rocky landscape. He gazed at the fort, tucked away behind the acacia trees lined along the street, on a mound almost in the shadow of the hill.

'This city is a specimen of architectural acumen. So these people have the skill to create such a well-structured castle!' He wondered.

'Magical. Awesome sight. Strikingly well-tended gardens!' The more he looked around, the more his pulse quickened. He was stunned. To him, Jaipur was like nowhere else, in the real world or the worlds of invention.

There were a lot of people roaming about within the fort premises, on the streets and in the markets; men selling roasted maize cobs, vegetables, bangles, footwear, sweet drinks; women scolding their children loudly; men talking to their friends, a family travelling on the camel cart with their possessions bundled up in cotton sheets.

He approached one of the passers-by and enquired about the residence of Roper.

An elderly man overheard his conversation. He came forward and took him to the same fort palace that he had been eulogising a few hours earlier.

'His house is over there, do you see? That white man holding a gun is standing. That is his residence.'

The Bishop thanked his informant and stood there for some more time like a statue, wondering at the beauty and majesty of the peacock gate, entry of the palace, and then he headed forward in his desired direction.

✳

Roper, who was posted as the British Resident in the Jaipur court, received the Bishop with open arms. He was looking for company, as he was quite disturbed by the events that had been taking place for the last couple of months.

On the evening tea table, the Bishop vociferously appreciated the capital of Kachwaha kingdom.

'You know Roper I have seen many royal places containing larger and more stately rooms, but this place is unique in many ways, its wild beauty, its hills and ruggedness. The picturesque quality of surroundings has a deep impact on me. These people in no way are uncivilised brutes as most of us think of them. And you know I spoke to some of them on the streets, I found them courteous and well behaved.'

Roper sat silent, listening to his guest. As the Bishop continued speaking his mind, he only nodded, as he was preoccupied with something grave.

Roper was an intelligent, sensitive and quite observant officer. His administrative acumen made him a quiet listener. He was not sure whether he should open in front of a man; he has just met a few minutes before. Second, he was not able to pinpoint exactly what was wrong, as he had just begun enquiring deeply.

Unmindful of his host's mind, the Bishop continued. 'Just look at the palace, gold painted domes and intricately carved spirals, single-floor houses. An extremely enchanting palace with its high front of seven or eight floors, diminishing in the centre to something like a pediment, and flanked by two towers of the same height and at the top adorned with cupolas. Wonderland! What an extraordinary creation in this remote corner! I must tell you my friend that I am completely in awe after finding such a marvellous town in a faraway place and country, Ah! I cannot compare any city with Jaipur. It is mesmerising.'

Roper smiled. He looked at the Bishop with amusement.

'Calm down, Your Excellency, Bishop Haber. You settle down. Whenever you are free I will tell you some interesting tales.'

Bishop nodded smiling back.

'This place is really wonderful, Your Excellency, Bishop Haber. The side of a lake, surrounded by a vast untamed valley, is the main area where a late king founded this city. No doubt, this place has some romantic vibes. The area surrounding the lake is spacious enough to accommodate the whole town. It takes you to another world. Overgrown trees and creepers have interlinked with towers and temples. The founders of this town were skilled town planners. No doubt about it. The crests of the hills on either side are crowned with gateways, whereas, the lower planes were meant for the dwellings of dignitaries and rich merchants.'

Roper stretched his hand, indicating towards fortified palaces at a distance, with balconies and verandas, connected with a long line of walls and towers, with an extensive castle on the hill just above the lake.

'Your Excellency, you have made the right observation. The fort and adjoining buildings are so planned that it seems as if they are emerging from the valley. Tomorrow, I will show you the best side of the town – imposing gateways, Divan-e-khas and Divan-e-aam, erected on the double pillars, carved cornices, foliated arches, latticed partitions, perforated parapets, pretty gardens and fountains. Right now, you have only a glimpse of the outer area. The palace complex is a marvel of architecture. It is as if a tiny town nestled in the lap of a large habitation. Oh! What a city, comprising of courtyards, gardens, buildings, temples, fountains, ponds, courts, stables, workshops and playgrounds.   Your Excellency must visit, *Jantar Mantar*, astrology observatory and many more… I will take you there. I promise.'

The Bishop heard him with an open mouth. 'Do you know, earlier this palace site was used for hunting by the late Ka…ch…awa… ha kings.' He pronounced the word with difficulty. 'There was a royal hunting lodge, still intact, at the bank of Tal-katora Lake. One of their forefathers, some Sa…wai…err…some Jaii S…iingh, sorry your excellency, actually I am not comfortable with their names,'

Bishop smiled. Roper further added, 'that's what I was told, the late king converted the chalet in Badal Mahal covered by lofty outer walls. Later, his successors added to it new structures as per their likings and fancy.'

Though Roper appeared enjoying chatting with his guest, but his thoughts were racing around somewhere else. It was Rupan; he hated most in this world, perhaps .

'There is always darkness under a brightly lit lamp. How should I describe what lies beneath the beautiful landscape? He did not know how to explain something for which he himself had no explanation?' Roper was puzzled.

He spent hours in the files , later in the evening after the Bishop took an excuse to rest.

✳

Roper was keeping a track of the activities of the queen and Rupan. In one year, many persons were killed in mysterious circumstances in the palace complex. He saw Rupan as a supporter and suborner of the Regent Queen.

Roper penned a long letter to his senior official.

'Dear Sir,

I am writing with a proof that it is not the regent queen, but a mere maidservant who is virtually ruling the state. I have the reports that require immediate attention. I am attaching the following herewith:

1. Rupan applies local drugs on the queen. I myself found once in a meeting that the queen was not in her senses. Her voice was wavering and her words broken. She appeared sedated.

2. I believe that Rupan maneuvered Fateh Kanwar to get herself appointed as *Raj Badaaran*, with all the executive powers to administer the zenana, though I have no proof to substantiate my doubts.

3. Most importantly, people vanish mysteriously and the royal court has no explanation of their disappearance and neither has any investigation been done so far.

4. I personally believe that those people did not disappear by some magic, but were killed. I suspect Rupan. As a responsible officer, I cannot let the criminals go unpunished. Justice must be given to those victims. It is quite possible that the queen might have ordered the killing of female attendants and other palace officials. Unfortunately, I have no evidence. I am giving this information only based on suspicion without conducting any enquiry, without any trial, without collecting evidence to cite concrete reasons.

5. Without getting any support from the royal court, I, in my own capacity would try to unearth the murder mysteries.

Yours' sincerely

Colonel Roper

Resident.'

Roper sent the letter through a special messenger. He had

decided to expose the murky political games by sending reports and accounts to the higher authorities in Delhi, whereas, the royal court accused him of producing false information and distorted accounts just to malign the image of the queen.

✳

Roper was called back after five or six months, of his reports, in the same year, in 1825. The British were not interested in the internal matters of Jaipur. For them, killings were an internal matter falling in the jurisdiction of the police and crime. The British were not accountable of any such thing as per their policy.

Authorities in Delhi thought that Roper was crossing the boundaries of his jurisdiction and it would not help him in any manner. Therefore, it would be prudent to replace him. Roper was asked to report back in Calcutta.

The Bishop was to leave Jaipur in the last week of October. When he came to know that Roper was to leave as well, he decided to accompany him.

'It is a long and arduous journey to Calcutta. I do not mind delaying my travel plans a bit. In your company, my journey will be comfortable. Provided you agree,' the Bishop expressed his desire.

'It is other way round, Your Excellency! I am obliged. Rather, I feel privileged. I am honoured.' Roper was delighted to have the Bishop as his travel companion.

Roper and the Reverend Bishop Haber left Jaipur in November 1825. He narrated the gory details of the killings to Haber, while travelling from Jaipur to Calcutta together.

'Your Excellency, can you imagine in your wildest dreams that two women could be on a killing spree in the palace?'

'Oh Jesus! What an evil thought! Who were these devils in the form of fair souls?' The Bishop questioned gasping in disbelief.

'There were cases that I investigated, but unfortunately, I could not do much in those cases. Fauj Ram, a *kamdaar*, a palace official, was butchered in his quarter. Second was Manbhaavan, who was a *badaaran* of a senior queen. Then Manbhaavan's assistant Radha and a Brahmin named Mandan were killed mercilessly.'

'Are you serious? Really?'

'Of course, damn serious! Your Excellency, it is a fatal combination of the queen and her *badaaran* Rupan. In the past one year, I have collected mind-boggling information. I spoke to hundreds of people from all occupations. I have spent hours daily in digging the past and present of these two women.' Bishop looked at him in appreciation.

'Well you seem to be an upright man. Would you mind sharing your knowledge with me?'

'Of course! Your Excellency, I am obliged.'

'Initially the queen and Rupan were working with good intentions, but having achieved the power, Rupan began to take undue advantage and within no time, she started exercising her authority openly without any fear and restraint. She had tasted power that intoxicated her entirely. A series of murders, then, were executed. The gullible queen oblivious of the killings, continued to trust Rupan blindly. Unfortunately, the ones upon whom the queen relied most committed the diabolical crimes right under her nose. Actually, I am still not very sure about the complicity of the queen, whether she was a party with Rupan or she herself was a victim of conspiracy.'

Roper stopped for a while, took a deep breath, and then added further.

'I thoroughly examined all the available documents related to deaths. No such records have been maintained and the officials are not even bothered, due to either default or design. Oh! Your Excellency, callousness is rampant all over the state, conspirators can wash their blood stained hands easily without any remorse and guilt. Somehow, I collected the details of some of the major heinous crimes that happened since I took over the reins of Jaipur residency in 1824. I noted the cases and carried out intensive investigation.'

Saying so Roper took out a slender notebook from his bag. 'I could investigate only four such cases in my own capacity, but of course, privately. I am sure there would be many more such cases to be unearthed.'

Roper ruffled the leaves of his notebook.

✳

Roper's narration:

'The first casualty was Fauz Ram, a palace official, who was working for me. It was a dark-moon night; everyone was in his bed, except the guards, Fauz Ram, was in deep slumber. He suddenly woke up. For some time he lay straight, and then turned right, then left. Nothing unusual. But he could not close his eyes. He felt uncomfortable. He guessed that there was someone in his room. The presence, he could sense was alien, intrusive, and predatory. He lay there quietly. Fauz Ram had already told me about the similar experience he had in the past . A few months back.

The room was dark, much darker than normal. He looked all around, peeped through the darkness of his room. There was nothing. No one in the room.

Fauz Ram got up. Left his bed, carefully, without making any sound, as he knew what he was supposed to do in such situations. He bent down to pick up a wooden log kept beneath his cot; suddenly a strong arm tightened his neck. Someone jumped on him from behind. The next moment his blood soaked body was lying on the floor. He was butchered in his quarter . Probably, he paid the price for knowing something he should have not known. His close friend, an occupant of the room, next door heard some stifled sounds. He put his eyes on a small crack in the door, but could not see clearly.

He stood there in a daze, for some time, unable to decide what to do. With a startle, he ran towards the adjoining room. He heard noises, but to his surprise, nobody was inside the room. The doors were open.

He looked around. 'There had clearly been a scuffle. Where the hell is Fauz Ram?'

In the morning, he found his body with multiple wounds behind his room in an open, but isolated area. The terrible sight made his heart sink.

'Perhaps, he bled to death. It means he was alive when he was looking for him in his room. Ah! What a fool I am! I should have searched in the vicinity. Perhaps, I could have saved him.' He howled like a wounded wolf. He reported the matter to me the same day. I surveyed the entire area, questioned the residents but nobody came out with worthwhile clue. Royal police also investigated the case . There was no witness of cold- blooded murder on record, hence the case was closed.

The second was Manbhaavan, who was a *badaaran* of the senior queen. At one point of time, Manbhaavan and Rupan were quite close friends and used to share their secrets.

Relations change with the changing times. Friends do turn into foes. They were not on talking terms and stopped seeing eye-to-eye for some time.

After a couple of months, again it was a dark moon night. Probably crimes and dark nights have some nexus. That night, the surprise entry of Rupan, quite late, into her small room baffled her. She used to live in her one room quarter, located in the area designated for *badaarans*.

Rupan spent some time with her and insisted that they must stitch up their rough edges. Manbhaavan readily accepted the olive branch extended by her. They had food together; Rupan spent the night with Manbhaavan. She spread a mat on the floor, covered it with a quilt, then she smiled. A nice bed for both, enough space as well. Yawning, she dragged Rupan to her bed and soon she began to snore.

After some time, Manbhaavan got up with a startle. She felt some movement, something passed across her cheeks. She knew it was not Rupan's chunar or braid. When you sleep with a known person, you develop a sense of the closeness of the other and upon waking, a trigger reminds you in an instant that that person is still there; the scent of skin, the sound of breathing, the warmth another body creates. The otherness beside you is comfort and familiarity.

She froze. This was neither comfortable nor familiar. Where was Rupan? She touched the space next to her. She was not there. Is she fine? How much time had passed? How long did I sleep? She felt like, it was probably not much. She noticed something. She stopped moving, even stopped breathing. She absolutely could not take her eyes off what was in front of her. A shadow was moving in her direction. Before she could scream, a familiar hand closed her mouth tightly. Then she recognised the familiar body odour. She was stunned. It was Rupan. Death came in the garb of her old friend. Her chunar tightened like a noose around her neck, before she could hit her enemy. Since that night, she was not seen, as if she had vanished. Again my all efforts to trace her ended up in failure.

Then Manbhaavan's junior Radha was killed in the most brutal manner. I was clued-up by an informer that she would be done away with. I did my best to save her, unfortunately, I could not. When I reached there, her body was drenched in a pool of blood. I picked up her arm to check her vitals. There was no sign of life and blood was no longer pumping from the gash that stretched diagonally across her throat. She was pregnant when someone took a dagger, forced upon her rib cage, hacked through several arteries and cut her throat.'

Bishop Haber was visibly shocked. His smile had faded. He was leaning forward, elbows on the window ledge of the carriage, staring out over the buildings towards the Bay of Bengal. Roper continued.

'The case of Mandan, a Brahmin, who was killed mercilessly, I found particularly chilling. That was some festival day. The first two or three hours were all fun filled. The streets were full of people on their way to join the procession. There were drummers, dancers and people singing and playing pipes in every corner, and many of the roofs and corridors had colourful flags and garlands hanging from them.'

Roper remembered how he felt lighthearted, full of happiness, walking through the city. Showers of crystals and silver and gold dust shot up in the air. It was spectacular. He further added,

'Mandan was tired because he had been preparing for the festivities for the last one week. On that particular day, since early morning, he had been busy in managing offerings in the temple. He retired early in the evening, with the consent of the head priest. In his room just behind the temple, he jumped on his bed and drifted into deep sleep. It was getting dark. Several shadowy figures jumped into his room through the open window. Crawling towards his bed, they tied up his feet roughly. His hand flew towards an iron rod lying under the cot, but they had already grabbed it, tied his hands so tightly that his wrists bled. They gagged his mouth, lest he should make noise. They huddled him off, to an unknown destination; travelled almost for more than one hour, until they arrived at a small mud house. When he questioned, who were they? And why had they taken him to a deserted place? They did not respond back. To-date nobody knows where was he taken and by whom? Was he a victim of petty criminals or he was eliminated by the royal order. After a month or so, one of my informers, somehow, encountered one of the villains, who unleashed violence on him on that particular night. He was told that it was Maharani *Sahib*'s order to imprison him there for his involvement in a crime. He was beaten mercilessly. It could not be ascertained whether the order emanated from the queen herself or it was Rupan, who ordered his execution in the name of the queen.

It is my gut feeling that he was not killed at the behest of the queen. I still believe that she did not know what was happening at her back. A trail of blood drops on the ground seen later by passers-by confirmed that he was dragged mercilessly before being bumped off. I knew it well that it would be a futile exercise yet I visited the crime scene to get some clue. Nobody was there, neither the prisoners nor the guards. To-date nobody knows what happened to him?

There is lot of muck underneath the magnificent Chandra Palace. The gang of the queen had tasted the blood. People had many tales hidden inside them.'

Both were quiet and lost in their own world. Roper remembered one more incident.

'Ah! There is no end to such stories. Do you know, she tried to poison Ukrur Kanwar, another queen of late Jagat Singh. It is believed that the Regent Queen asked Ukrur Kanwar to give up the *patta*[10] of the *jagir* of rupees sixteen thousand that was given to her by Jagat Singh in lieu of a *jagir* worth rupees three thousand. Ukrur Kanwar refused. Then they tried to force her consume poison and imprisoned her entire staff. When she refused to drink the poison, she, too, was imprisoned in the fort with other prisoners. After keeping her in captivity for many years, when they failed to get her *jagir*, she was freed,' sighed Roper.

'And who are they? The queen or somebody else?' the Bishop asked.

' I am sure it was Rupan and her gang. Its name should not be Jaipur. It should be *Jhuta durbar*, the lying royal court. There were no reasons for hoping that the plotting, crimes, killings would ever stop,' he added with remorse.

'How did you collect all this information?' the Bishop stared at

---

[10]Papers of land deed

deeply perturbed Roper.

'My informers! My people! There are many persons, who hate them. They know the secrets, but where would they go when a protector turned into a terminator.

I tell you, I don't like that place, even with its pomp and glory.

I rather hate that place. I hate those people.'

But Bishop Haber loved the place.

He adored its habitants. He will always love them.

He felt bad for those unfortunate souls and prayed for them.

The Bishop was engrossed in Roper's narratives that seemingly failed to create a dent on his thoughts. He looked at Roper. Silent.

The real settings of tales always hold a fascination. He thought about the city, the astonishing sight, the first glimpse of Jaigarh rising out of the dusty winds, the first sight of the birds hovering over the palace walls. In addition, those domes touched with gold and gleaming in the sun, the first sight of graceful arches of Chandra Mahal. The first encounter with the locals, their faces with those memorable sharp features, the prominent nose, the hauteur of expression, tanned skin, thick black beard and moustaches. Their long walks after having meals through squares, where all you heard were the sound of footsteps on stone, because carts and horses could not ply around the palace.

Now having these strange stories on his plate! Haber was intrigued, wondering how such brutal killings originated in a place, which was known for valour, honour and sacrifice.

---

[11]British representative at Jaipur court was designated as Resident, though officially, he was called the political agent. The first British resident at Jaipur was Captain Sturrock during 1804 to 1806. After a long interval, this position was revived and Major Steward as a political agent was posted in march 1821 and he continued till April 1824. Colonel Roper, his successor was on the seat from 23 April 1824 to November 1825. Captain John Low had the longest period beginning on 12 November 1825 and ending in 1830. After Low's tenure, political agency was closed by William Bentick as a useless expenditure. In 1832, the only British officer at Jaipur was an humble news writer, akhbarnavis at the salary of 100 rupees per month. He used to collect news and send it daily to Delhi. In Jaipur, people believed that he was a British spy.

*

Roper's hurly burly tenure, less than two-years concluded not with a happy note. Then Captain John Low, the succeeding Resident took over his charge.[11]

Captain Low continued to follow the policy of Roper, and kept a tight vigil on the palace activities like a hawk. Low was watchful and he put his people on the job of collecting information about Rupan and her gang's activities.

In the night, Captain Low, crouching on his table covered with lots of papers glanced through the disturbing figures; the accounts of the state were worrying. The arrears of tribute were twenty lakh rupees and the debt to bankers was more than eight lakh. The annual income was reduced to twenty-three and a half lakh, while the annual disbursement was to be made of thirty and a half lakh rupees. The state was not in a position to pay its employees' salaries regularly.

Low had completed the report based on available figures, kept it safely in the cupboard, locked it, and then asked his servant to get something to drink.

In fact, Low was waiting for someone. Generally, this was the time, when his spies used to give him the valuable piece of information.

A completely covered figure, from head to toe, entered the room. It was difficult to know whether, the figure was a male or a female. The voice was like a whisper.

'Juntharam will visit Rupanrai tonight at any hour. He is likely to be with her for an hour or so.'

Low jumped off his seat. He rushed into action. With the two guards, he moved into the direction of *Roop Niwas*, her residence. They entered the premises of her mansion under the cover of darkness. There was no sign of anyone in any corner of her house. Was the information correct? He wondered.

He spent some more time there hiding behind the bushes, hoping to get his prized catch. A few minutes more, as he decided to return, he noticed a flickering light near the window in the far corner of a room, at the ground floor in the backyard. Across the window pane, he saw two shadows. He came closer to the window. He overheard the conversation:

'RupanJi, what did you want to talk about?' asked Juntharam, standing courteously, a few feet away from her. Rupan moved towards her desk and sat on her chair indicating Juntharam to take the place beside her.

'I know all there is to know. Now is the time to act. No more discussions,' she declared.

Juntharam was surprised. I thought you had solved all your issues with Prince Jai Singh.'

'JuntharamJi, you are getting old. You are no more alert and vigilant. Why? Please do not live in your comfort zone for so long. Always keep your eyes open. Don't get fooled by his mannerism. He is a hard nut to crack. Someone has poisoned his mind with all kinds of absurd ideas. He thinks, once he becomes a full-fledged king then he will deal with us. I had made out his intention by indulging with him in leisure talk.'

Suddenly, Rupan was quiet. Was there some sound outside the window? She froze. She got alert. She put her index finger on her lips and indicated Juntharam to leave with a leather bag. There were a large quantity of jewels and coins in the bag made of cotton cloth lying on the table. Rupan herself pushed the cotton bag in the leather bag and handed over the bag to him and instructed him to carry it safely. Juntharam escaped from the rear window. Rupan, now, was in action.

Low tried to arrest Rupan, but failed to catch her red-handed. While he was hunting for her in the house, she had escaped through a secret tunnel and reached the palace. She was alert and always kept her defence ready for any such eventuality. She knew that Captain Low was keeping an eye on her activities, ever since he arrived in Jaipur.

✳

Within no time, her supporters spread the news that Low had dubious plan to remove the Regent Queen that is why he had come at this odd hour to arrest Rupanrai, who was the right hand of the queen.

Low was surprised to see a large mob heading towards him when he was about to leave *Roop Niwas*. The people in large numbers had assembled around her house. They were shouting and screaming.

'How can a British dare put his dirty hands on our *Ranisa*?'

'Kill him. Don't spare him.'

Captain Low and his guards somehow managed to escape from the rear gate.

Actually, people had all the reasons to believe Rupan's side of the story. Once, the British did try to oust the queen. A meet to vote was held and, twenty-eight of the total presence supported the policy of Fateh Kanwar, while twenty-two voted against her. The British failed to remove the queen from the seat. On the contrary, Rupan was successful in usurping the entire management of state affairs.

Low's anxiety was further intensified, as Rupan began to wield increasing authority in the affairs directly linked to the British. Her authority extended from advocating re-allotment of administrative posts to taking command of tax collection in the kingdom.

The British government wanted to hold a meet with the minor king along with the nobility, *thikanedaars*, and *jagirdars* of the state to advise him on the state matters, but Rupan and her gang already created a scare in them. Rupan and Juntharam became so powerful that they did not allow anyone, not even the nobility to meet Jai Singh, who was kept under their constant vigil.

CHAPTER 16

1834-1835
The Beginning of an End

It was the first quarter of the year 1834. Fateh Kanwar was not keeping well. Her lungs and liver were completely damaged and she was languishing in great pain. She was clearly diminishing, her appetite had gone and she had lost almost half her body weight. She was confined to bed, and had lapses of memory and moments of confusion. At times, she had bouts of consciousness.

'Another year has begun, I am feeling so weak...so sick. I have ruled over Jaipur for almost fifteen years, still I am far away to fulfil my most cherished dream. Jumwai *Mata*, kindly give me one more year. Let me see, my Jai on the throne.'

Jai was one year away from attaining majority. His smooth ascendance to the throne weighed heavily on her mind. The assurances by most of the major *thikanas* to support the prince had done little to relieve her anxiety.

The queen's terminal decline had been so rapid that even the medical practitioners were taken by surprise. Kunwar Jai Singh and her daughter-in-law argued with attending physicians many a times over the medicine to be administered to her. Medicine practitioners too quarrelled with one another frequently. They could not diagnose the cause of her ailment precisely.

People were , however, making wild guesses in a hush-hush tone.

'Rupan had been administering her own prescription on the queen for the last four to five months. But no one knew what powder she had been giving her by mixing in milk.'

'Rupan is solely responsible for poor health of the queen; she might be giving her slow poison.'

'It is an open secret; she had been giving opium to the queen for years.'

All kinds of rumours were doing the rounds in the corridors. Nevertheless, no one had the guts to voice their opinion, openly.

The queen's personal medicine practitioner for long, had come to a definite conclusion that the end was near, but had great difficulty convincing the royal family of the inevitable, even in the final days when they saw the queen drifting between delirium and clarity. They were certain that routine doses of opium and such other drugs, in the past, had taken their toll. Gradually, her body organs showed the signs of crumpled stage.

Her courtiers and close relatives though noticed her deteriorating health, but they were not prepared for any bad news so soon. Not before Jai Singh's ascendance to the throne.

✳

The queen had been as reluctant to accept her death as those around her had.

'Am I better?' she asked the royal *vaidya*, 'I have to live a little longer, as I have still a few things to settle.'

He assured her, 'Of course, *Maji sahib*! You have been passing through a bad phase of health, but now you seem to be better. I see speedy recovery.'

Events took a dramatic turn for the worse from the beginning of the year, as Fateh suffered a series of strokes. Her illness left the queen unable to carry out her royal duties. She was not able to see that proper orders were being issued and complied with diligently. Resultantly, everything had come to a grinding halt.

On that particular day, she was not in her usual self-right since morning. Jai Singh was seated beside her bed. She opened her eyes with great effort in order to have a glimpse of Jai, as she pulled herself towards him out of natural affection, although, she had been experiencing excruciating pain. Her restless mind recalled past events. She uttered a few words in a low voice and then the name of Jai. Jai Singh came closer to her, but failed to comprehend properly the words she spoke.

'Don't torture yourself my son. A mother feels fulfilled in the growth of her progeny. I got status because of your father, but your glory is the source of my satisfaction, complete contentment; you have given meaning to my worthless life,' she muttered. She tried hard to bring a faint smile on her face.

Jai was speechless. He was perplexed and filled with apprehension at the sight of his mother, lying in the bed, not able to speak coherently, as if she was in the grip of some great pain. The queen began to sink, as the family crowded into her small bedroom.

Jai Singh sat on her right holding her hand. The queen gained consciousness, for a while, but unable to see clearly, lamented repeatedly. 'I am very sick.'

Each time he replied, '*Masa*! You will soon be better.'

A young nurse knelt on the back of the bed, supporting the queen's head.

Her family and nobles were prepared for her final departure.

✳

A short while later, a *sewadaar* walked down to the entrance gate where a large crowd was waiting, and declared solemnly.

The Regent Queen, Maji Sahib of Jaipur, Fateh Kanwar RathorniJi breathed her last in the afternoon. She closed her eyes finally and bid adieu to this mortal world forever. Her last moments were in the company of her son, daughter-in-law, grandchild and close relatives.

What followed was chaos and confusion.

With the announcement, wild rumours began to fly thick and fast...

' *Maji Sahib* had not eaten anything for quite a few days. Most of the time she was bed ridden.'

'She was unconscious for the last couple of days.'

'*Ranisa* was sinking and her trusted ally Rupan was busy in stealing and filling her coffers.'

As the room was filled with the sound of sobbing and wailing mingled with the chanting of *mantras* by the priests, her son and grandchild were summoned to perform the last rites.

Across the city, people from all occupations gathered in small groups. Shops and public places were closed. Crowds lined along the streets to pay their last respects to the queen.

Preparations for the last rituals began. A pyre was prepared in the royal burial ground at Gaitor.

The body of Fateh Kanwar was cleaned, bathed and dressed in her traditional wedding attire, red and golden lehenga and chunar that she liked the most. Holy water was poured into her mouth and gold coins with basil leaves were put on her lips. Similarly, some leaves and gold coins were put in her nostrils and ears. Her hands were put on her chest. Both her thumbs were tied together. Her toes were also tied together.

Sacred *mantras* were whispered into her ears. Priests summoned Jai Singh and the close kin, to lift her body. Through all this, Jai Singh remained outwardly cool, calm and composed.

The funeral procession lasted two hours, with the queen's body kept on the wooden stretcher on the carriage drawn by horses through the crowded – yet eerily silent – streets.

✳

One year passed by. It was the beginning of the spring season, in 1835. All around the palace, flowerbeds were blooming. People of Jaipur were looking forward with great expectations. With the coronation of Jai Singh, a new epoch would begin. The past few years proved to be a terrible time, nothing else but gloom and dismay of one kind or other advanced like a torrent and swallowed up the whole of Jaipur.

Jai Singh had completed seventeen years, yesterday. He had crossed his status of a minor king; he wouldn't have needed any regent to control him. He would rule his country in his full capacity as a king. But..., alas! What boggled his mind was the fact that the most dependable persons , who cradled him in their arms, betrayed him. For the last so many months, he had been preparing a dossier on his own officials and ministers through his reliable sources.

Vasant panchami, the spring festival fell on 6th February. The fifth day of the spring season. It was unusually a wet day and cold night for this time. Half past midnight. The sky was overcast with thick dark clouds. It was just starting to rain, as Jai Singh the crown prince entered his bedroom.

The drops were gentle, almost pleasant, but dark clouds overhead indicated him not to expect a light spring shower. Not a single star was visible. Breeze had given way to fiery winds and Lo! Heavy drops began lashing the windowpanes. The two quarters of the night had passed peacefully.

Jai Singh needed his space and solitude. Tomorrow will be

different. It would be good if dawn driving its chariot emerges late on the horizon. Seated on a beige velvet cushioned long armchair in the balcony, he was enjoying nature's mild fury. As he had decided to skip dinner, he told the chef to take rest.

A solitary owl perched on the mulberry tree hooted ominously. It was so eerie that a strange feeling gripped the prince. But he brushed it aside soon.

Sewadaar came forth holding a golden tray with almonds and cashews in golden bowls and a glass filled with saffron milk. Jai Singh indicated to keep it on the side table.

Jai Singh's day was spent fervently in making a public spectacle of his own, in conducting crucial meetings and assigning significant duties to his trusted band. He rode through the city on a heavily decorated elephant, at the head of the royal procession.

Little did he make out that after the death of his mother, he had emerged as a direct threat to those, who were once confidante of his mother, Rupan *badaaran* and *sanghi* Juntharam. Now he was a grown-up young man, ready to take on responsibilities as the king of the state, without the support of Rupan or Juntharam.

Unlike his father, Jai Singh was alert, enthusiastic and in the past, on many occasions, he had displayed his own mind. Courtiers, nobles and elders in the family were sure that under his rule Kachwahas would soon regain their lost glory. But precisely that was the reason that proved fatal to him.

Rupan and Juntharam were aware that, now their days were numbered. Their vice like grip on Jaipur would weaken soon. Within no time, they would lose their powers. They felt threatened. They knew that luck and time were running out for them.

Therefore, once again, they hatched a cruel conspiracy.

✳

Jai Singh had planned to offer prayers in the early hours of morning to the goddess at Nahargarh, as he would be wearing a new robe of responsibility the following day. He made a conscious choice to spend his night in the serenity of Nahargarh.

Nahargarh, the abode of tigers, had always been fascinating to him, since his childhood. Surrounded by the dense jungle of palash, *sheesham, babool* and *khejri* trees. Bushes and foliage that easily grow in hot and dry climate. The ramparts looked like green-coated walls, layer upon layer, huge green precipices pressing down, leaving no room for light and air, even during a hot and humid daytime.

The fort, earlier called Sudarshangarh, nestled comfortably on the lofty summit of the Aravalli hills; was well connected to Jaigarh Fort through its extended ramparts. The rooms and courtyards were linked by corridors with delicate frescoes. Nahargarh was generally used as a retreat and hunting destination by his father. Later, when Jai Singh visited the place, he was strongly fascinated by its locale and surroundings.

The flames of torches flickering in the houses, at the foothills were seen from the doors and windows of the fort. They looked like stray twinkling stars, studded on the dark blanket of patchy land. Serpentine steep stairs were lazing around the hills and royal flags waved whenever breeze caressed them. From the distance, the fort looked like a magnificent abode. Four layered walls covered it from all sides. At the top was the king's chamber, just below, on the left, the third portion was meant for close relatives, princes and princesses and the forth was intended to be used by the army and courtiers.

✳

Far below, at the main gate of the third section of the fort, there were two torchbearers, alert and looking around cautiously. One of them began to move forward slowly, placing each foot carefully and expecting at any moment to hear a hiss from a protesting snake. A dusty track, not much in use, enough to make some one slip; a hill, a tumble of boulders, and above, stretching horizon, the empty dark sky, insects singing in the darkness of the night.

In the light of the torch, the bridge joining the third and fourth portions was visible clearly to the torchbearers and just below the main gate, under their feet, there was a deep watery gorge filled with venomous snakes and crocodiles. Both the torchbearers began to climb a zigzag narrow lane, paved with stones in the direction of the top most portions.

'Why JuntharamJi? Why are you breathing so fast? Is it aging or something else?' asked the female figure.

Juntharam, holding a torch in one hand carefully, a spear in another, followed Rupan without answering. He could not afford to fall behind. Not when he had a heavy price to pay. He tramped his way through the twisted web of roots and vines and darkness.

He had always been scared of snakes.

A snake frightened of snakes!

As their shadows, visible in the light of their torches, gently crept in, Rupan and Juntharam crossed the long corridors of the top most palaces and stopped at the main entrance of the residence of Jai Singh.

✳

There were two guards, as alert as hawks. Why have these two come to meet the prince at this odd hour, so late in the night? The guards looked at each other sceptically. They were alarmed to see both of them together. Their sudden arrival, without prior information, was disquieting. They tiptoed behind them and suddenly appeared in front of them like apparitions. It was thinning of the fog that alerted the guards to their presence.

'Has Maharajkunwar Jai Singh *Hukum* already retired?' Juntharam asked. For a moment, the guards looked uncertain, what brings them here? Should they be allowed to proceed further? Then they answered cautiously.

'No. *Hukum* is still awake,' said one of the guards.

'Fine. Now open the gate and leave. We do not need you here anymore. We are here on a crucial mission, not suitable for your ears.'

Without waiting for their response, hurriedly they entered the room of Jai Singh. The handsome young prince, reclining on the cushioned sofa, glanced warily at them for a moment.

He was surprised, why were they here? Without having his permission? What is so urgent? Still he offered them a seat.

✳

Tragedy was all set to spread its cruel claws on its prey. They talked, and talked on various issues. However, the issues to be discussed were not so important as to be discussed at that odd hour of the night. The prince was annoyed, but maintained his calm. His world of solitude was disturbed. What brought them here? He tried to read between their lines staring at them with his sharp eyes. Yet, he was too young to suspect any foul play. How could he expect any wrongdoing on their part, who had always been there with his mother?

Breeze, drizzle, fragrance of wild flowers and the coronation ceremony scheduled in the morning, all made Jai Singh more forgiving and tolerant for their uninvited intrusion. Young mind trusts, it tends to be less vigilant, while experience always questions and treads carefully.

Finally, Juntharam suggested, as he could not wait any longer now.

'Maharaj *Kunwar*, I request, you must refresh yourself with a different drink.'

Jai Singh agreed happily.

Juntharam himself brought glasses. Wine was poured. Carefully, he mixed a powder into the drink; he had brought along – a powder that promised to knock him out forever. Time favoured Rupan and Jhuntharam. Things happened exactly the way they had planned.

The deadly exhalation of the darkness thickened, the rain lashed further. Jai Singh's eyes drooped. After a few seconds, he tried to get up, but he stumbled and dropped his wine glass. His eyes became sleepy and his body slumped. Jai Singh lay there engulfed in darkness, his drugged body co-operating smoothly with their wicked and ruthless plan.

Juntharam and Rupan moved closer to him noiselessly, and with a look of caution, which quickly deepened into diabolical glee; they carefully surveyed their prey. Juntharam touched his robe; there was no response, no movement of that still majestic figure. Poison was covering him slowly; first, his lips turned blue, and then face, arms and finally his whole body. He was breathing his last. He could open his eyes with enormous effort. Then his head bent down, his eyes still, face white and blue, his body began to shudder and then his lifeless body slumped on the floor.

Juntharam spoke something, first softly, then loudly; there was no reply. Bending on his knees, he lifted his inert left arm, and then he let his arm drop lightly at his side. 'Huh...! Finished...! Now, you go there,' he said, indicating his finger towards the sky, 'and enjoy your coronation in heaven or hell, whatever...!'

The four cautious eyes roamed around inside the room, as they stepped out and soon vanished in the darkness.

✳

The fourth quarter of the night was over. Both the devils returned soon with the guards and a company of soldiers. Juntharam with his sullen face and tearful eyes was busy in taking the soldiers into his confidence, narrating how the young king died of a urinary infection.

Hurriedly, arrangements were made to cremate the dead body. He was aware that it could be disastrous to wait until morning. Poison would make its appearance on his body, turning it blue. If the people could see his dead body, they would make out in no time that their prince had died of poisoning, then, there would be havoc.

'Guards might insist on calling the medicine practitioner. We cannot lose a winning game. Make haste Juntharam Ji!' Rupan was getting impatient.

Just before the dawn, the funeral was conducted amid a cordon of soldiers at Gaitor, the cremation ground meant for the royals, where his mother was also cremated a year before. His body was carried there secretly.

The same hands, who murdered him, lighted the pyre. Thus, the duo of devils, in order to execute their plan with perfection, denied Jai Singh even the last rights according to royal tradition. While the greed for power had killed a young king, and the urge to taste such power soon killed humaneness.

The roar of falling water adjacent to the cremation ground was filling the deep gorge. The flames near the water shot a thousand diamonds on the walls of the fort.

Rupan gazed deep into the flames, which were to consume soon the lifeless body on the pyre greedily. Her face was as hard as a solid rock. Her eyes were as red as the burnt amber. With her accomplice, in the swirling, ash-laden smoke, Rupan cast a look at Juntharam; their eyes met and she smirked at him. Why had she chosen to kill the prince? Rupan had absolutely no answer. However, she had a clear idea about fulfillment of her ambitions following the death of Jai Singh. Therefore, she just could not bother about everything else.

Nobody smashed the pot filled with holy water before Juntharam pushed the log with the flame into the pyre. Nobody walked around the burning pyre.

The devils departed hastily and vanished into the darkness of night. The flames of the pyre had not died out completely. Smoke had covered it. His body was reduced to ash, but not fully. The next day nobody came to collect his remains. Nobody performed the last rituals. Nobody came to sprinkle pious water to extinguish the remains of the pyre. Nobody was there to set his soul to be free of all worldly bonding.

In keeping with the dark political ambitions, conspiracies and intrigues of those times, Jai Singh was killed mercilessly more or less in the same manner, others were killed. It was clear to all the people, who could have done such a heinous act, but a meaningful lull pervaded all over. See the irony of fate, those very hands that once rocked the cradle of the prince had turned it upside down. None of her formidable rivals could defeat Fateh, but her own blind trust in a wrong woman did.

✳

As the news of sudden death of Jai Singh under suspicious circumstances broke out, the whole of Jaipur state erupted in a boiling surge of uproar and anger. Jai Singh's death in less than a year's time of the demise of Fateh Kanwar virtually rocked the royalty. Chandrawati, the young widow of Jai Singh holding her one and a half year infant cried incessantly. She cursed the perpetrators of this heinous crime.

'Just yesterday evening, I saw him off. How would I know that I was bidding him adieu for the last time. And today he is gone. Vanished in air. Just like that. Who killed him? How? Why did he go alone? I should have gone with him. I should have...' She broke down completely. Her cries and wails were heart-rending; pain immeasurable. Who had the nerves to console her? For her, heaven had virtually been fallen.

The guards of Nahargarh had spilled the beans. The intriguing questions agitating everybody's mind were – how did Juntharam and Rupan sneak past the guards, made their way to the prince's room and how after a couple of hours, the prince was found dead in the same night and how come they performed the last rites in a tearing hurry without involving the family, relatives, courtiers, nobles and *thikanedaars*?

People created havoc on the streets of Jaipur city. They out rightly discarded the version advanced by Juntharam, as the people were convinced that their prince had not died accidentally, it was a well-planned plain murder.

✳

Bansidhar, a very popular musician and singer along with Vidyadhar, a Brahmin from Bengal working as a senior official in the department of accounting, decided to make the people of Jaipur know what had happened that night.

He composed a song based on information that he gathered through his sources and assembled a group of folk dancers. With his group, Bansidhar and Vidyadhar walked down all the streets, performing a street play, singing loudly recreating the incident of that fateful night.

People in large numbers followed him beating drums:

Here comes vasanta(the spring)! Vasanta!
Young prince rejoiced festivity and laughter,
Evils were ready to a brutal slaughter!
Oh! What comes with the arrival of vasanta!
Colours, flowers bloom and groom,
Prince was to play with colours soon!
Here comes vasanta! Vasanta!
He, born to adore the throne,
Devils' skills to kill, they hone.
Here comes vasanta! Vasanta!

Fifth day of fun and celebration
In the dark night, he was done away with poison,

Oh! What comes with arrival of vasanta!
In the dreadful night , pyre was laid.,
Embracing the woods, alone he departed!
Oh! What comes with the arrival of vasanta!

All alone in the wilderness!
He recognised the cruel face, moaned in sadness
Oh! What comes with the arrival of vasanta!
Who will punish the wrong?
Who will bring back dreams and hopes?

When devils dance, and play their song.

As the true story of the death of Jai Singh unfolded, the whole city rose against Juntharam and Rupan.

A large crowd, highly incensed, began to hunt for Juntharam and his associates. A section of the crowd that traced their hideout began hurling stones at them. They sprinted towards a safe place, panic-stricken. They had to move fast; there was no time to even change clothes or carry their belongings. He promised to answer later the questions the family members may like to ask, but first they had to flee. Therefore, they ran and ran, as fast as their legs could take them. There was no time to look back, even as his ancestral *haveli* faded away from their sight.

The *haveli* of Juntharam was ransacked; the rioters did not leave anything behind. Overnight, Juntharam had gone from being a wealthy businessman and powerful minister to a powerless pauper.

✳

Somehow, Juntharam with his gang sneaked into the premises of zenana and pleaded for mercy from the queens. He and his family were sheltered. Throughout this ordeal, Juntharam and his family members took refuse in the safe quarters of zenana and stayed there in hiding for four days.

People's fury was not in a mood to subside, as Juntharam and Rupan, the main culprits continued to remain hiding away in a safe haven; people therefore unleashed their anger on Jain temples.

The Jain community bore the brunt of his deeds. The first incident occurred in the early morning when a priest of the Jain temple was killed and his body thrown from the top of his one-storey house. The sound when his dead body hit the ground reverberated throughout Jaipur. Fear and panic spread like wildfire – the madness of the mob had no limits.

In one day, the situation had gone out of control. There were riots on the streets and houses of Jains and their temples had been looted and ransacked.

Rampage continued unabated for two days. Third day, late in the evening, the mob moved forward in the direction of a large Jain *haveli*, situated at the outskirts of Jaipur, near Puranaghat. Within few hours, the *haveli* with its temple was turned into a mound of dust and stones and a *Shivalingam* was installed at a marble altar in the centre of its courtyard. Many more of the Jain temples were attacked in and around Jaipur; statues of *Tirthankars* (Jain munis),were either destroyed or replaced by the idols of Lord Shiva.

✳

The British decided to intervene at this crucial juncture as on their part it was astute to resolve the issue instead of remaining mute spectators.

First, the British Government undertook the guardianship of the eighteen-month-old infant son of Jai Singh. It was another blow to the widow of Jai Singh. A council of Ministers under the presidency of Berisal was formed and the security of infant king as well as Jaipur was put under the administration of the council until the infant king attained maturity. Thus, a full stop was put on the rule of regent queens.

Second, Major N. Alves, Political Agent for Rajputana, who was posted at Ajmer, was sent to Jaipur to investigate the case of Jai Singh's death thoroughly.

Alves acted prudently. In order to review the situation, first, he called Berisal Nathawat and asked him to reveal whatever knowledge he had.

'I personally believe, Juntharam and Rupanbai have committed a heinous act! It is not my belief. I know for sure that Juntharam and Rupan are the culprits. Majority of Jaipur can vouch their role in the death of the prince. Both are known for their infamy and notorious activities. Security personnel had seen them at odd hours in the fort, where the prince was resting. Why they were there, where they should not be? It is really unfortunate that both are being shielded by the queen, as they have earned the confidence of *zenani deordhi*.' Berisal made his statement cautiously.

The presence of Major Alves in Jaipur had sent positive signals that the culprits would not be spared. Fresh cases of riots and violence did not erupt after his arrival.

The next move of Alvis was to set forth a system of governance in the state. For so long, Jaipur with armed gangs fighting on its streets had been reeling under anarchy. For the time being, it appeared as if unabated tumult had ended and peace would prevail thenceforth because of relentless efforts of Alvis. However, the eerie calm was the sign of arrival of thunderstorm.

✳

It was a very hot and humid afternoon on 4th June1835. Alves and Martin Blake, a British official with his team had fixed a meeting with Chandrawati, other queens and the nobility, at the royal court. Before the meeting, they visited the crime scene. After collecting information from the people in the course of investigation of the case, they proceeded for the fort.

Juntharam was not a man, who would have accepted his defeat easily. With his word having been sent around, many of his supporters, duly armed, along with mercenaries from the nearby areas assembled around the fort.

During his shelter in the zenana, he had garnered the support of the *zenani deordhi*. Officials and his supporters incited the crowd spreading the news that the British were intervening in the internal matters of Jaipur. Within no time, an armed assault was launched.

The meeting was over. As Alvis and his team crossed the court premises and he was about to get into his palanquin, the crowd encircled them cagily, like fighting dogs. Slowly, the gang approached them and when they came closer to them, they launched a fierce flurry of fists. Alvis responded with speed, evading the blows, sometimes using his palms to deflect his opponent's blows. The fight seemed to go on for a long time. An agitated crowd with stones and logs rushed towards him from a narrow lane.

A man from the crowd pounced on Alvis carrying a sword and injured him severely. Gravely wounded, he made a narrow escape. The security personnel overpowered the attacker. Officials moved Alvis to a safe place. Cornet McNaughton, his secretary escaped death but suffered severe injuries.

Martin Blake, another British officer, who was trapped in a deserted street, however, succumbed to the injuries.

Additional force was rushed. A contingent of hundreds of soldiers descended in Jaipur. British officials were saved. The culprits arrested.

Both Juntharam and Rupan were captured from their hide out, but the turmoil in Jaipur did not end even after their arrest. Mayhem continued unabated for weeks.

✳

In the ensuing investigation, although hundreds of people were interrogated, yet strong evidence against Juntharam could not be gathered. First, because people were still scared of Juntharam and his supporters. They believed that Junthram is one person who would not remain imprisioned for a longer period. Once he is out, he would make their life hell. Second, Jhuntharam was a seasoned schemer; he did not leave a single trace of the crime having been committed by him.

Nevertheless, after an enquiry, the court sentenced Juntharam and his supporters Hukum Chand, Amar Chand, Hidayatullah Khan and several others including Rupan, to death by hanging for their involvement in the brutal murder of the crown prince and the carnage that followed in the city.

Diwan Amarchand and Hidayatullah were hanged. At the last moment, the Governor General changed the death sentence of Juntharam, Hukum Chand, Sheolal Shah, Manik Chand, Rupan and other minor culprits. They were condemned to life imprisonment in the absence of concrete evidence. Juntharam was exiled to Dausa, where he died in 1838, just three years after his imprisonment.

Rupan was sent to Pushkar jail. She spent the rest of her life there until she breathed her last. Most of the time, she used to collect stones and spend the whole day in counting and recounting them. Whenever anyone passed by, she hid stones in her shawl. In her last few days, she used to howl like a wounded animal in her cell. She got her hands badly injured, as she used to hit the iron door with her fist, as if she was brandishing someone. Her hands were mostly bleeding, fingers broken. The prison doctor had to bandage her wounds by force. The next day, she was found in the same condition.

At times she shouted, 'Go away! Go away! You cannot catch me. Come…catch me if you can.'

What an irony! Her life changed when she was on her way to Pushkar with her family in her childhood and her life altered once again at Pushkar, when she languished in jail there and turned a lunatic. Her torment, her suffering ended, after a long period, almost fourteen years, she breathed her last in 1849 and was laid to rest in peace, in Pushkar.

The fifteen-year rule of Fateh Kanwar coupled with Rupan and Juntharam ended tragically. Perhaps, Rupan and Juntharam had never realised that one day their deeds would culminate into fiery flames that would annihilate the entire Jaipur, including the two of them.

And Fateh Kanwar, she witnessed, how the great Kachwaha dynasty lost all its glory within her life time and was annihilated by an unparalleled catastrophe. She remained highly concerned about security of her son until her last breath; yet, she could not ensure his safety after her death.

✳

Back to the same dark night of 6th February 1835. The spirit of Fateh Kanwar descended on the land of mortals, where she belonged to once; she took a quick peek around, forlornly. In Jaipur, the land of Jumwai Goddess, where Kachwaha principality rules.

'Just one year ago, I was in the midst of a bustling Jaipur, in the centre of royal turmoil, struggling with all kinds of political storms. Today, I am no more even a smallest particle of those power corridors.'

Who I am today? Merely a suffering soul, tormented by my own guilt. I cannot tread the same lanes and royal corridors again that I left behind a year ago; so what if I want to rectify today, something that I destroyed yesterday. Ah! No way to tame the time.'

Even the dead gets nostalgic.

She came to the room where Jai Singh was having his saffron milk on the fateful night. The final moment for the coronation of her son was just a few hours away. She started dissecting her past.

'In this vast stretch of the rugged terrain, the king and his honour, his desires, his whole world revolves around only two things; first, his kingdom, his territory, his land, and second, his women, not all women, only those who matter to him. The position of a queen, in his eyes, depends on the need of the hour. At times, a woman occupies first position and the land becomes second. Truly, the king is an absolute authority, his last word counts and strict adherence to his dictate is mandatory. He could unleash unlimited power over the needs, aspirations and sexuality of his women, whenever and wherever he wanted to. Common wisdom over the years had stamped that women have no control over their own emotional, mental and sexual desires, though it is the other way round. It then becomes mandatory that he must carefully guard his women. This total control over the women has nothing to do with love, only with the fear of the loss of his honour. That's why, for ages, kings have been pushing their women behind the closed walls of *zenani deordhi* and placing eunuchs to guard them. His supremacy is boundless; survival of his queens, concubines and children depends on his desires. Having ascended the throne, he is always a king even behind the closed doors, enjoying the pleasures of intimacy with his queen or a concubine. My king, my man, Maharaja Jagat Singh was the same. No different.

'I, Maharani Fateh Kanwar, queen of late King Jagat Singh, could dispel darkness from my life only after the demise of my husband. Perhaps yes. Perhaps no!

What a paradox, I lived a suffocated life because of a man, my husband.

And I could liberate myself because of another man, my son! Hah!

Mother of a son.

Mother of a male child.

Whatever I wished, was at my feet.

A magic wand fulfilled all my wishes.

My man was not there to control my desires

I was the mother of a male child.

I thought.

I believed.

My all miseries vanished.

Really?

'That was the time, when my word used to be the last word. And, just look at the irony, at this moment, I know that my son is going to be killed very soon, but I cannot do anything.'

'Long back, I left this mortal world, never to return. But a mother cannot rest in peace even in heaven if her progeny is in pain, down on the earth. I have descended on this soil again to be with my son at the last moments of his journey, when he is about to leave this cruel world.'

'Ah! The youthfulness of my handsome child is all set to be curtailed callously. My soul could not rest in peace… For the last one year, I have never been at peace with myself. I knew that the bloody hands would snatch away the life of my promising son. Just look at my helplessness, I could not even warn him against the advancing enemy. It was my mistake. I did not bother to show him the true colours of the devils at the right time. How could I be so imprudent, thoughtless, absolutely foolish, knowing well that the snakes and scorpions, who had wiped out many in the past with their deadly stings, would ever spare my son in future?'

'Why did I believe them all my life? Why did I fail to understand that those who change their loyalty like changing seasons would be devoted to my son after me? Oh treacherous duo! I am to be blamed for watering your noxious ambitions. Rupan! My heart bleeds! You could have treasured our relationship, precious friendship, a bond of trust, but you chose power and possessions. I, a fool, gave you a long rope, Rupan!

I pray, my Lord! Let time stand still eternally. Let night never descend. Ah! I beat my chest! Tear my breast! I pray God to spare the life of my child!'

Alas! The wails of a suffering soul were not heard, not answered, no boon was granted.

Rupan and Juntharam were ignorant of the fact that they were not alone in the chamber of Jai Singh. Someone from the other world was there, beside the prince – the invisible soul of his mother. She witnessed the completely devilish drama that Rupan and Juntharam devised and demonstrated in her presence. But neither were they aware of her presence nor she could do anything to save her son, the only purpose of her life, her son, who she lived for, till she breathed her last.

Today, she was merely a silent spectator.

With a muffled cry of horror, the invisible witness of the evil act, looked wildly at her son, then realising that she was not able to provide any help, she fell down at her son's feet, and there crouching, covering his face with her palms, howling despairingly.

She helplessly watched her son dying.

He also saw her shadow moving towards him.

'Who is there?' as if he whispered.

A shadow of a woman came to him and stopped beside him. He took some time to recognise her, and then, he, bewildered, tried hard to get up. There were furrows on her forehead. Her untied long hair was dry that had covered her shoulders. Her face was pale and her lips quivering.

'*Masa!* You!' he exclaimed.

'Yes, I, your mother! I have come to take you along with me. It seems that today my unfortunate life in the real sense has ended. My life, my motherhood, all was a meaningless pursuit, when I see you in this miserable state, a victim of utmost treachery.'

In the pale yellow light of the lamp, Jai Singh glanced at the face of that feminine shadow, which was engraved with umpteen painful lines of memories. His mouth, his heart, and his eyes, all were stock-still.

And that female figure! Today she witnessed his death; he was killed in front of her eyes. She was there, the whole night, to embrace her son, sitting near the lifeless body of her son. She held the head of her son lightly and kept him in her lap.

She was there when the mortal remains of her son were put on pyre, turning into ashes.

She was there to console his betrayed soul and then both mother and son would leave this tortuous world forever.

For most people, an element of mystery shrouds the departure of the soul from its earthly home of bone and blood. During her lifetime, over the years, she had seen death, smelt death, weighed, and caused death. She had become accustomed to death. Still, the death of her son was far too painful to bear; this time her soul was trampled under a great burden.

Mother please take me across the Pushkarini River, in that world, far away from this dark and dirty planet. Please take me in your shelter.

Mythology says that Pushkarini or Vaitarni River is the last bridge between this world and other world. It is said that Pushkarini was originally based in Vaikunth, the abode of lord Vishnu. It is commonly believed that Garuda brought down the river on earth; People get salvation simply by taking a dip while crossing the river and they get rid of their sins.

'Alas! Little did I realise that one day I would pay the price for my *karma*. Then, I also paid the price for my blind trust. I became the victim of my own trust – trusting wrong people blindly. I did not perform my dharma diligently as a regent queen. The trail of killings started by the people, whom I allowed to grow larger than life, culminated in the death of my own son, Prince Jai Singh. Lust for power and money of Rupan and her accomplice could reach such dizzy heights just because I watered this poisonous ivy to grow.'

With the rising sun, both mother and son left this mean, mundane and murky world. Leaving behind all – their everyday desires, their sufferings, their glories, and Jaipur. Only their morbid tales remained behind to be told and retold.